turquoise

Books by Marilynn Griffith

SHADES OF STYLE
Pink
Jade
Tangerine
Turquoise

turquoise

Marilynn Griffith

Revell
Grand Rapids, Michigan

Published by Fleming H. Revell
a division of Baker Publishing Group
P.O. Box 6287, Grand Rapids, MI 49516–6287
www.revellbooks.com

Printed in the United States of America

Library of Congress Cataloging-in-Publication Data
Griffith, Marilynn.
    Turquoise / Marilynn Griffith.
        p.   cm. — (Shades of style ; bk. 4)
    ISBN 10: 0-8007-3043-7 (pbk.)
    ISBN 978-0-8007-3043-7 (pbk.)
    1. Women fashion designers—Fiction. I. Title.
PS3607.R54885T87 2007
813'.6—dc22   2007017283

For Mair.
Thank you for helping me find the right shade of blue.

There is a time for everything,
    and a season for every activity under heaven:

a time to be born and a time to die,
    a time to plant and a time to uproot,

a time to kill and a time to heal,
    a time to tear down and a time to build . . .

Ecclesiastes 3:1–3

It was you who set all the boundaries of the earth;
    you made both summer and winter.

Psalm 74:17

Prologue

I'll love you forever.

Lyle Rizzo didn't say it with his mouth, but with his eyes. Two blinks and an intense gaze that cut right through his wife's soul.

"I love you too, babe. For always."

It was the end for them and they both knew it. He'd known it since his cancer diagnosis, and he had accepted it. His wife, Chenille, had not. She'd ridden the wave of treatment and remission with a white-knuckled grip, always hoping, always believing . . . until the cancer came back again, this time burning through her husband like one of those wildfires she'd seen before on TV. Only no firefighter or doctor could put out this blaze. Only God could stop it, and for some reason, he'd chosen not to, just like he'd decided that her baby wouldn't live.

She took a deep breath and held on to the bed rail, always so cold against her hands. God had decided, and there was nothing more to do but accept and be grateful for the time they'd had together. That's what Lyle had said when he was still able to talk. It was what she would have said too if this were someone else's husband. But it wasn't anyone else's husband. It was Lyle.

He'd closed his eyes for a moment, not sleeping exactly, just sort of hovering between earth and heaven, between Chenille and Jesus. She watched as a smile passed across her husband's lips, knowing that he was leaving her, slipping away. She should have let him go at home or maybe at the hospice where everyone liked him so much, but something in her had still wanted to try and save what she knew could not be saved. It seemed selfish now to have inconvenienced him, to have caused him more pain, but no matter how hard she tried to be like her husband and just fall back into God's hands, it wasn't so easy for her. It seemed as she watched her husband's eyes open and shut that nothing had been easy lately, not for a very long time.

Lord, send somebody. Please. I thought I wanted to be alone, and maybe I did. Maybe I do. I'm just tired. So, so tired . . .

"Mrs. Rizzo?"

Chenille turned and stared at the door. A doctor whose name she couldn't remember stood in the doorway. His eyes were swollen. He was wringing his hands. She thought to answer him, to invite him in, but couldn't summon words. Instead, she lifted her hand a few inches in a strange sort of wave.

Dr. So-and-so took that for an invitation. He stood quietly for a while, then began to speak. "You probably don't remember me. Megan and I—forget that." He shook his head and started over. "I've become pretty good friends with your husband over the Internet. I just wanted to come down and . . ."

She clenched her fists. Come down and what, say goodbye? That's what she was trying to do. Chenille had prayed for someone, anyone, to come, but perhaps she should have been more specific. If she could just gather the strength to get up and go out into the waiting room, Flex or Nigel might come in and talk to her about Lyle in low soothing tones. They could do that because they knew Lyle in real life, unlike all the people in cyberspace who considered themselves Lyle's best buddies. Her husband's online cancer journal had been a blessing in a lot of ways, but it had its downfalls too.

"Thank you." It was all that came to Chenille's mind to say. She glanced down at his name tag as he walked around the far side of the bed. He gave her a slight smile and then focused on Lyle. Chenille's mind finally processed the letters on the doctor's name tag: *Loyola*.

Dr. Loyola leaned over Lyle's bed and whispered something. Chenille didn't quite catch it all, at first.

". . . it's pretty cold out there today. Again. It's been a long winter. Really long for you, I guess. You said that in a post once, about it always being spring in heaven, only without the pollen. Well, I think it's going to change to summer just for you, man . . ."

Chenille didn't hear more because she was crying too hard. Too loud. It had been a long winter for Lyle, a long time of pain and weakness. And yet, he'd endured to the end. Dr. Loyola was right—what flower would be able to refuse Lyle's sweet spirit? She closed her eyes, imagining a field full of roses on the verge of bloom. Well, she tried to imagine it, but the visual never came through. Instead, she saw a forest of trees with stark branches jabbing into the cold. She hugged her own shoulders. Lyle's winter was ending, but hers was just beginning. Tears that she'd held in over so many months, so many disappointments, washed over her face.

She was about to totally lose it when she felt the doctor's arms around her, rocking her gently from side to side as though she were a newborn. His arms felt sure and safe, like a wall to lean against so that she could go on, so that she could stay in this chair until her husband took his last breath, so that she could take out the list in her purse and make the calls to the funeral director, to Lyle's cousins . . . So that she could survive this day without dying herself.

As quickly as the embrace had come, it dissolved, taking the doctor with it. "Thank you," he said. "Thank you for letting me be here. I shouldn't have come, but thank you anyway. He told me that you were amazing. I shouldn't have expected any less."

The doctor disappeared before Chenille could reply. She grasped the railing again. Her friends had come to be with her, to be with Lyle. She needed to go and tell them that things were the same, though in reality, things were changing every second. She forced herself first to let go of the rail, to put one foot in front of the other. As she left the room, Chenille looked back and caught her husband with both eyes open. He blinked twice and stared at her for a few seconds before closing his eyes.

Chenille paused and closed her own eyes as the first of many snowflakes landed on her soul.

1

Winter's first wind can bend even the strongest of people, wresting treasures from clenched hands, blowing broken promises across parking lots like the snowflakes not far behind it. Chenille Rizzo felt it coming. She steeled her back and staggered once when it blasted against her. She focused on each step, on holding on to the baby quilts in her arms. Her moves came slower, serpentine, until she lifted her head enough to make out the letters at the hospital entrance. She was halfway there when another gust forced her to reach up and save her hat—her best friend Raya's sad, yet precious, attempt at knitting.

The blankets, like so many other things she had lost at this hospital, escaped her grasp and blew away. Winter had returned when she wasn't looking, just when she was starting to dream of spring.

She knelt and gathered the blankets, quilted from scraps of her life, by her own hands and the hands of her friends. They'd told her not to come tonight, her friends; they'd said that it was too cold and too late, that

11

the recent warm spell had only been an Indian summer, a ruse with the keys to winter's cage, waiting to unleash its hungry wind. And they'd been right, as usual. Not that it'd do much to help her now.

A snowflake fell onto her mouth like a bitter, icy kiss.

She shoved her hat down farther, working her hand back and forth through her hair and praying her curls would stay where she'd pinned them, instead of springing out like a red jack-in-the-box as they had done many winters before. Tonight though, even with all the wind, something felt different. She hoped so. She'd come for just that reason, to make a difference.

She stared at the last blanket she'd picked up as the snow blustered around her, wondering if she had them all. Did her arms feel lighter or was it her imagination? Oh well, she'd have the nurses check the parking lot later when things calmed down—

"You missed one," someone said behind her. A male someone. "I'll get it for you."

It was a summer voice, his. One she'd heard thrown across beaches through the cupped hands of husbands and sons. It was the kind of voice that would cause a woman to forget herself and run toward it. Her own husband's voice had been that way. Beckoning.

She turned to face him with a cautious pivot. She frowned, unable to make out who it was until he was several feet away. Recognition washed over her in a towering wave. It seemed as though she might turn to stone as she faced him. It was the craziest thing, the way she reacted whenever she saw him, since the day he'd wished her husband a forever summer. It was usually at a distance. First, there'd been an inexplicable anger, probably because he'd been present when Lyle died— moments too intimate to have shared with a stranger.

Next came a feeling of shock at the sight of him—why that reaction, she had no clue. This time, there was only a raw nervousness so taut that she almost dropped the blankets and ran inside. A year ago she would have done so. Now, she was too tired of running away and was just trying to walk toward God, toward life.

"Thanks, Dr. Loyola," she said, her voice scratchy from too many meetings and phone calls. She should have moved closer to the building, gotten out of the wind, but she didn't. Neither did he.

"Sergio," he said, and then flashed a smile. "Let me help you. Please." He leaned forward, his bare hands touching her gloved ones as he placed the blanket he'd rescued on the top of her pile.

His touch, though muted by the fabric between them, felt reassuring. His sincerity was both comforting and painful. For a fleeting moment, she allowed herself to remember . . . She'd once had someone to help her, someone to hold open the door for her, to carry her load for her. Lyle would have loved this, to bring something to the babies.

But Lyle wasn't here. Chenille wasn't sure she wanted the doctor to be here either. She'd made it this far on her own. He was getting too close—physically and otherwise.

She heaped the wet fabric in her hands and jerked her hand back, determined to stand on her own two feet.

"I've got it, thanks." She swallowed hard, hoping she didn't sound rude, thankful for the cover of snow disguising her tears. Through the gusts, she could see Sergio's face come and go, still smiling. He had dark skin like her late Italian husband, only a richer, deeper tone. He looked the way she did after the first day of vacation in a warm place, before her skin burned and peeled if she wasn't careful.

Sergio. It was a fitting name, she thought, as images of

sheiks and Mediterranean tycoons rifled through her mind. Even Zorro flashed by, followed by a Spanish explorer with a pointy beard. At night, when others slept and she could not, she watched movies that he could have easily starred in. With a better haircut, of course. His was a little too plain, sort of Mr. Spockish around the ears. Or maybe it was the ears themselves . . .

She clicked her teeth together, reminding herself that she was doing it again, ripping a guy apart at first sight. She thought of Nigel, one of her partners at Garments of Praise. What had his army buddies called him? The Conquistador. She stole another look at Sergio. Yes, it fit nicely.

Her freezing fingers, however, did not fit nicely into her cold, soggy gloves.

While she prepared her polite good-bye, he struck a thinker's pose, despite the wind blowing back the sleeves of his jacket like wings. "You probably don't remember me. I was a friend of your husband's. Well, sort of, anyway. He was an amazing guy. I still read his blog sometimes. His prayers. He loved you so much . . . Anyway, I know it's been awhile now, but I am so sorry for your loss. Forgive me if I sound strange. I've seen you before and wanted to say something. I came to seem him at the end, but—"

"I remember." Chenille finally forced the words welling in her throat past her lips. It had been a long time since anyone had paid their condolences or wished her any sympathy. Life went on without Lyle, often without her too. People tried to understand, but time had healed their wounds. She had been surprised to find that it had healed some of hers too. This man, though, with his everywhere voice and wishes out of season made Chenille want to rip off her bandages and inspect her scars. He made it seem as though it would be all right to do so.

"Right. I guess you would have remembered. I just wasn't sure. You always look away . . . It's probably bad etiquette to bring it up now. Sorry if it is. Your husband just meant a lot to me."

"He meant a lot to me too." She felt stupid for saying it and angry at this Zorro doctor who was stealing her strength before she could make it to the door. He had no right to act as if he'd known Lyle because he'd read some online journal. Sometimes she hated the stupid Internet. She still read her husband's blog too, but she didn't like to admit it. Not with half of New York still reading too. In these moments, she longed for something of his that belonged to her alone, knowing that it could not have been. It wasn't her husband's way—not then and not now. He knew how to belong to people. Lots of them.

She turned toward the entrance and started walking toward it. The overhang was piled high with snow. Not sure why, she turned back, watching the doctor shivering in a jacket fit for a fall walk instead of a winter snow. He evidently had been fooled by the previous week's warm weather too.

She blinked away the sting of the cold, the pain of the memories escaping the box in her mind where she kept them. The wonder of Lyle in the eyes of a stranger, in the mouth of someone she barely knew. She took the blanket he'd just given her, the top one, and held it out to him. "You look colder than I am. Thanks for your help. We'd better get inside before we freeze."

He raised an eyebrow. "For me?"

"Yes. Keep it." Chenille turned to walk briskly toward the entrance.

Another strong wind and the hail it brought with it caught her off guard, but what surprised her more was a hand on her back and a familiar blanket landing on top of her pile of quilts.

The doctor picked her up like a rag doll and ran for the entrance just as the sky went white with pelting ice. He slowed as the automatic doors opened.

"I didn't see that coming," Sergio said as he lowered Chenille to her feet just inside the hospital entrance. Chenille recovered quickly from the surprise and handed him the blanket to warm himself.

She laughed. "I'll do you one better. I didn't even see *you* coming." She made a mental note to get another optical exam. Her night vision wasn't what it once was. To be honest, nothing about her was what it once was. The beauty of widowhood: nobody to care if you got fat or worked too late. It was the pain of it too.

They were inside now. Separate again. Emotions tumbled through her, pushing her toward a hasty retreat. She bid the doctor a good night and hurried down the hallway. She needed the quiet of the nursery.

She pushed through the doors leading to the nursery, but not before she got a glimpse of the doctor, blanket wrapped around his shoulders, a gentle smile on his face as he watched her.

Dr. Sergio, with his frozen fingers and haircut from outer space, was the type of man who would care, who would take a woman's hands from the computer keyboard and kiss them where it tickled, right in the center of her palms. She'd only known him for a cold, dark moment, but she knew it, just like she knew it about the married or soon-to-be-married men on the train, checking their watches and making nervous calls to check in when they would arrive late. She'd once been the one on the other the side of the phone, angry about overcooked chicken or missed arrangements with friends. What she wouldn't give for a call like that now.

Now, she cut up her pain and stitched it into rainbows

for other people's babies because she'd never have another child of her own. No longer Mrs. Rizzo, part of a whole, she was now Chenille, the lady who lost her family. Only here, at the hospital, where everyone lost people all the time, did things seem normal.

It didn't make sense really, spending so much time at the place where she'd lost the people she loved the most, but when it worked, it worked. Walking to the nurses' station and seeing a familiar face made Chenille smile. It would be a good night.

The head nurse, alone at the usually busy desk, waved as Chenille approached. "Hey, there you are. We thought you weren't coming. You probably shouldn't have. It's late and they say it'll storm. Didn't you hear?"

She shrugged. She'd heard, she just hadn't listened. She piled the soggy quilts onto the counter. "Oh, it's storming all right, believe me." She handed the baby quilts to the nurse. "They'll probably need a toss in the dryer, but they'll be fine."

The nurse held one up to the light, turning it around and around. "I can't believe you haven't been quilting all your life. I've been knitting since I was six and quilting almost as long. This is excellent work. Worthy of a high price. Speaking of which, did you bring one for us big babies like you promised? We're already fighting over it."

Chenille stared at the ground. The big quilt. The one she'd given to—

"It's mine, I'm afraid, but maybe I'll rent it to you." It was the doctor, looking drier than before, but still chilled. Goose bumps ran along the tops of his hands and disappeared into the tangle of black hair at his wrists. Chenille bit her lip, but not before she imagined what kind of hair might be on his chest. As a newlywed, she hated that, the hair. Hair left in the sink after a last-minute shave, the scratch of the beginnings of a beard, the tangle of chest hair under her head when snuggling up for a movie. She'd thought back then that she'd hated the hairiness of men, but she didn't now. Not at all. Like everything else, she missed it.

The nurse winked. "Ah . . . I see how it is. I didn't think you two had met officially, but I see that you have. Probably for the best. Dr. Loyola here is now in charge of the Pajamas for Preemies project. He'll be the one to take your blankets from now on."

Chenille stared off into the distance for a moment, her head leaned a little to the side. She righted herself and grabbed for her hat, not knowing what else to do to fill the silence. Her hair made a splatting sound as it smacked against her ears and shoulders. A knit hat hadn't been the best choice. Raya's stitches had created a fashionable water sieve. "Um, okay. I'll try and remember that—I mean, him."

The nurse laughed.

The doctor didn't. He did something worse. He beamed as if a lightbulb had been turned on in his face.

"I don't think you'll have any problem remembering him, not from the look on both your faces. I'm glad of that, for both of you." The woman looked from Chenille to Sergio and back again. "You're two good people."

Chenille started eyeing the bathroom but knew there was no way to avoid this runaway truck. It was coming straight at her, and not for the first time. Though Lyle was dead, people still thought that she was like him—good. Better. Not perfect, of course, but better. She wasn't anymore. She thought things, said things, did things . . . Well, she'd learned anew how much grace God had to offer. It was the learning to accept it that got tricky sometimes.

The doctor gave voice to her thoughts. "I can't speak for

Mrs. Rizzo, but I'm not good. I just haven't worked this shift long enough for you to know it." He chuckled, then his eyes settled on Chenille again. "I agree with you about Mrs. Rizzo though. She's good. Very good with babies." He held up his wet blanket behind him, one fist at each corner. "I've seen you in there, rocking, singing. Wrapping them up. I sort of envied those little ones and their blankets. Their redheaded angel."

Both Chenille and the nurse stared at him with their mouths open.

The nurse spoke first. "Slow down, Doc. Save a few lines for the first date. Sheesh. I think that's the most he's said since I've met him. Men." She reached over for the blankets. "I'll make sure they're dry for you next time. Now call yourself a cab. You should go on home. It's nasty out there."

Good with babies. Chenille was still tangled in those words until the nurse had mentioned her leaving. "Wait. Give me the one on the bottom. It's Erica's. I know she's sleeping, but I just want to whisper to her about it. Let her know I came by."

The nurse got a troubled look. "Oh, honey. Didn't they call you? I told them to call. She's gone. Middle of the night last night. The mother is in there now. I'd never met her until tonight. So young. Fifteen. Looks smart, though. Lots of big books. She's taking it hard."

If not for Sergio dropping his blanket on the nearest chair and running for the nursery door, Chenille might not have moved at all. She tried to comprehend what she had heard, tried to tell herself that Erica, the special baby that had seemed so much like her own, was gone. There were others, of course, babies that she came and prayed over and covered up, hoping not to be seen or noticed while doing so. Babies who, like the friends she worked with, had become her family of sorts, a testing ground for her love to see if it still worked.

19

Again, her love had failed. Or had love failed her? It didn't even matter anymore. The effect was the same.

She looked like a baby herself, Erica's mother, with a giant backpack weighing down her birdlike frame. Her jeans had a hole at each knee, poverty masquerading as fashion. She stood in front of the empty bassinet, balancing on one foot, then the other. Sergio was there already holding her hand. They were speaking in hushed tones as Chenille put her belongings on a chair and approached them.

"I wanted to come last night, but nobody would bring me. They said she was dead already and there wasn't nothing I could do." She shook her leg, rattling the chains belting her waist.

Sergio took the young mother's hand. "You're here now. That's good, right?" He spoke to her easily, like an old friend.

She didn't look convinced. "I don't know. Maybe. Rico had to play with his band, but he's coming too. At least his mama says he's coming." She buried her other hand into a pocket so threadbare that Chenille wondered if it would rip apart.

She must have stared too hard at this girl, this mother, because the girl narrowed her eyes at Chenille. *What are you staring at? This is none of your business*, her eyes said. And she was right. Chenille fumbled with her coat, dug into her pockets for her cell phone. What had the nurse said? A cab. Home. Anywhere but here.

The doctor wouldn't let her get off that easily. He kept the young woman's hand and walked her around the little crib to Chenille. He took Chenille's hand, held them both on either side of him. "Jessica, this is Mrs. Rizzo, one of our volunteers. Erica was her special assignment. She makes blankets—"

Jessica, whose name fit her much better than her jeans,

20

looked up from her sneakers. "You? You made all those little blankets? I've seen other babies with 'em. They nice." She rocked forward on her toes. "Real nice."

The nurse from out front approached with Erica's blanket, still warm from the dryer. "She made this one to give your baby tonight. I'm sure she won't mind if you have it."

Sergio squeezed Chenille's hand gently, massaging her fingers, rolling words up out of her broken heart like toothpaste at the end of a tube. She cleared her throat. "Yes, please. I'd love for you to have it."

It was true and she was glad he helped her say it. Erica had been too fragile and underdeveloped to be touched or exposed to much noise, but her oxygen levels always rose when Chenille sat quietly, praying with her hands stretched wide outside the plastic bassinet. Despite the highway of wires and tubes coming in and out of her, Erica was often alert during Chenille's visits, with talking eyes she'd obviously inherited from her mother. Eyes like her own son's might have been, Chenille imagined, if she'd ever seen them open. But his eyes hadn't opened. He'd never taken a breath or made the cry that makes mothers' bosoms heave with relief before they count fingers and toes.

Erica had reminded Chenille of him, Lyle's boy, who'd died looking not quite finished with elongated limbs and a tiny, angular face. It was a look that made a mother cry through her smiles, wishing she could somehow get the baby back inside, for even an hour.

The girl bit the inside of her cheek and held out her hands to receive the quilt. She ran a hand around the satin ribbon along the edge, jerking her other arm out of her backpack so she could touch it with both hands. Her backpack clunked against the backs of her calves before hitting the marbled floor. A worn copy of Shakespeare's sonnets tumbled out. Jessica didn't seem to notice. Where was this girl's mother, Chenille wondered. What had happened to her? What had happened to each of them, standing there together?

Jessica's nostrils flared as she clutched the blanket to her chest, held it to her face. She rocked back and forth, as if in agreement. "Yeah. You got it. You got her. She was like a sunburst of words even though she couldn't talk yet, like a poem to end all poems." She closed her eyes, bowed her head. Sergio and Chenille did too. The young mother's prayer had no words, and perhaps that made it even more powerful.

As Jessica lifted her head, Chenille saw Sergio's Adam's apple bobbing in his throat. His eyes looked moist, but his grip was steady. Strong. Maybe he was just doing his job. Unsure, Chenille cried for both of them, for all of them. No sounds came out, just tears winding across the bridge of her nose, navigating her freckles like a rocket among the stars.

Her voice was hoarse as she spoke. "You're right. It is a sunburst. The yellow is from one of my husband's yellow shirts. He wore it to church a lot. The orange is a dress I bought for our second honeymoon. My husband died before I got to wear it. The pink is from my baby, when I thought we were having a girl. The blue is from my baby. I lost him too."

The girl looked surprised, even sorry. Chenille made a fist with her free hand, and then loosened it. She'd been trying to console Jessica, not get sympathy from her.

Sergio gave Chenille's hand a slight squeeze and let go. Chenille understood and reached across the empty bassinet to touch the blanket, still not quite dry at the edges. Chenille held on as she explained. "It's okay. Those clothes made me sad sometimes, but they made me happy too. Just like your baby made me happy. You shared her with me. Let me share this with you."

It was a sweet moment, like when the music stops in church but everyone keeps singing. Chenille felt something brush over her at the crease of her elbows, behind the backs of her knees. As warm as the wind outside had been cold, it came sweetly, cupping her chin, kissing her temples. It was a Jesus breeze—and Lyle was in it.

You did good, Red. Real good.

"Oh." It came out breathy, the way her friend Raya sometimes answered the phone after her husband had been on a long trip. Sergio's eyes were closed and his hands open, palms facing up, as if he'd felt it too.

"I told you, Jess, no funeral or nothing." The voice was as brash as Sergio's was smooth. Gravelly even. Instead of the young boy they'd expected, a man in his twenties with a guitar and a sad look turned out to be Erica's father. He'd thought they were putting the baby to rest, having a service. And maybe they were, but they hadn't planned it.

"They're just giving me her blanket, babe. That's all." She stuffed it into her backpack along with the book of poems and gave Chenille a hard look.

Chenille didn't take it personally. She knew there was just no one else to blame. She understood that. Totally. It made her sad to think that her friends would have understood too. She'd been hard to love lately, but they'd loved her anyway. This love she gave now was because of them.

"Whatever. Let's go." He looked Chenille over with a flat, assessing glance, dismissing her instantly, and then squinting at her eyes. He must have seen something, because he gave a small nod. "Thanks. I seen you before, rocking her and thangs. I used to come and look. Didn't wanna hold her. She was just too little, you know."

She did know. "Yes."

Sergio handed the guy a card, then pulled it back and

scribbled something on the back. Probably his personal number. "Call me. I'd like to hear you play sometime."

The guy didn't even look at the card before handing it to his girlfriend. "For real? Okay. We can do that."

The couple left in a close tangle, tight and slow, coming together already against the cold, against the pain. Chenille stared at the floor, not wanting to look anymore at the little bed where Erica had slept. It was stripped clean now as if she'd never been there. Even the name card had been removed.

The name card. The only evidence she could access on hard nights to prove to herself that her son had really been born, that she'd really been a mother. The thought of it being lost to that girl forever . . . She pushed the baby bed back on its wheels, shoved her hands into all the compartments, jerked out the stiff metal drawers.

Sergio reached for her hands, but she dodged his grip. She snorted in frustration, looking up as the couple pushed the button to exit through the double doors. "The card. Where is it? The one with the baby's name?"

"Here." He'd stuffed it into the pocket of his lab coat, but it wasn't bent too much. "I tried to give it to her. She didn't want it."

In a panic, Chenille grabbed it, stunned by the ordinariness of it, a three-by-five card written on in marker. Simple, yet powerful. "One day she'll want it," she said, squeezing between him and the baby bed. She was running now, smacking the button and chasing them down the hall.

She caught them as they stepped into the snow. The boyfriend took it. This time he didn't say thank you. He didn't say anything. He just held the card up in the air, up in the swirling wind, took a deep breath, and let it go.

2

Chenille went back to the nursery to collect her coat with her gloves stuffed in the sleeve and her yarn ball of a hat. No one looked at her oddly when she returned after running out of the room and chasing down Erica's parents. Chenille was thankful that there had been no other visitors around and hoped that her fuss hadn't bothered any of the other infants. but it didn't seem as though it had. The staff in the NICU didn't chide her for her unusual behavior. They were used to grief.

She'd once been used to grief too, but it had been awhile. For some reason, this loss, someone else's loss, hurt almost as much as her own. Perhaps it was the young couple's unwillingness to grieve that made her hold her sides as she passed through the other babies. These little ones, still so close to heaven, seemed to know that now was a good time to rest. Chenille envied the babies that, their peacefulness. Probably the way the doctor had envied the babies when she rocked them.

The doctor. He wasn't in the nursery

anymore. She'd thought she'd heard him behind her when she went running for the parking lot as though her life, her love, had depended on it. Who knows? Maybe her love had depended on it. Maybe what mattered wasn't what people did with your love, but whether or not you let them know you cared, even if you had to make a fool of yourself to do it. She wished now that she'd turned back from the train some of those mornings when Lyle went his way and she went hers—that she had run him down, taken his lapels in her fists, and kissed him for the world to see.

Wherever the doctor was, she prayed that God would bless him. He'd called her an angel, but he'd been the one with the wings she'd needed this night. She whispered good-bye to the nurses and exited slowly through the double doors, inching along while she tried to remember the number to the cab company. She rummaged through her coat pockets for her cell phone, only to put it back when she found it. She needed to sit down for a minute and pray, think. Ahead of her, the sign read WAITING ROOM. She took a deep breath and tumbled into it, thinking about how desperately she needed some time to pull herself together.

Sergio must have needed the same thing, because he sat just inside the door with his head in his hands. He looked cold again, like he'd stood outside for a while in just his lab coat. He'd taken cover under the quilt she'd given him. Someone had been kind enough to throw his quilt into the dryer with the others, but it didn't look like it was helping much yet. He looked good with it draped over him, though. It looked like it belonged on him.

He gave her a weak smile. "Hey, this is my spot. You're going to have to find your own."

She wasn't sure why, but that made Chenille laugh. Probably because it was something like her late husband might have said. "Well, sorry, but this was as far as I could get without breaking down, so you're stuck with me." Chenille wiped the corner of her eye, thankful that her friend Jean had made her switch to waterproof mascara. "I'll try not to cry on you."

"Oh, that's okay. It's my own tears that worry me. I'm supposed to be way past this by now, not to mention that I'm a guy." The doctor stared up at the TV that was playing a sitcom from the seventies. He stood to turn off the television. She was about to say that he needn't bother, that she could tune it out, when she realized how good the silence sounded. He sat down again, picking up the quilt and smoothing it around his shoulders. For a few seconds, Chenille regretted giving it to him. Comforting a baby was one thing. Comforting a man was quite another. Of that she was certain.

"You have black stuff on your face."

She sighed. "Oh well. The goth look is still hot, right? I could always starve myself and become a runway model."

He threw his head back and laughed, though she hadn't thought it to be that funny. "You're really something, you know? All serious one minute and totally hilarious the next. And you've got great timing too. I really, really needed a laugh just then."

"Glad to be of service." She didn't say it, but he had great timing too, his shoulders moving up and down in laughter as though the scraps of her husband's shirts had worn off on him. She joined him with a giggle of her own. When Sergio let the blanket drop and peeled off his wet lab coat, she stopped laughing. He wasn't as scrawny as he'd looked earlier. There was a lot hiding under those oversized jackets. When he started tugging at his T-shirt, she closed her eyes, not wanting to spoil what her imagination would come up with later. She could live off the T-shirt image until spring.

And then . . . she peeked. A colossal mistake. A patch of

silky, black hair the size of her two hands was centered in the middle of his chest. He pulled the dry blanket around him and pushed the wet clothes aside as unashamed as if he'd been alone. When he spoke again, the laughter had drained from his voice. "That guy Rico. I know he's not going to call me. I talked to him before. I heard him playing once, to the baby. He's good. I know somebody in music. Well, I used to . . ." He lowered his head. The quilt swallowed his words.

Chenille was glad when he went quiet. She felt tired all of a sudden, like she didn't want to talk. The things that she did want to do, like investigate Sergio's chest hair, moved her to prayer, but the words wouldn't come easily. None except one. *Help*.

Sergio reached behind him to turn off the light. "You'll have to excuse me, but I'm going to try and get some sleep. Wake me up when your cab comes and I'll walk you out."

She didn't move.

She didn't speak.

He didn't care.

Still sitting up, he closed his eyes and fell asleep almost immediately. Or at least it seemed so. After several minutes in the quiet darkness, he threw the quilt open like a cape, extending one arm to her as he had earlier that night. "Come," he said softly.

She swallowed hard and closed her eyes, his voice echoing in her mind. With anyone else, anywhere else, it would have seemed crazy for her to even consider it, but here, now—as she moved toward him—it made perfect sense. Still, as he closed the quilt around her, she couldn't help wondering if she'd lost her mind. Chenille's idea of taking a risk was coming to the hospital at night alone. This was something else. Something crazy.

Crazy or not, Chenille closed her eyes and sighed against

him, realizing that she'd been freezing to death even before winter's birth tonight. As his touch on her hand had felt familiar earlier, his body against her felt the same, as though it fit. Her body slumped against him as if something had been made right. Chenille felt herself again for a moment, like she'd once felt after a night of sleeping in her own bed. She rarely slept in it now, not deeply. She mostly tossed and turned and watched bad movies.

He smoothed her hair and nudged her head to his shoulder. She shivered, but not from the cold. His sleepy hands in her hair felt somehow like the way Lyle used to throw his leg across her in the middle of the night. For a moment, she felt like a wife again.

She felt like a woman.

Then his cold fingers touched hers and brought her back to reality. He mumbled something about tests and charts, even smiled as she rubbed the back of his hand until it was warm. Like the rest of him. She should go now, she knew. And she would go, but there was just one more thing. Chenille let her head fall over to one side until her ear was against his chest. She listened to his heart beat. It was a beautiful, amazing sound. She meant to get up, to slip away. Instead, she started to cry.

"I didn't see that coming," she said softly.

He wound his arms around her back. "Me either," he said in a drowsy voice. "If I'd known tonight would be like this, I'd have dressed warmer and taken my vitamins. I figured you'd run off from me like you usually do—"

Chenille kissed him quiet.

Like everything else tonight, it felt crazy. Crazy but wonderful. He tasted like Chinese food and peppermints. Smelled like baby soap. He kissed her back reluctantly at first, as though he were asking a question: *What does this mean?* She reached up into his hair and ran her hand through it, giving her answer: *I have no idea.*

It must have been the answer he was looking for, because Sergio didn't ask any more questions. His mouth answered hers in a quiet softness that made her eyes blurry with tears. And then he kissed her eyelids in the ticklish space just below her brow. First the right and then the left.

It was incredible. A little too incredible for this widow to take all at once, even if she was the one who had started it. Chenille felt herself snap awake, come alive to see what her crazy side had done. He was right; she should have run off. It was definitely time to run again.

Where was her coat? Chenille shrugged off the blanket . . . and the wonderful warm man underneath it.

He pulled the blanket around his shoulders, closed his eyes. "It's okay. I understand."

She turned in circles, saying nothing, just trying to get her arms into her sleeves. Chenille wanted to yell at him at the top of her lungs, to tell him—like she told her friends—that he didn't understand. That he couldn't understand. Yet, somehow, she knew that he did. And she didn't know what to do now. She'd never gotten to this part before. Maybe Erica's parents were smarter than she'd thought for letting winter swallow their memories. Maybe by some miracle, she would close her eyes tonight and forget Sergio with his minty mouth and hairy chest. Probably not. Still, she needed to get out of here and talk herself off this ledge. And, of course, there was no way to fool God.

And Lyle. She clenched her fists, squeezing the guilt between her fingers.

Sorry, babe, she thought.

"It's okay," she could almost hear him say as she pulled on her gloves. Lyle was wrong, of course, just like Sergio was wrong for sitting there all quiet and beautiful and tragic like the movies she hated where everybody died at the end. She was just leaving, that's all. It was best for both of them.

Not trusting herself with his mouth again, she kissed his forehead. Or at least she tried. He grabbed her around the waist and pulled her down to him, this time kissing her gently on the cheek. "Be careful. I'm usually around here. Call me if you need me. I'll call you when I wake up."

Chenille nodded and stumbled into the hall. Her calling him? Him calling her? Her heart began to race. What had she done?

He did call. Late too, probably the end of his shift. He didn't apologize for the hour or seem surprised that she was wide awake. At the sound of his voice, Chenille was both afraid and relieved. It had been real. All of it.

Sergio still sounded a little out of it, but he was definitely in a lighter mood. "I'm headed home. It took me half an hour to get your number from the nurses. You sound surprised to hear from me."

Chenille smoothed her own quilt against her bed. It felt cool against her hands. "I am surprised. By everything." She wasn't sorry that he'd called. She was glad. She just didn't know where to put him. To put this. She was the CEO of a fashion design firm. People depended on her. She couldn't keep this foolishness going.

"I was pretty surprised myself. Kiss and run. That's new. For me, at least. You might do it all the time."

His tone was playful, but it wasn't funny. She already felt bad enough. Still, she felt herself smiling. "Not hardly. I haven't been kissing anyone—or talking on the phone with anyone, for that matter."

"I know. Me either."

There was that knowing thing again. And again, it rang true. Not that it mattered. The line was quiet, and then came a snore, building and bursting like a crescendo.

She pressed a button in his ear. "You're not driving, are you?" She felt breathless waiting for his response.

He laughed. "No, I'm leaning against my front door, believe it or not."

Okay now, that was crazy. "Go inside, go to bed. Call me tomorrow . . ." Why had she said that?

"Will do. Anything else?"

"Yes. Pick up some sweet potatoes and apricots tomorrow. It's good for the circulation. Some chicken soup too. Can't have the doctor catching a cold." She sounded ridiculous, using the language of mothers with a grown man who was far from her son. The words ran out all at once, revealing the truth of her concern.

"Got it . . ." There was a pause. She heard the door shut at the other end, then lock. "Anything else?" he asked in a blurry voice. He seemed glad to have someone care about him.

She closed her eyes and pulled her own quilt up around her chin. It didn't do much, even with the extra blankets she'd piled on top. Sergio would sleep like a baby under his quilt though. "Nothing else. Just cut off your phone and go to sleep."

"Night, babe." He sounded like a drunk teenager instead of a tired doctor.

She shook her head. She wasn't prom queen material. She wasn't even dating material. He'd really lost it. Still, she wanted him to get to sleep. They'd straighten it out tomorrow if she hadn't gone into what her friends called a code blue, a total meltdown. After this night, it could happen. "Night, Sergio."

As the phone went dead in her ear, Chenille sang a hymn

to herself. Her own lullaby. And then she kissed her fingertips and touched the place under her brows where Sergio had kissed her. She could sense Lyle all around her now and all the sadness that came with him sometimes. Worse yet, she could feel Sergio too, could still hear the beating of his heart in her mind.

Comfort was all the kiss had been. Nothing more. She'd nearly convinced herself until she remembered that her friend Raya had shared her first kiss with her husband outside Chenille's hospital room when she lost her baby. A comfort kiss was what Raya had called that too. Now they were married with three kids. She really hadn't bought the concept when her friend tried to explain. She hadn't thought something like that could happen. Comfort had meant friends and family, not strangers. But that was before she'd felt for a moment her late husband's touch from another man's hands. And then, the touch of the man himself.

It was Sergio that worried her now, his fresh memory searching her heart for a place of its own. She'd been so sure, so confident that there was no room in her heart for even a thought of another man, and yet so easily he'd found a corner . . .

Oh, give me a break. It's been two years, honey. I'm just glad all you did was kiss the guy. Cut yourself some slack. That sweet baby died, you had a bad day. And let's face it, you're about due for a good kiss. Better a stranger than you attacking the postman one afternoon. Now that'd be awkward.

It was Lyle, funny and honest as ever, rushing into her heart as morning arrived. As the sun rose, sleep fell upon Chenille. She welcomed it like a gift.

3

Chenille was dreaming of a beach with giant peppermints when a buzzing sound sliced through her sleep. She slapped her alarm, knocking it off the table.

The buzzing continued. Somebody downstairs, trying to come up. Her shoulders tensed, hoping that Sergio hadn't gone so far as to show up in person. He should still be sleeping anyway. They would definitely have to talk . . .

"Come on, girl. It's cold out here!" They were the voices of her girlfriends and co-workers, all three of them.

She'd had an intercom installed in the bedroom for Lyle. Today she appreciated it. "If it were summer, I wouldn't let you up, you know," she said, pressing the button to let them into her building.

"We know," one of them said. "We know." It sounded like Raya, but Chenille was so tired she couldn't be sure. What she was sure of was that they were going to try to get her up and out today and she wasn't up for it. She wasn't really up for explaining why she couldn't go either. "I was up all night kissing a strange man" wouldn't sound very good, not even with friends as understanding as hers. She decided not to say anything until she figured it out herself.

She tugged at the top blanket on her mountain of covers and pushed the others on the floor. It was a little warmer this morning. Upon inspecting the blanket she'd kept, Chenille frowned. It was a crazy quilt made from her maternity clothes, the last thing she wanted to sleep under right now.

A key jingled at the front door of Chenille's apartment. There were voices outside, loud and anxious. For the first time, she regretting giving them a key.

"If you'd move, maybe I could get it open." That was Raya.

"If you'd give me the key, maybe I could get it open." That was Lily, who was pregnant and should have been at home.

"I know one thing: somebody had better do something to get this door open. I'm having a power surge, and in about ten seconds, I'm going to start peeling off my clothes. So unless you want the building super to be traumatized, I suggest that one of you put that key where it's supposed to go!" And that was Jean. Definitely Jean.

Chenille pulled her pillow over her head, but she couldn't help but laugh. They were a crazy bunch, but she loved them. They loved her too, and their way of showing it was by butting in. She chuckled a bit before heading to the door to help them.

She could almost imagine Lyle laughing with them as they all tumbled in after they pushed and Chenille pulled. She'd pushed herself into their lives too—first, trying to play matchmaker with Raya and her husband Flex, who'd attended her church. She'd probably overstepped her bounds there, but even Raya had to admit they were a good couple. Then with Lily and *The Next Design Diva* reality show and her old boyfriend . . . Jean with her old husband that none of them had known about . . .

All four of them had their stories; Chenille had just thought that the ink on her story was long dry. Now she was starting to think that it was just beginning.

I guess they learned from the best on that one. You reap what you sow, Red. Hard to be on the other end, isn't it?

Lyle again. As if having God in her head wasn't enough, she now had a dead husband to deal with. "You just be quiet, okay? You haven't talked to me for months and now all of a sudden it's blah, blah, blah. Don't you have something to do in heaven right now?"

Her friends looked at each other and then at Chenille.

Jean spoke first. "Lord have mercy, is she in there talking to Lyle again? Give me my purse—"

"No purses unless you're pulling out credit cards." She walked to the door and twisted her doorknob. "You all almost broke my door again."

Last spring, someone had broken off the key in the lock, but no one remembered who. Quite convenient. They'd offered to pay for it, but Chenille had taken care of it herself. She ought to start a fund for the next time—they'd come close today.

She smiled at her friends, lined up on her couch like rainbow sherbet: Lily in a lime-colored jumpsuit, Raya zipped into a pink parka, and Jean with a bright orange cape. Chenille folded her arms across her chest. "For crazy people, you sure do look good. I have to give you all that."

Jean, the oldest and most outspoken of the group, unzipped her boots and pitched her clip earrings onto the table. "And you look like somebody put you on the spin cycle and let you rough dry. I guess it's my turn to get you together. I'm burning up anyway; I might as well have a shower myself." She gave Chenille a playful shove, then looked up at the ceiling. "Lyle, you coming too? I hope not, even if you are dead."

Chenille started laughing then. She laughed so hard that she dropped to her knees right in her living room. She'd always thought that going insane was some sort of long, torturous process. It was turning out to be a very short jaunt.

Lily gave a look of concern and disapproval. "Cut it out, Jean. Now you've got her hysterical. This is not how intervention works."

Chenille laughed harder, this time holding her side to keep it from splitting. "So—so this is an intervention? Who are you supposed to be? The Rainbow Coalition? Or the Powder Puff girls?" She tried to get up off the floor but couldn't.

Raya shook her head. "Neither. Just friends who have decided that all this making quilts and visiting babies is officially weird. Good deeds are, well . . . good, but you only go to work, church, and the hospital. You need a new pair of boots. Let's go shopping."

Jean gave Chenille a hand up. "Go shopping? She's as far away from leaving this apartment as I am. It's a good thing I brought my tools," she said, patting her oversized leather purse.

A buzz sounded on the speaker. "Chenille? Are you up? I did try to call. I need to talk to you. About last night. About everything."

Chenille's friends leaned forward on their seats, getting as close to the intercom as they could get. She jumped into the silence, before they did. "I, um, have company right now. Can I call you later?"

Jean leaned in close to the speaker. "Don't mind her. You

can come right on up, Mr. Mystery Man. Our work here is done."

He laughed. Chenille tried not to melt, not to react at all. Not in front of them. They were going to pounce on her anyway, but they wanted to see him for themselves, no doubt. Whenever a mystery man appeared, they were all on notice. Raya had taken a picture of Jean's ex-husband—who was now her husband again—with a digital camera so that the rest of them could see. Chenille had enjoyed that at the time. It'd been fun then, but it wasn't now.

"Keep him talking," Raya whispered to Lily. "I'll try to get a shot out the window ."

Chenille rolled her eyes. At times like these, they thought they were spies instead of professional fashion designers.

"Sounds like you've got a full house up there," he said. "I'll catch up with you in a few days, the next time I'm off."

Relief sounded in her voice. "All right, then. Talk to you soon." Chenille turned off the speaker.

Lily held up her hands. "A few days?" she whispered. "Are you crazy?"

Jean dashed out of the bathroom armed with a blow-dryer and a brush big enough to tame a lion's mane. "On second thought, a few days is probably a better idea. We got excited because there's a man about, but it's against the rules. You can't let a man just come to your house unannounced, even if he does sound like Clark Gable on the Spanish channel."

Chenille shook her head. She was thankful that Sergio seemed to have given up and left. Jean was in rare form, dashing about the house looking for beauty implements. Chenille just wanted to go to bed. It was Saturday, after all. She paused as Jean went by again. "That must be some hot flash you're having, woman. Sorry I don't have any ice cream."

"It's a power surge, not a hot flash! How many times do I have to tell you?" Jean shouted from the bathroom.

"Not many," Raya said, coming back from Chenille's bedroom, holding up her digital camera like she was a reporter for the *Times*. "You don't have to tell me twice. That man downstairs almost gave me a hot flash, though, and I'm a happily, happily married woman. Zoom is a beautiful thing."

Lily groaned. "We know, we know. Now let us see."

Raya gave her best smile before turning around her camera. Chenille's stomach tied in a knot. There he was, with dark circles and stubble, looking like he'd just rolled out of bed. Looking better than he had last night if that were possible. She hugged her sides again as her friends started in.

"Oh my goodness! Here we are trying to take her shopping and Big Red done gone and got her a man," Jean screamed from the bathroom where Raya had gone to show her Sergio's picture. She couldn't stop smiling. "I am so happy for you, hon. Aren't you happy?"

Chenille groaned. She and Sergio really did have to talk. By coming over, he may have ruined her life. She had to work with these women, and they were going to tease her to no end. She blurted it out. "It was just a kiss—"

That brought Jean out of the bathroom with a pair of tweezers still aimed at her chin. "Did she say 'kiss'?"

Too stunned to speak, the other two women nodded.

Jean slumped onto the couch between them. "Oh well, it's been a good run. I guess I'll have to keep the bathroom door closed now when I'm over here. There's a man afoot."

They all had patterns. Lyle had a special knock—once, twice, and then seven times fast. Raya's husband Flex knew how to pick the right flowers, always getting some for everyone when he sent them to Raya. He'd once sent Lily baby's breath; while Chenille searched the box for the rest of the flowers, Lily had gone nuts over it. For Jean, there were usually zinnias in chocolate brown or burnt orange that seemed perfect once she held them. Nigel could eye clothes on the rack that would fit perfectly without trying them on. Doug, well, he could cook and sing, not to mention sketch a perfect pair of pants in one try . . .

Chenille had always been content to be with them, even if she wasn't always one of them. Even Doug, who shared the passion that she and Lyle had for missions, didn't quite grasp Chenille. No one did, not even Lyle's sweet family who invited her for pasta now and then, usually when a single friend of the family was visiting. So when her friends thought she needed a new pair of boots, but all she really needed was a good nap, she went along anyway, because this was how they loved each other, because she needed all the love she could get.

She returned home from shopping with her friends to find a vase full of snow with yellow daffodils. A crocus rose up through the middle. Chenille dropped her bags and knelt down to embrace the handful of summer, the little bit of hope. She wasn't sure who had made the delivery, but she was sure of the sender. She was also sure that she had no frame of reference for him. No box to put him in. A card was taped to the outside.

> Hope springs eternal.
>
> In the Bible it says that faith is the substance of things hoped for. Many times my faith wavers, but you are everything I have ever hoped for. I pray that I have not offended you in any way. Though I was tired and upset, it is no excuse.

I hope . . . and pray that we can start again,
preferably before we're both snowed in. I left my
number on your machine. Call me when you're ready.
I'll be waiting for you, like I always have been.

Serg

Though her friends had teased her mercilessly about her visitor, at the sight of the flowers they retreated with only smiles and good-byes. Thankful for their hasty retreat, Chenille wandered inside to put the flowers in water instead of snow, but found herself staring at them on the counter instead. Sunshine didn't come into her life enough, she decided. She would have to accept more of it and give more of it too. Her friends needed it; so did the people she worked with. So did Sergio, she knew, but she couldn't help but wonder if he hadn't just let her off the hook. Call him or not? He'd stepped back, put the ball in her court. She wasn't sure she wanted to serve. The replay of what had already happened would be enough to get her by forever.

Or at least for a very long time.

She moved the flowers into another vase. She held a chilly daffodil between her hands, rolling her palms together against its stem. Beautiful. Just like the man who'd sent them.

She'd forgotten all about her new boots, her old friends, everything, it seemed. And yet, there was Lyle, urging her to be brave, daring her as he always had to believe God even when she didn't understand.

Chenille pulled out her treadmill from underneath her bed. It would be good for her—not to become Super Girl or anything—but it was a start. It was acknowledging that someone besides God and her girlfriends might ever see her thighs again. She tried not to think about it as the motor turned on. Then she did think about it. And about *him.*

She started running. Chenille started sweating, going at it hard and thinking harder. She thought about Erica and how badly she had wanted that baby to live. She'd wanted, needed, a miracle. She'd been so sure that this time would be different, that she'd come away with something . . .

The flowers on the table caught her eye. Had her miracle passed over the NICU for a cold waiting room with bad TV reception? Had that doctor, wrapped in her blanket, been her daffodil? Her always summer?

Chenille pressed her eyes together tight and ran faster than she had in a long time, as fast as she wished she could run away from her own questions. She wasn't ready to deal with the answers anyway. She didn't want to know.

She leaned over the rail of the treadmill and picked up the remote to her stereo system. Lyle had been a gadget person, and the two-year-old system was top-of-the-line back then. Everyone at work had long since given up CDs for MP3 players and other gizmos, but the CD changer still suited Chenille just fine, especially at home. She pressed the button and praise music poured out from a CD Lily had mixed for her the year before, when Chenille was having a bad time. Though Lily had her own design firm now and no longer worked for Chenille, she was still a great friend.

Lily had been discovered when Jean "borrowed" one of her designs and sent it in to a fashion reality show. Lily had ended up winning the show and marrying the fashion mentor she'd been assigned to. The couple's new line, Worlds Apart Fashion, was a fashion-forward, socially conscious firm that had everybody talking . . . and buying. Still, somehow, Lily found time to do sweet things like burn a CD like the one playing now, a deliciously eclectic mix of Gregorian chants, urban gospel, jazz, and old-school rap.

Chenille slowed to a walk as Kirk Franklin gave way to Dizzy Gillespie. She threw one arm over her eyes and began to cry. How could she ever get to know someone all over again the way she had known Lyle? Who would ever understand all these different sides of her but her friends? And even they didn't get it all. No, it was too late and she was too tired to try. She looked at the flowers again, now drooping over the sides of the vase she'd put them in. Though they were beautiful still, the snow, the winter, had been too much. She wondered if her own winter would prove too much for summer too.

It's too late. It's a cute thought, but it's just too late.

It was just a kiss, she'd have to accept that. Sergio would have to accept it too.

If she ever saw him again.

4

She'd looked for it everywhere, that little card like the one Erica's father had thrown to the wind. That small piece of paper with her son's name in fat print, written with baby blue highlighter. The last time she'd had it out, she'd laminated it because the writing was starting to fade. This time she couldn't find it at all, but she found something better. Or maybe something worse.

The hallelujah shirt. Hidden beneath squares made from Lyle's church suits, triangles from her wedding veil, back pockets from his favorite jeans, was the amen to all her husband's prayers, a simple oxford shirt that had always signaled celebration. By wearing it, he said volumes without ever speaking a word.

Chenille wore the shirt tied at her waist as she danced between the boxes strewn over her bedroom. At church the previous morning, the praise dancers had performed the same movements she did now, bending low and leaping forward, raising her hands to heaven. Today, she'd have to head for work, despite her wrecked room and her heavy heart. Despite the terror that seized her the night before when she could no longer recall Lyle's face from memory, but Sergio's brown eyes came easily, even in her sleep.

Not that she'd slept much the past few days. She'd spent time with contacts in California and London, talking through every time zone, working long past when Lyle would have shot out his hand from the bed and grabbed her wrist. "It'll keep," he would have mumbled into the pillow that she always worried would suffocate him, sleeping facedown the way he did. In the end, what had killed him had been much worse. She realized now that in some ways his cancer had killed her too. God was offering her a new life now, a life she didn't quite understand.

She was trying to understand, though, starting with her new boots and old shirt. It'd been three days since losing Erica, since kissing Sergio. It was time to get up and go on. Three days had been enough for Jesus to leave his tomb; surely she'd managed to get some "emotional work" done in the same time.

Chenille put a pack of Kleenex in her purse, just the same. Grief had a way of washing up on the shores of her heart, unexpected, uninvited. It had a way of hitting her out of the blue. And into it too. She dropped another of Lily's CDs in too, along with three Ziploc bags of cheese curls—flaming hot, baked, and white cheddar. She topped it with a handful of butter candies. Lily had been the one who taught her how to really pack a purse. She was still grateful for the lesson. The woman was a genius. Sometimes Chenille regretted letting her get away from the company.

A minute later, though, she smiled and shook her head, admitting to herself that she would never have wanted to keep Lily from her destiny, even though she knew that her friend would have stayed if she had asked. Chenille had known what Lily could do, what she could give. It was more than Chenille could offer her.

She stared at her drooping daffodils as she put on her coat and grabbed her keys. It'd been a long weekend, and she could have easily slept for a week. She wouldn't though. She couldn't. Chenille wasn't a doctor like Sergio, but she had lives to save too, namely, her own.

The phone rang as she gathered her things to leave. Chenille knew without looking who the caller was. She dug into her purse for the iPod that she never used, plugging her ears against the sound of the phone. She tucked a daffodil into her coat pocket before stepping out into the cold, carried off on a musical chariot driven by a group of chanting monks.

By the time she got to work, she'd forgotten about the shirt she was wearing. Everyone else seemed to remember it.

Nigel Salvador, Jean's husband and the company's president, stopped her at the front door, his silver hair smooth against his brown skin. He straightened her collar and gave a slow nod. "He told me that if he lived long enough, he'd wear that shirt to see Jean and I married again. I never saw him in it. It looks good on you."

Her friend Raya joined them, rebuttoning Chenille's cuffs. "He wore it to my wedding. He was sick, but he came anyway." Lyle had discovered his cancer in the midst of Raya and Flex's budding romance. He'd even told the two of them about his illness before telling Chenille, asking the couple to pray for her, and for him too. That had angered Chenille then, the way Lyle had given away some of the things that she thought should have been hers alone. But that was who Lyle was, what Lyle was. A giver. It was all he'd known how to be.

46

Nigel rubbed his chin. "I know that you gave away a lot of the clothes. Made all those quilts. Are you going to keep this one? I think you should, but if you're going to cut it, let me know. I think I'd like a scrap myself."

Chenille touched his kind face, thankful for his concern. He had a lot on his plate now, with running much of the day-to-day operations of the business in addition to heading up the veterans' recovery ministry at their church. Not to mention being Jean's husband. That was a job in itself. A job he took great pride in.

She thanked him for his offer but admitted she wasn't sure what she'd do with it. Raya hugged her and set off for her own office. Chenille did the same, leaning against Nigel's shoulder as she went down the hall. Though her father had looked very different than him, Nigel reminded Chenille very much of him. They had the same spirit, the heart of a protector.

They stopped at her office door. She smiled, but her voice wavered. "I know you didn't know him that long before he died, but he talked to you so much at the end. I was a good wife to him, right? He knew that I loved him?"

"Of course. He knew. I think he worried that you loved him too much. He wanted for you to have a good life, a happy life, even without him."

She retied the shirt at her waist, as if trying to restrain the ache settling in her stomach. In that moment, she knew she couldn't part with this shirt or with her husband. Chenille had given away all that she could part with. There was no room for anything else, anyone else. "He wore this to the baby's funeral, you know. He said that heaven was a celebration, no matter what. I didn't speak to him for two days because of it. Two days. What I wouldn't do for those days now."

Nigel shook his head. "Don't do this. You're not playing fair."

Fair? What did that have to do with anything? "God doesn't play fair either." She gasped as she said it, surprised by her own words. Despite her years as a Protestant, the Catholic guilt of her childhood rose up in her throat. There were some things that weren't to be said out loud.

Her co-worker evidently didn't agree. He held both her hands and raised them in the air. "Yes, now we're getting somewhere. I've waited two years to hear something like that from you."

Chenille stared at her fingers, yellowed from eating cheese curls on the train. Nigel smelled of plums and bay leaves and imported coffee. She could smell Jean's perfume too, lingering on his shirt. It was a good smell and a good start to her day. She surprised herself again by not crying. "Thanks," she said. "For everything."

"Anytime," he said before leaving. "One thing though. There's something in your office for you. They delivered it early this morning. First thing."

There was something in her office, all right. A whole lot of something. She might as well have walked into a rose garden. The flowers circled her desk in rings of yellow, pink, and red before taking over the couch in a sea of closed, white buds. Whoever had made the time-consuming arrangement had been kind enough to leave a path to her desk with just enough room for her to squeeze through. On the cushion of her office chair was a note.

Chenille,

I don't know when I'll see you again in person, but I see you all the time. When I am awake or

48

asleep, you are with me, blooming always. Last
night, I dreamed of roses, a garden. Then I realized
the garden was you. The white roses are for your
sorrows, for your losses. And for mine. Do not
spend too much time with those though. Smell the
others too. There is more to living than losing. You
reminded me of that. I've drunk too deep of sorrow
in my life, but perhaps there are other things in
God's cup for both of us. When I'm praying tonight,
I'll meet you at the Father's table. His cup is never
empty.

    Serg

    P.S. I read through Lyle's blog again last night.
He was truly a remarkable man.

Chenille held the note for a long time before tucking it into her pocket. It was a fitting companion for her daffodil. Raya hadn't mentioned the flowers, so she probably didn't know about them yet, but there'd be no way to clear them before other people would see. If she was honest, she wasn't sure if she wanted the roses moved. She wasn't sure if she wanted them to stay. She'd made, in her grief, an unattainable, isolated place, somewhere that she could go alone where no one could reach her. Sergio had no respect for this wall, reaching right into her heart and bidding her to come to him. Beckoning, she'd thought when she first heard his voice. It described him in every way.

Speaking of beckoning, she might as well get the flower

show over with, so they could all buckle down and do some work. She pulled herself up to the desk and clicked on her computer, dashing off an email to Raya and Jean to come and see. On Mondays, the creative hour—sixty minutes of employee free time—came first in the day, so she didn't feel too bad about it.

Evidently, her friends didn't either, because she heard heels clicking down the hall a few seconds after she hit Send. Chenille wrapped her arms around her shoulders and gave herself a hug. How she loved these women.

Jean half-slid through the doorway with a plastic container of simmering spices. Chenille knew without asking that it was some of Lily's husband's famous Thai chili. The stuff was guaranteed to clear your sinuses and produce a few tears, and it was full of protein, everything Jean looked for in a dish. She almost dropped it, though, when she saw the flowers. "Okay, that man looked young in that picture Raya took, but he has an old soul. This is a man's gift. I like him already."

Raya came in next, both hands on her mouth. "Oh," she said. "Oh my." She looked at Chenille with disbelief. For a moment, she was speechless. That didn't happen often—Chenille almost paused to record the time and date. She found her voice soon enough. "Okay, so we don't know him yet, so I'm not going to get ahead of myself, but this has The One potential." She turned to Jean. "Don't you think?"

Nodding and taking a bite of her chili, Jean agreed. "Definitely."

Chenille shook her head. "You two are incorrigible. I'm right here, you know. Anyway, take what you want and then tell all the girls on the floor to come and have their pick too. I can't carry all of this home."

Raya whipped out her camera. "Say cheese!"

She didn't say anything, but her friend took the picture anyway. She had a thing about preserving images before they were messed up. She did the same thing with her kids' cakes at their birthday parties. It never bothered Chenille before, but this time she wasn't sure if this was an image she wanted to preserve. It was almost too beautiful, something that you just have to be there for.

Fitting or not, Raya snapped her shot just in time. As quickly as Jean shouted "Free roses!" into the hall, Chenille's office was overrun. They'd expected the women to come, but quite a few guys came too. The three ladies figured most of the men were getting bouquets for their wives, but when a few single guys showed up and snatched a bud or two, they all smiled. Maybe men liked flowers too. Chenille kept some of each color rose, mixed in a vase on her desk. Except for the white ones. There were still a lot of those left. Too many.

Chenille tried not to think about it. Staff meeting was tomorrow, and though Nigel handled it now they usually consulted on Mondays. She started to email him, but picked up the phone instead. He had a thing about at least hearing people's voices. He'd also rather look into people's eyes, but Chenille didn't want to see anyone else right now, not even her friends. She pressed his extension. "Hey. Do we need to run through the schedule for the staff meeting tomorrow?"

"There are a few things, but I've got it pretty much. Some charity items for our consideration. Should I just put them on the agenda?"

She took a white rose with her free hand and lifted it to her face. "Sure. That's fine."

Nigel sighed. "Are you okay? Do you want to talk about it? The flowers? The guy who sent them? Anything? I can spare Jean if you want—"

She didn't want to discuss it with Jean or with him. Her

other line rang before she could tell him so. "Look. I'm fine. There's another call. I'll come down later if I need to."

Chenille took a deep breath and clicked over, hoping it wasn't Sergio. She didn't want him to have to call her again. This time she would call him. Maybe even send him some flowers.

Why not just let it die on the vine? You're headed for trouble.

"Chenille here." She spoke into the phone evenly.

The receptionist, who normally spoke quite articulately, rambled into Chenille's ear. "There's a client up here insisting to see you. A Megan Ariatta? She's not on your schedule. Should I send her away?"

Chenille closed her eyes. If it'd been Sergio on the phone, she'd thought it might have taken her forever to think of what to say to him. With Megan around, the next hour would definitely be an eternity. They'd started her latest wedding dress half a dozen times before she called off the wedding, supposedly for good this time. Though the company had gotten a lot of publicity out of the account, sometimes Chenille wished they'd never commissioned the Ariatta gown at all. Still, she was a customer and deserved to be treated like one. "It's okay. I'll see her. Go ahead and send her back."

5

The timing couldn't have been worse. Just as the receptionist's voice sounded in the hall announcing Megan Ariatta's arrival, Chenille's computer announced an incoming email. She caught the title of the message as she stood, preparing to greet her guest.

[LyleLines] New Blog Post

She gasped as her office door opened. Her late husband's online journal updated? Impossible. Was this some dirty trick from her friends? Had someone hacked into his site? As she forced a smile while Megan greeted someone in the hall, she drafted an apology in her head so that she could get away and call their Internet Service Provider. Something was definitely wrong. And yet, there was Lyle, in Chenille's head. In her heart.

People first, Red. Always people first.

"Mrs. Rizzo?" The receptionist stepped into the office first, with a look of concern. She was fairly new to the position and probably hadn't met Megan before, but their client's abrasive personality was legendary. Chenille wouldn't be surprised if the previous receptionist had left a special note about her. She had a way of getting what she wanted . . . when she wanted it. "I'm sorry, I tried to tell her that all clients need an appointment. I could have referred her to someone else, but she insisted on speaking with you."

"It's okay, Courtney. Megan, come on in." The quicker she did so, the quicker Chenille could figure just what someone was trying to pull, both with her emotions and her computer. Megan showing up around the same time as the message appeared didn't seem like a good sign either. Though her infamous million-dollar wedding dress had gotten the firm off the ground, it had also almost destroyed Raya and Flex's relationship before it started. It seemed as if they'd redesigned, refit, and remade Megan's gown a hundred times, only to have all the weddings cancelled. All time that Chenille could have been spending with Lyle. Oh well, that was in the past. At worst, Megan was in love with being in love, as all Chenille's friends and co-workers said.

Until today, Chenille might have agreed, but when her usually snobby and slim client waddled into her office in a pair of off-the-rack maternity jeans with a fresh face and hair swept back into a ponytail, Chenille didn't know what to think.

"Hey, Chenille," she said. "Sorry if I caused a problem in your schedule. I won't stay long. I'd just really wanted to come by and talk to you and didn't want to put it off anymore."

Chenille ran a hand across her forehead as understanding came to her. This was why Megan had called off the wedding, why she'd been so distant through many of their final design sessions. After a while, it was as if Chenille were designing the gown for herself. Now she knew why. "You're fine. Really. Come on in."

When Megan tried to lower herself into one of the chairs, Chenille scrambled around the desk, pushing her office chair in front of her former client. The other chairs had been murder on her back when she was pregnant. "Sit here. Those chairs are pretty but they're not the most comfortable."

"Pretty things are seldom comfortable. I'm learning that the hard way. The makeup was the first thing to go." Looking beautiful but vulnerable without her usual mask of perfection, Megan took the seat Chenille had offered. "Again, sorry to just drop in on you like this. I know you all hate to see me coming."

Lord help us, but the truth is the truth.

Still, it bothered Chenille for Megan to think that they felt that way about her. Especially now. "I wouldn't say we hate to see you coming, Megan. Anxiety might be a good term to describe our feelings." Chenille managed a smile. "Today is different though. It looks like there's all good news. I'm glad to see you. Congratulations on your pregnancy. If you'd let us know, we could have sent something over. Please leave your registry at the desk when you leave. How are you doing?"

Megan shifted in her chair. "You'd have done that too, wouldn't you? Gotten me a gift after the way I've treated you, all of you. Every time I see Raya and Flex together, I want to climb under my chair. I can't believe that I ever tried to come between them. I came up with the whole wedding dress thing in the first place just to embarrass her. It was all my mother's idea. Now look at both of us. Mommy has AIDS and I'm pregnant and alone."

Chenille dropped into the chair she'd tried to spare Megan from. With her not being pregnant, it sat just fine. Megan's words were a different story. Her former client definitely hadn't stopped by to talk about seam allowances. Chenille leaned over and pushed the door to her office shut. She took one of Megan's hands in hers. "How is your mother, by the way?"

Megan licked her lips as if trying to find the right words. "She's in an AIDS hospice in Englewood. It won't be long now. She's okay with it, though. She's made her peace with God, and she's helping me to make mine. At least she was, before I went and did this." She pressed a hand to her belly. "Here she is dying of AIDS and I go out and do something that could land me with the same fate. I keep trying to get to God, Chenille, really I do, but it's like I don't know how to be right. To do right. I just keep doing the same things over and over. I don't know any other way."

Something in Chenille's back tightened. Although the subject was different, there was a familiar ring to Megan's words, something that struck home. Wasn't Chenille trying to get to God too? Wasn't everyone? So many things to say came to mind, but Chenille stopped herself from saying any of them. Like Nigel had done for her that morning, she curled her arm around Megan's shoulder. She even took it a step further, reaching over to kiss her head the way Sergio had done, the way her own mother had done for her each night. It was hard being a woman without a mother. Chenille knew that very well. Megan must have been learning it too. Her tears soaked Chenille's blouse.

"I'm sorry. I'm so sorry, God. I'm so sorry . . ." She repeated the words over and over into Chenille's shoulder.

Though she had no tears left to cry and she didn't say the words out loud, in her heart Chenille said her own "I'm sorry, God" list too.

I'm sorry that I've been angry at you for taking Lyle.

I'm sorry that sometimes I doubt you.

I'm sorry that sometimes I don't trust you anymore.

I'm sorry that I'm mad at Lyle for dying, even though I know that makes no sense.

I'm just sorry.

The two women hugged again.

Megan pulled away first. "I'm not sure why I'm here. I don't know what I expected from any of you. I've put you all through so much. I just respect each of you, especially you, Chenille. You're strong. Your faith is strong too. Even though I didn't act like it all the time, I saw that in you. I saw Jesus."

Chenille let her hands go limp at her sides. If only what Megan said were true. "God is strong so that I don't have to be. And I'm glad of that because I am weak in every way. I was praying with you just now—not for you, but for me, because I'm sorry too. We all have things to be sorry for. It doesn't stop when we believe. We just have somewhere to go to get forgiven. Maybe you need to stop trying to get to God and just be still and let him get to you. He's very good at that."

Sounds like a plan. You might want to try it yourself.

Megan sat back in the chair and pulled her purse into her lap. It looked straight out of Target. Unbelievable. Megan saw Chenille looking at it and held it up. "What a difference a few years make, huh? With Mom being so sick and me being pregnant, all the things that used to be important to me just aren't anymore. I bought this right off the street. Ten bucks. Can you believe it?" She pulled out an envelope and extended it toward Chenille.

After the recent flurry of deliveries, Chenille wasn't sure if she wanted another envelope. "What's this?"

Megan offered a weak smile. "Money. Now that I'm pregnant, Daddy's concern has kicked in. I've sort of lost interest in a lot of the things I had before, so I'm trying to make good on my debts, if nothing else. That's the rest of the money I originally agreed to pay for the dress. You all did an amazing job every time, and I could have been married ten times for the work you did. I talked it over with my father, and we agreed that we should pay you."

Chenille just stared straight ahead, not knowing what to say. When she didn't move, Megan opened the envelope for her. Chenille gasped as she counted the zeroes, all five of them. Half a million dollars. The other half was long gone, doled out in many checks over the past few years, but this was unexpected. "This—this is too much."

Megan shrugged. "It really is too much, but it's fair and your firm definitely earned it. I never should have put so much money into a dress, even for a wedding. It doesn't matter now; nobody's saying it, but I know what they think. You probably think it too."

Chenille set the check aside. "We probably think what?"

Megan rocked forward in the chair. "You probably think that this is my punishment for all the things I've done. All the men I've been with. I mean look what I did to Raya. First I ruined her wedding, then she gets with someone else and I tried to break that up too. Then I find someone whom I really love and want to be with and everything, and I go and do this—"

"Stop it." Chenille's hands were shaking now, from anger instead of pain. "Don't you ever, ever say that again, do you hear me? Babies are not punishment, and it takes two people to make one of them. I don't care what anybody tells you, this is the biggest blessing of your life. You hold on to that—you just—just hold on to it." She didn't know what else to say.

Tears were trying to come now. More tears than Chenille had room for. Having cry days at home was one thing, but work? Well, that was another thing all together. Today was supposed to be an easy day. Tying up some loose ends and warming up for travel and meetings. This whole estrogen fest and crying jag was not part of the plan. And yet, the tears came anyway. Soon, she'd be turning into a sprinkler—and it was November.

Megan took a sharp breath and covered her mouth. "Oh my goodness. You lost your baby. I wasn't thinking. How could I have been so insensitive? I mean, I didn't forget exactly; I was just wanting to talk to somebody, and it didn't occur to me. I feel doubly stupid."

Chenille tried to stop crying, to tell her it was okay, but she couldn't. It wasn't okay. It hadn't been okay when Raya was pregnant this last time or now when Lily was about to deliver. Chenille loved them, she'd even made maternity clothes for both of them, but it didn't always make things okay. And yet, it wasn't anybody's fault. There was no one to blame. It just was. She hadn't really been thinking of it until Megan pointed it out.

"I'm so sorry," she said to Megan over and over. She was thinking of her computer now. Her message from Lyle. She had to get that figured out. "Thank you for the money. I'll have to talk to the board. Someone will send your father a receipt . . . or the check back. I still think it's too much. I'll have someone call . . ."

Megan was crying now too. "It's okay. Keep the money. Do something nice for everyone, especially for yourself. Thank you. For everything. I'll make an appointment next time." She got up slowly, and then stopped to scan Chenille's office.

Megan frowned. "Headed to a funeral?"

"Something like that." It occurred to Chenille then how it must look. All those white roses. Chenille's voice faltered a little as she held the door open for her guest. She stood still for a moment, watching Megan go, trying to make sense of what had just happened. One minute, someone had sent a message from her dead husband's blog, and thirty minutes later, Megan left her with enough money to ensure the company's solvency.

Shoot, with that much cash, she could turn the company over to Nigel and the others and just serve on the board. If she kept the check, that is. Even though Megan's father had originally agreed to pay a million dollars for the dress, they long since amended the agreement with him, charging him only for their actual work. As much as the check would be a blessing, Chenille wanted to do things in the best way and not just take the money because Megan was pregnant and feeling guilty.

"You've got mail," her computer trilled again in a voice so happy that Chenille wasn't sure whether to hug it or bash the machine into pieces. She kicked a trash can instead. She remembered Lyle complaining about people posting spam into his guestbook and even hacking into blogs of people he'd known. Why would anybody do something like this, though? Didn't they realize how much this would hurt her?

She could hear Raya knocking on the door she'd just closed behind Megan. "Did you just get that email? What's going on?" She'd been signed up for Lyle's blog feed too, receiving notification every time he had made a new post.

Chenille didn't open the door. "I don't know what's going on. I'm going to read it and see if I can get any clues. I'll let you know when I know something." She grabbed a fistful of roses for courage and clicked the link.

The words she read took her breath away.

Chenille,

You are reading this, so by now I'm quite dead.
I have a lot to say, but Flex will only let me

sit up for a minute, so I'll be brief. You're in the kitchen with Raya now, laughing. When you do that, it makes me happy. And angry too. I want you to laugh and have babies and go to dinner in your green velvet dress. So do it, okay? If you haven't already, find a guy (the bum!) and fall in love. That's an order.

Love,

Your First Husband

PS Don't break the garbage disposal. I can't fix it anymore.

She dropped to her knees in the office. A sea of arms reached in to pull her up, but she seemed to melt through their fingers, slipping away from them. She could hear her friends whispering above her, her employees moving around her watercolor paintings. "Is it real?" she asked someone with a pretty necklace. Probably Jean.

"It seems so, baby. We're checking into it now. Apparently you can set blog posts in the future. We're trying to get Flex on the line to see if he remembers anything."

Chenille closed her eyes. It was real, it was him. Lyle. She was sure of it. "He was right about the garbage disposal. I've had three already. He was so good with it." Someone tried to pry the roses from her hands. She held on to them even tighter.

"Do you think he knew? That I was going to kiss somebody? Why did he think I'd be with someone already? I was a good wife, right?"

"You were a good wife." Strong arms lifted her into her office chair. A man's arms. He smelled like baby detergent. He kissed her right between her eyes. "You still are."

Chenille straightened herself, loosened herself from Sergio's grip. She wasn't sure what Sergio had come for, or how he had been able to come considering his work schedule, but she was glad to see him.

Sort of.

The sight of him made her angry too. She had told Lyle time and time again during the early part of his illness that she'd never love anyone else. He'd given her a look, a patronizing stare. "Sure you will, Red. Sure you will." She'd been so sure that she wouldn't, yet he had known her better than herself, even pinned down the timing. It made her wonder just how much her husband had known about the timing of his own death. Still, it made her angry that Lyle had been able to measure her love so easily, so accurately.

Didn't Lyle know that sometimes she felt physical pain when her friends' husbands held their wives around the waist with a strong, easy grip? Did he know that sometimes she went to their old restaurants and made reservations for two, just to have another chair at the table? No, he didn't know, couldn't know. Sergio didn't either. This email was just a letter from a dying man who'd hoped to spare his wife some pain, and Sergio was only here to benefit from being in the right place at the right time. She saw right through the both of them.

She pushed away from Sergio, though part of her wanted nothing more than to have him take her home. "Thank you. I'm fine, now. Sorry you had to come in on all that. There was a message . . . well, I'm sure you know about it. Anyway, thanks for the flowers." It was time everyone stopped trying to protect the Good Wife. Including herself. She stood to her feet.

"I'm glad you liked the flowers." He smiled on one side of his face, the way Chenille's brother had when they were young. "I see everyone else in the place liked the flowers too. I guess I went a little overboard, huh? I didn't really think about how you'd get them home. I just wanted to show you—"

"Right. Well, thank you. You showed me. We'll talk later." Chenille realized how sharp her words sounded, but everyone in the room was hanging on to Sergio's every word. He was a nice man, a wonderful man, but he wasn't her husband. Regardless of what Lyle or anyone else thought, she wasn't ready for love. She might not ever be.

Sergio didn't look as understanding as he had that night in the hospital waiting room. He looked a little irritated with her, hurt even. He turned and left without saying anything else, not even good-bye. Chenille could hear the rumors starting to buzz even before everyone milled out of her office. Her friends lingered behind, offering everything from lunch to a ride home. She turned them all down, waiting for the last person to leave.

Alone in her office, Chenille unbuttoned Lyle's shirt. She slipped it off her arms until she was only wearing the angora shell she'd worn under it. It'd been stupid to tie the shirt up anyway, as cold as it was. She held it to her face, hoping to smell some trace of him on the dark cotton cloth. Nothing. Just fabric softener. Unlike his friends, Lyle hadn't been one to wear much cologne.

Chenille moved her hands down both sleeves and pulled until the first seam gave. It ripped easy from there, leaving a jagged gash. She'd trim it later and get some good squares out of it, maybe even save some scraps for a small blanket for the next baby that stole her heart. Maybe she'd even do another full-size quilt, one for her bed so that he'd always be with her. Or maybe she'd give it to Flex since he and Lyle had been prayer partners.

Maybe not.

If he'd had a part in all this, she was mad at him too. Chenille buttoned the last button on her coat and wound a scarf around her neck. She stuffed the two halves of her husband's shirt into her briefcase and pulled the strap high on her shoulder. She stared at the flowers, knowing she'd probably never get any more from Sergio. Maybe it'd been good that Raya took a picture after all. There was no point trying to take any of them, no point in trying to hold on.

As she turned to leave, a white bud that had been closed earlier in the morning opened before her eyes.

Chenille ran for the train, deciding as she went to make a quilt from the shirt and to keep it for herself. Maybe she could still be Lyle's wife, if only in her dreams.

6

Good news travels fast. Bad news travels faster. Chenille had never been more certain of both facts as she headed toward the weekly staff meeting the week after Megan's visit. She stood just outside the conference room door, knowing things might be said that she didn't want to hear, things that she'd gotten wind of already. As usual, there was nowhere to escape.

Even though Garments of Praise employed a lot of believers, everyone knew that as sure as there'd be worship during the meeting, there'd be gossip too. It was a Tuesday tradition that continued despite all Chenille's efforts to the contrary. Being best friends with the other designers who had their own dramas didn't help things. Having Nigel at the helm for the past couple years, however, did seem to be having some effect. Just not this morning. Though the meeting didn't start for another thirty minutes, employees huddled around the conference table in clusters, giving input on their own agenda.

"I heard they found her on the floor in

her office." One of the new girls from patterns talked out of one side of her mouth as she pinned something on her lap.

Someone whose name Chenille couldn't remember at the moment, a new hire, clasped her hands behind her back. "Her husband was a real romantic though, you have to admit, planning ahead like that to talk to your wife. He must have really loved her."

A blonde from production shook her head. "I think the guy was a little weird, if you ask me. A real nut. I'm alive, and I'd never put down all my business for the whole world to see. No wonder Rizzo's losing it." She was visiting from their new factory in New Jersey, here only for training. Chenille made a mental note to make sure she didn't return.

"You shouldn't talk about things you don't know about or people you don't know about. Take your seats, please." Chenille didn't have to peek around the corner again to see who that was. She knew that voice anywhere. Jean Guerra, Nigel Salvador's wife and his partner in the head of the menswear division. Chenille took a moment to thank God for her friends. She sighed with relief. At least now she could walk into the room without stopping someone midsentence. Her friends. What would she do without them?

Not much, seeing as how she hadn't even looked at the agenda for this meeting. It'd been enough trying to catch up on her rest and the backlog of work over the past week. This whole blog thing with Lyle had Chenille so distracted that she was just really getting back on track a week later. She'd called Sergio a few times to apologize for how things had gone when he'd come to her office, but he hadn't returned any of her calls. This morning, she'd had a bunch of daisies sent to the hospital for him. She thought later of how wrong it probably was to send a man daisies. Oh well, just something else to apologize for.

She took her seat and opened her notepad. She wasn't prepared, but she'd take good notes. Nigel had taken over running these meetings almost a year ago, and he always did a great job. Today wouldn't be any different, she hoped, and although she sensed that the employees' lack of confidence in her and her abilities was probably the most urgent issue, it would never appear on the agenda.

Nigel cleared his throat and took his seat next to Jean, a few chairs down from Chenille. Raya took the seat to her immediate right.

After a short call to order, the meeting started with a short prayer and a hymn Chenille had never heard but would have to ask for the lyrics to. As she unfolded the agenda on her lap and began to read it again, the door creaked behind her. Chenille didn't turn to look, not wanting to distract the group even more than the rude person had. That was until she saw who it was—a tall, dark man with raven hair and a boyish smile . . . and a daisy tacked to his lab coat. He'd obviously forgiven her, but his timing wasn't the best.

"Sorry I'm late," he whispered, leaning in to give her a quick, warm hug. "Something came up at the hospital. Something good, actually. I'll tell you later." He moved away quickly, taking the scent of oranges and cinnamon with him.

Chenille sat stunned, listening to the sound of her own breathing. Had Sergio just hugged her in front of every single one of her employees? He had, and just a week ago some of them had seen her nearly faint from her late husband's message. They probably thought they worked on a soap opera set instead of a fashion design firm. She blinked a few times, hoping that this was a bad dream. From the smirks and smiles looking back at her, she could rightly assume that she was awake and this was all really happening.

"Dr. Loyola! Good to see you again. So glad you can join

us." Nigel wiggled his tie and reached across his wife to shake the man's hand. "We had you down third, but please, go ahead. We wouldn't want to keep you from the hospital."

The man nodded, winking at Chenille before standing. Both Jean and Raya kicked Chenille under the table. This was getting worse by the second.

"Hello, everyone. I'm Serg Loyola. I'm here today to talk to you about the Pajamas for Preemies initiative to gather blankets and pajamas for the many premature babies who come through our NICU every year."

He paused to smile at Chenille. "Your boss has been kind enough to supply us with many of her own fabulous quilts, but we need more. In fact, we could even use some of the scraps you throw away from manufacturing. People around the city are signing up to make quilt squares from the fabric and patterns we provide. You're all welcome to help on that end as well. It's pretty easy." He reached into his pocket for a lopsided quilt square. "I've even made a few myself."

He laughed at the looks on some of the employees' faces. "Okay, it's not that bad."

He walked over to the projector in the center of the room and motioned for someone sitting near the door to hit the light switch.

Nigel spoke out from the door. "The presentation you sent me is loaded. You can go ahead."

Sergio did just that, clicking through photos of babies from the nursery and their parents. Some pictures showed the nurses, doctors, and other volunteers as well. The final shots seemed more recent, showing doctors and nurses whom Chenille recognized. She even laughed a few times, until a picture of her holding on to Erica's bassinet scrolled by with her name in the caption and her title at the company. Next came images of nurses swaddling babies in Chenille's quilts. The last photo, one of shirtless Sergio wrapped in her quilt and napping in the waiting room, made Chenille grip the table. The caption "The staff loves 'em too!" hit her just as hard. She wondered if the shot had been taken the same night Erica had died or if Sergio made it a habit of strolling about the hospital with no shirt on. She also wondered why the thought of someone having taken that picture, no matter the circumstances, made her more than a little angry.

Needless to say, she moved her feet to elude the rain of kicks underneath the table. Poor Nigel started coughing as though he'd swallowed a ball of fire. Chenille must have started sinking down in her chair, because Raya leaned over and nudged her in the shoulder.

"Sit up, girl. That was nice to see. You've helped a lot of people," her friend said.

"So have you," Chenille whispered back. "You worked on a lot of those."

Raya shook her head. "Not really. We just got you started. You did that work. All you."

Nigel cleared his throat, his sign for Raya and Chenille to be quiet.

Even more embarrassed now, Chenille apologized.

Sergio went on. "I'm leaving behind some pamphlets with more information. We hope that you'll all see this as a worthy project and think about how you can help, both as a company and as individuals. We'd love to have some of you as volunteers as well."

Chenille pressed her eyes shut, praying he didn't mention her again. She'd probably never go back to the NICU again. What had begun as trying to be helpful had become too personal, too complicated. That made her sad, but this was way more than she could handle right now, not to mention this whole thing today being totally unprofessional.

Dr. Loyola seemed more than happy to deal with Chenille though, smiling in her direction as he gave his final comments. "Again, through the kindness of your employer, we've been able to have many more beautiful, handmade blankets on hand. The one you see me sleeping with in the slide show was made by her, and it affects me just like the babies. I can't sleep with anything else." He took his seat to a round of hearty applause and pecked her cheek with a light kiss before starting to gather his things to leave.

Great. Just great.

Jean tapped her pile of papers against the table looking very, very pleased with herself and with her husband. Nigel seemed a little flustered, but amused. Chenille crossed her arms, trying to remember how many more workdays she had until Thanksgiving. This was way too much drama for any workplace, especially her own.

Before Nigel could continue with the next agenda item, one of the employees who'd been letting off steam before the meeting raised her hand. Chenille sighed. What was this, a press conference?

Nigel leaned forward in his chair. "Can it wait until the meeting is over, please?"

The young woman shook her head. "I have a question. For the doctor." She pointed to Sergio, who almost flinched a little, but then turned on his megawatt smile. His Vulcan haircut had been traded for a short, layered style. As Chenille looked at him, she wondered what she'd been thinking to kiss him that dark, sad night. He was gorgeous.

"Your pregnant fiancée was here last week. How does she feel about you flirting openly with the designer of her wedding gown?"

Fiancée? Megan? Chenille held on to the arms of her chair, sure the room would begin to spin at any moment. Though she definitely didn't like the woman who'd asked the question and wasn't sure she wanted to hear the answer, she turned to hear Sergio's response, just like everyone else in the room.

He looked as puzzled as the woman who'd asked the question. He turned to Chenille and then back to the soon-to-be-fired-employee. "First of all, I apologize for stirring any controversy. It was not my intention. I'm just an intense guy who can get a little carried away. To answer you, I'm no longer engaged to Ms. Ariatta, and until I saw her leaving here last week, I had no idea she was pregnant. I'm sure that, like all your company's clients, she'd think that my relationship with your boss is about what Garments of Praise is about—clothing the world with kindness and beauty. On that note, I'm going to have to leave." He stood, avoiding Chenille's eyes.

Nigel sighed with relief. Only a publicist could have coached him on a better response. "I think that about covers it for charity projects this week. Thanks for joining us, Doctor. You can look forward to hearing from us soon."

"I'll bet," someone whispered from the back.

Chenille held up a hand, signaling for Nigel to stop again. She stood slowly and began to clap her hands slowly. "Let's give the doctor a hand. Thanks so much for joining us today." She leaned over and shook Sergio's hand, although she almost kissed him on the mouth just for spite. This whole thing was more than she could take. No one should have to explain anything to her employees. Their careless gossip had gotten them all in a mess today. "Mr. Salvador, please shut the door after Dr. Loyola. I have a few things to say."

The room became quiet, punctuated only by the thud of the door closing. Chenille moved around to the front of the desk and unbuttoned her suit slowly, then cuffed the arms of her jacket as if preparing for a long meeting or a good fight.

71

Today it might be both. From there, she stepped forward into the middle of the U-shaped table and began to speak.

"Some of you don't really know me very well. You were hired by someone else while I was doing something else. And that's okay. We"—she motioned to Nigel, Jean, and Raya at the head table—"always knew that things would get to this point, that the business would get to this size."

Chenille walked to the woman who'd asked the insinuating question, and placed both of her hands on the table in front of her. "But make no mistake, people. Though I did not hire you, I can fire you. Though you don't know me, you may want to get to know me. Why? Because when my baby stopped moving and took its last breath, I was here, making a future for you. Because my husband sat in this room bleeding, to make sure that there was someone to take this place where it needed to go. Because the four of us have laid on our faces in prayer, in tears, and have taken the losses to make this place happen."

She turned and walked back to the front. "Those aren't the things I tell people because I've never felt they needed to be told, but obviously I was wrong. The doctor who left here today comforted me last week when I went to the NICU and found that a baby I'd been praying for—for weeks—had died. In my mind, she was my hope, almost the same as my own child."

Chenille paused and shook her right leg a little, fighting back tears. "Though I didn't realize at the time that he was the man who'd been engaged to our former client, Megan Ariatta, that man who just left here extended me more courtesy than many of you have today. It's been a hard week for me this past week. And a hard month and a hard year and a hard year before that. But you know what? Profits are up seven percent. We've hired twenty new people in the past six months and given $300,000 in clothes and other goods to people in need. You know why? Because it's not about me when we're here. It's not about you. It's about the work. If you can't deal with that, please turn in your laptop, cell phone, pager, or anything else that has been assigned to you."

She turned and collected her things from her seat, bowing low in Nigel's direction. "Mr. Salvador, please forgive my intrusion upon your meeting. I beg your leave."

"I'm proud of you." Raya looked straight ahead as she drove, turning down a side road lined with barren oaks, their boughs hanging over the road like outstretched hands. It was girls' night out, but with only two girls this time. Lily had been put on bed rest and Jean was at one of her granddaughter's school meetings. Chenille hadn't cared to ask for the specifics when Jean declined the invitation. In fact, since making a fool of herself in the staff meeting earlier in the week, she hadn't said much at all.

"Did you hear me, woman? I said that I'm proud of you."

"That makes one of us." Chenille stared out the other window, trying to decide where she'd spend Thanksgiving. Last year she'd gone to Raya's grandmother's apartment and eaten until she was sick. Despite the wonderful food, this year she didn't want to be around a lot of people. She wanted to think through this thing, this mess that was called her life.

They crossed the bridge to Staten Island, and Chenille immediately knew they were headed to a pizza place Lyle had loved. Italian all the way. A month ago, Chenille would have squealed with joy at the chance to go there. Tonight she just felt numb.

Raya shook her head and drove on, drawing closer to their

destination with every second. "Look, sometimes you just have to pull rank. There are a lot of new people, and in your efforts to be humble, people may get things wrong. True enough, you've had a lot of personal incidents at the office lately, but you see that none of the old heads were trying to trip. We've all been through it. I mean, Jean, Nigel, and I didn't have a clue what was going on, but we knew better than to disrespect you."

Chenille chuckled. "Perhaps it's I who have disrespected myself. All the things I'm doing now—going out at night with blankets and stuff. I probably never would have done those things when Lyle was living. Not even when he was sick, you know? It's like I'm just different now. Maybe people sense that and don't think they have to afford me the same respect. I can't say. I'm not proud of how I handled the situation. If you have to wield your power, you really don't have any."

The car went silent for a moment as they pulled into the shopping center where the pizza place was. Chenille knew that Raya would much rather have gotten pizza from the city if she was going to splurge on the calories, but she knew she'd get her turn too.

Raya stopped the car but kept the heater running. "On the other hand, Chenille, if you can never use your power when you need it, what's the point in having it? I think the difference you're experiencing is switching marital status. It's sad to say, but people really do treat single people differently sometimes. It hasn't been so long ago that I've forgotten. Not to mention Lyle did a pretty great job of protecting you."

Chenille sighed as they went inside. Her friend was right. Lyle really had put a wall of love around her, and as much as he could, he was still trying. She just didn't like his methods. She wanted to talk about Lyle's email tonight, to get Raya's thoughts on it, but she just couldn't bring herself to bring it up. Swapping husband stories was nothing when Lyle was alive, but now it felt like Chenille was sharing her last meal with someone who had her own restaurant at home.

Once they sat down, the owner and his wife rushed over to give Chenille a hug and a kiss. Was she well? She looked thin. Had she met another wonderful Italian man yet? If not, they had some friends . . .

Chenille managed to talk her way out of being set up, but there was no way around the extra cheese they put on her pizza.

Raya was more than happy about the special treatment. "It tastes much better like this. Anyway, have you called him yet?"

Stringing the pizza back to her plate, Chenille gave her friend a funny look. "Called who? Serg? Not exactly. A few short emails. He's been working straight through. Lots of double shifts. I'm glad. I'm still not sure what to say. Now that I know he was engaged to Megan, that puts a whole different spin on things. She and I are totally different."

Raya pushed her pizza away and checked her phone for messages. Flex was babysitting, but the little one could be a handful, especially at night. "I still can't believe that none of us recognized him. He does look different, and that was awhile back. Three or four years, I guess. A lot has happened . . . Wait, did you say that you are totally different from Megan?"

"Pretty much. Yes, I'd say that we're very different."

"Oh. So you're so much different from Megan? That's not what you said you told her when she bopped in your office with a bellyful of baby. So which is it? Is God a respecter of persons or what? I'm just curious . . ."

Too curious. That's the downfall of having smart, spiritual friends. They think too much and pray too hard. Chenille dug into her purse for her copy of Lyle's email. Analyzing that would keep Raya quiet for a few minutes at least.

A chorus of "Happy Birthday" struck up in the booth behind them, and Chenille felt like her brain was splintering from the noise. Was she the same person who'd once gone to rock concerts and enjoyed them? It was official. She was getting old.

"Here." She grabbed the envelope from her purse and slid it across the table. She kept her face on Raya's expression. It was Chenille's turn to be curious. What did her friend really think about what Lyle had said? She figured that her friend had definitely read it already on her own computer, though Raya hadn't mentioned more than how thoughtful Lyle had been to do it. From the way her brows were furrowing though, Chenille wondered if maybe she was wrong.

When Raya stood up and started putting her coat on and tossing out bills for the tip, Chenille was totally confused. "Hey, wait. What's wrong? Are you mad because he mentioned Flex in it? I talked to him. He didn't know what was going on, just thought Lyle wanted to make a post. It was actually your birthday, I think. Speaking of which, what do you want this year—?"

"Some honesty, maybe?" Raya stared at her until it seemed her eyes would bore right through Chenille's skin. She unfolded the letter, an invoice, and the check that was attached. The check from Megan's father for half a million dollars.

The wrong envelope! Chenille had meant to give that to Nigel . . .

Raya blew out a breath. "As for Lyle, he's dead, God rest his soul. You on the other hand, are supposed to be alive, supposed to be one of the partners of this firm. The founder, for goodness' sake. How could you be walking around with a check in your purse for this much money and not tell any of us?"

Chenille opened her mouth but no sound came out. "I was going to talk to you guys about it. I got caught up in everything else going on . . . I wasn't sure whether or not I was even going to keep it. After what happened in the meeting, I've decided not to. It's too much. I'm going to give it back."

A sharp laugh came from Raya's mouth. "You decided not to? You're giving the money back? What happened to all of us being partners with equal votes?"

People were staring now, including the restaurant's owners. Chenille dropped a twenty on the table before matching Raya's stride and heading for the car. "I guess I made the decision. I didn't think—"

Raya unlocked the car doors with her keychain before getting in and sliding under the wheel. She held a finger in the air. "You nailed it right there. You didn't think. Lately, you're not thinking at all. We're supposed to be a team now. CEO or not, we're all supposed to have a say in these types of decisions. If that's not how this thing is going to work, then you need to let me know now because, though we don't all make speeches, all of us have made sacrifices for this company."

Chenille buckled her seat belt and thought about how much pain Raya had endured just agreeing to make the wedding gown for Megan in the first place. She'd been caught kissing Raya's intended at the rehearsal dinner just months before Megan called with the offer. As spiritual as Chenille wished she were, the dollar signs had blindsided her. The company had needed the money, she thought, especially with her having a baby. It pained her to remember it. Could she have designed a dress for a woman who had wrecked her marriage? Chenille knew the answer. All her friends were better women, stronger women, than she was. "I'm sorry,

Ray. I really am. You're right. I'm still working the old ways. Can we pull over somewhere and pray?"

Raya ran a hand through her golden afro and backed out of the lot. "The only place I'm parking this car, Chenille, is in the garage by my house. If you want to come over and pray, you're welcome to join us. I'm more than happy to seek God, but I think you need to know that it's going to take some human action too to make this one right. We've been loving you the best we can, all of us, but maybe it's about time you returned to the land of the living."

7

Hearing the truth was hard. Admitting the truth was even harder. And yet, it had to be done. Sergio Loyola punched his hands into his lab coat and faced a hard truth—Chenille Rizzo wanted nothing to do with him. When he called her office, there was always the same kind but firm message: "She's in a meeting." He was starting to think that she'd be in a meeting forever as far as he was concerned.

He swallowed hard and went through his rounds, checking charts and children. Listening to heartbeats and talking with nurses and other doctors about cases, dictating his cases for transcription. He tried to go through the motions, to wield the confidence he'd had during residency, when he was engaged to Megan. Strangely enough, the feeling in his heart that they'd never make it to the altar had been a sort of weird security, allowing him some intimacy with no expectations.

He'd prayed for Megan, shared his heart and his faith with her, but all to no avail. For her, life had been all about the cold, hard cash and what it could buy. She'd thought marrying him would keep her with plenty of money to spend. That thought made him laugh. Everyone assumed doctors were rolling in money, but it wasn't always true. Student loans for a medical student were as much as some small corporate startups. So much that sometimes it woke him up in the night in a cold sweat. Yet on other nights, he slept peacefully, dreaming of the Scriptures he'd read before going to bed, often in a corner or on a bench in the waiting room somewhere. Though he was no longer a resident, the hours were almost as long. And evidently, so was his imagination. He'd sure fooled himself into thinking that Chenille was the woman God had sent to be his wife. She'd been like Rachel at the well, watering the sheep, only Chenille's water had been blankets and her flock a bunch of sick babies. Or so he thought.

That's where the similarities ended. Instead of being a young, innocent virgin who lived at home, Chenille was a big-time businesswoman and a widow. A good-looking one at that. Add in that she'd been married to the infamous Lyle Rizzo, known as much now for his dying as his living. He'd been dead two years and people were still going to the guy's blog for encouragement. To think that Chenille would even consider being with him had been a long shot, but Sergio had felt strongly that being with Chenille was part of God's plan. The feeling was just as strong as his conviction that he wouldn't end up marrying Megan.

Maybe he'd had the whole thing backward. Maybe Megan was the one after all . . .

Nah.

He'd fought too hard with his old life and his old ways to go back to being greedy and striving to get as much as he could. Not to mention the sexual part of their relationship, or lack thereof. Having a woman pretty much walk out on you because you want to wait to get married to make love is enough to wreck any guy's ego. A few years before he'd met Megan, he might have caved in, just to be able to say he wasn't a punk or something stupid.

Now he knew that what others mistook as weakness was something else all together. Meekness. It was one of the things Sergio really admired about Jesus, how he didn't try to explain himself or defend his position. Didn't flash his "Son of God" ID badge at anybody. Sergio ran a hand over the plastic identification hanging around his neck. How many times had he worn it when it wasn't necessary? Plenty. How was that really any different than Megan's lust for material things? His desires were rooted in the same thing, only he wanted approval and recognition. Though he'd considered himself the more spiritual of the pair, even Megan had picked up on his need for affirmation. He had a long way to go, that much he knew. He just didn't want to make the trip alone.

"Dr. Loyola to the nurses' station," the intercom droned.

Sergio checked his watch. His shift was over, but he'd planned to stay awhile and help cover once he got a nap. It wasn't like he had anyone to go home to, like many of the other doctors and nurses. He let a cold stethoscope bang against his chest and walked out of the nursery. What—or should he say who—awaited him there took his breath away.

"Megan?" He said her name like a question, but already his arms were open to her, his eyes taking in her distress, her need for acceptance. It was a look he'd often seen in the mirror when looking at himself. He hoped she wouldn't brush him off like she had the last time he saw her at Garments of Praise. Probably not, since she was here to see him and not the other way around.

The nurses, who'd been quiet when he first arrived, began to whisper in low tones as he took Megan's hand and led her down the hall. None of the nurses who'd known Megan during their engagement had cared for her, but her showing up more than a little pregnant got everyone's attention. One of the other male doctors gave him a look of warning as he passed by, but Sergio kept going anyway. Though Megan hadn't become his wife, she was definitely still his friend. His steps were sure. He knew exactly where he was going.

"I'm sorry for coming here," she said in the softest, most beautiful voice he'd ever heard come out of her mouth. "I know all this is a surprise. I should have called to warn you I'd be coming. I had an appointment here and was a little overwhelmed. Alone. I got the wild idea to come down and see if you were working. Which was silly in the first place. You are always working. Or at least you used to be."

They turned into the waiting room, the place where Chenille had kissed him. Sergio watched Megan sit down, stopping himself from reaching out his hands to help. He'd done enough of that lately, and it'd gotten him in plenty of trouble. He took a good look at Megan's belly and tried to calculate her due date. He stopped himself when the months got too close to the end of their relationship. He didn't want to know.

Megan must have read his eyes. "It was after. Some sort of rebound maybe? I don't know. That really doesn't make sense either, since I know you never really loved me. You just went along with my nutty wedding scheme because you were too much of a gentleman to make a fool of me. I will forever be grateful to you for that, for trying to love me, even though I was a total shrew."

Sergio's throat felt thick as he watched this new Megan, without her three-inch heels and four layers of lip gloss. Her hair, braided straight back into black, glossy cornrows, had tendrils poking in every direction as though she'd had them in for several days. Before, Megan had never allowed a hair to leave its place. Her former pink claw nails were now natural length and sporting clear polish. She looked and sounded . . . real. It was like meeting someone you thought you knew for the first time.

Rethinking his new hands-off policy, Sergio searched for words while putting an arm around her shoulders. Soft shoulders, not muscles and bones jutting through skin like before. There was a give to Megan now, a surrender in the way her body relaxed under his touch.

Meekness.

Somehow, she'd found it before him. And without him. Maybe he really had gotten things mixed up after all. "If you'd have asked me six months ago if I really loved you when we were together, I probably would have said that I thought I loved you. Today, though, I see the real you, the part you only gave me glimpses of before throwing up your walls and shutting me out." He leaned over and gave her shoulders another squeeze. "This person that I see now, someone willing to go through the hard times without knowing how God is going to work it out, that woman is someone I loved."

Someone I could love again.

Megan's lip started to tremble, and Sergio thought that she was going to cry, to tell him the whole story of what had happened since he'd last seen her, to answer all the questions he didn't want to ask. But she didn't. She didn't cry and she didn't stay. She pushed up out of the chair with one hand and reached out to shake his hand with the other.

Her formality seemed strange, awkward. "Hey, we were engaged, remember? Don't shake my hand or treat me like some stranger. I want to help you."

"You just did. " She smiled and grabbed her purse, one he'd never seen in her collection before.

When he tried to say more, she kissed a finger and held

it to his mouth. "Don't. You've done enough. You gave me Jesus. He'll see me through from here."

Sergio nodded in agreement as he watched her go, fighting off feelings of jealousy and anger. Now Megan was depending on Jesus? When she'd gone out and gotten pregnant by some other guy? Faith had been the one thing that stood between them, the thing that finally pushed Megan away. Now that her cruise ship had run aground, it was Jesus she held on to, but as usual, Sergio was left high and dry.

Chenille must be giving lessons.

"Thanks for coming." Chenille said the words in a tired voice, but she meant every word. She'd had another long weekend, one without her friends. She'd been in a battle, but she hadn't fought alone. She hadn't fought at all. That battle—and this one, the one that had led to today's meeting—had been the Lord's.

There'd been no staying in bed or eating junk food, just praying and praising, pushing and pulling. She'd thought a lot about what Raya had said, about what her friends had been through in the last couple of years while she'd been cutting up clothes and running to the hospital. Lily and Doug had lost their first baby not long after she'd lost Lyle. They spent several months and methods trying again before starting the process to adopt a child from China. That too fell through, even after several trips to a Chinese orphanage. They'd come home changed, though. Content. A month later, Lily had missed her period. Lily's perimenopause turned out to be a baby, just as her mother's health seemed to be taking a steep decline.

Now, as a major stockholder in Garments of Praise and a member of the board of directors, Lily held a protective hand over her belly and smiled at Chenille. It was a knowing glance, an understanding look. "Glad to be here."

Jean lifted the glasses from the chain around her neck and held them up to her eyes, peering over the documents Chenille had given them concerning the payment Megan's father was willing to make. Though Chenille knew that both Jean and Nigel had been working around the clock on the spring menswear collection, she watched as they pored over the pages, noting every number. This was their company too, and they cared about it. Chenille leaned on the back of the chair in front of her, wishing that she'd cared about them lately half as much.

Like Lily and Doug, Nigel and Jean had a lot going on. They were struggling to parent their adult daughter and teen granddaughter, who was a senior in high school and headed for college. It looked like the two of them would be footing the bill for the teen's education if a basketball scholarship didn't turn up from somewhere. Nigel had been diagnosed with post-traumatic stress disorder by a Christian psychologist but resisted any treatment other than going to the VA hospital a few times a month for Bible study and prayer with others like him who'd served in Vietnam. He and Jean were also training to do prison ministry in the facility where Nigel had done his time.

After over twenty years apart, they said they were still learning how to be married. Chenille had to laugh now, looking at them pinching each other under the table. If they were still learning, they certainly were good students. They shared a quick kiss before turning to Chenille with their full attention.

Chenille asked Flex to lead them in prayer before she got them up to speed on some items they all needed to vote on. Flex stood to lead them in a short prayer, something out of

Lily's prayer book. He opened his mouth to begin and then closed the pages, leaning his head to one side, like a puppy trying to catch a scent.

That made Chenille bloom inside like the white rose she'd seen in her office. How many times had she come upon Flex and Lyle sitting in her living room that way, heads cocked like two hound dogs? Too many times to count. Too many times for her not to know that this wasn't going to be a regular prayer.

Flex let silence speak to each of them, unafraid—as he might have been a few years ago—to just stand there for a moment to see what God wanted him to do. Finally, he moved, but not in the way that anyone expected. In a suit of the best cut and cloth, freshly cleaned and steamed to perfection, Flex took a step back from the conference table and lowered himself onto the ground, first on one knee, then two.

Long past questioning, Raya joined him quickly, a step ahead of Chenille. Lily tried to kneel but her belly wouldn't quite cooperate. She rested on the floor on her left side, knee curled up to her chest. Nigel and Jean disappeared for a moment under the table's edge then bobbed back up so that Chenille could see both of their heads, a sleek mass of silver hair and a short crop of auburn curls that made Chenille think of the burning bush.

Evidently Flex had the same thought.

He moved silently and solemnly, removing his own shiny loafers. "Father God, we thank you for Garments of Praise, for the partnership that you have brought us into. This ground is holy, fertile. Ripe for a beginning. This ground is good, but we've got to be willing to die to get the seed to grow. Give all of us a heart to die to ourselves, to do whatever you want us to do, even if it doesn't make sense. May each of us be radically and relentlessly obedient to you, today and for always. In Jesus' name, amen."

Chenille felt breath leave her as though someone had deflated a balloon. Radical and relentless obedience. That's exactly what God was requiring of her today. She had almost decided against sharing with her partners and board members the resolution that had come to her in the night like a touch in the hollow of Jacob's thigh. She had wrestled with God, trying to get some understanding, trying to get some truth. What she'd come away with was not what she'd come for, wasn't anything she would have ever chosen herself. But as she opened her heart to it and closed her mind to her own fearful, angry thoughts, she knew it was the only way.

Lily tried to get up off the floor but made a funny face. Chenille snatched a pillow from a couch nearby and told her to stay put. What would it hurt to have a meeting on their knees? It had been Chenille's posture for the past three days anyway. "Well, I guess we're just going to do things down here on the floor. It'll be fun. Not to mention that it's probably wise with all the decisions that need to be made."

Nigel laughed. "I'll say. There are a lot of zeroes on those papers. Not to mention that the company who prays together stays together, right, Chenille?"

"Sometimes." She tried to smile at the corny phrase she'd used to explain the blessings and hymns before all the staff meetings. Now, however, the phrase tugged at her heart, shaking her confidence. Had she really heard God? Would she really go through with the plan that had come to her in the midnight of her soul?

Radical and relentless obedience. It was time for Chenille to stop second-guessing herself, time for her to stop second-guessing God. She straightened up an inch or so and grabbed the piles of papers off the table and passed them around. Someone handed her a pen. A pink Sharpie, Raya's signature pen.

Chenille smiled and gave her friend's hand a quick squeeze. Raya held on a second longer. That said everything.

"You've all looked at the documents provided by the billing department and an offer of what Mr. Ariatta is willing to pay. I was concerned about the integrity of the situation, so I talked with Mr. Ariatta's accountant about it. His statement is among the documents. Many of you have probably already read it. It seems that Megan isn't taking any money from him herself outside of what's left of her trust fund and current investments. She's taken a job—"

"A what?" The thought of Megan working got Raya's attention. Everyone in the room looked a bit surprised. Chenille wondered what they'd think when she dropped her bomb.

She continued. "Yes, Megan has started a foundation for mothers with AIDS and their children. That's not what we need to discuss. First, I need to apologize to each of you for taking this payment under consideration without input from all of you, the partners, board members, and major stockholders. This is no longer my company. In fact, it never was. This is God's thing, and if he wants to bless us, who am I to stand in the way? I hope you can all forgive me for acting without you and doing things that are not in the best interest of the firm."

There were nods around the room. The door opened and Lily's husband Doug came in with a briefcase and furrowed brow. He sat down and crossed his legs, placing one hand on his wife's stomach. He didn't miss a beat in saying what the rest of them were probably thinking, what they'd been saying among themselves. "We forgive you, Chenille. I heard most of it coming up the hall. We know that you've been running this place for a long time. And doing a great job of it. But if the business is going to expand, I suggest putting more thought into your management structure. There need to be more defined layers of authority and room at all levels for both group and individual decisions. This one, though . . . well, it's a big one and affects us all."

Didn't Chenille know it. "Right, well, if no one has any more questions or needs any more discussion, I move that we take this to a vote." There was a quick second followed by ayes all around. Chenille wasn't surprised at all. "All right. Nigel, will you work this out with the finance department to make sure that there is one person in charge of dealing with this? At the budget meeting, we'll have to decide how to allocate the money, but it sounds like we might be able to do some of the expansions that some of you suggested when you came on board."

Everyone was smiling as Doug helped his wife up off the floor. "I'm not going to ask how you all got down here, but my old bones can't take it. Can we take this party back to the table, people?"

Nigel laughed. "You'd better keep some BENGAY in your pocket, old man." A momentary flinch as he pushed up off the floor gave away his own discomfort.

Everyone else made it to the table easily, each with a look of joy and relief. Someone asked how they were going to celebrate. Chenille interrupted. "Before we celebrate, I have one more thing to discuss with you all, something that's not on the agenda."

Everyone froze as if posing for a still photo. Raya's eyes darted around the room as though she were looking for something. Chenille was at it again.

Chenille reached into her briefcase and retrieved six letters, all sealed in gold foil. Each one looked like the envelopes passed to the hosts of award shows, announcing the winner. In this case, she felt the same, as though she was finally going to win. She wasn't sure if her partners would agree.

"Before you open the letters, let me say that I could not have survived the past two years without each of you. Your love, faithfulness, and hard work remind me every day that God is still here. That love is still here. For that, I thank you."

Flex left his envelope on the table. Raya pushed hers away, reaching for Chenille's elbow instead. Chenille patted her friend's hand and nodded to Nigel for him to read the letter aloud. He'd ripped into his first but had no change in his facial expression. He shook his head at her notion to go on, but handed it to Chenille instead. "You read it."

She gave him a quick nod of agreement, acceptance. It was only fair. She was supposed to be the big cheese, after all. It was her turn to let God be her wall. And though she was sure there'd be mixed reactions, she was ready too.

She held the paper on her lap, thankful that she'd gone for the heaviest, brightest paper stock they had in the office. "'After prayerful consideration, I, Chenille Rizzo, founder and chief executive officer of Garments of Praise Fashion Design, am submitting my resignation, effective immediately. My partner shares in the company will be offered for sale to the firm's partners to be shared equally among them. I will retain my private holdings of the firm's stock and be available for consultation as needed.'"

Chenille had read the letter out loud to herself the night before and then again this morning, trying to read fast in case someone tried to interrupt. She hadn't read it fast this time. She couldn't. And no one had interrupted. In fact, no one said anything at all.

8

He should have called first. That thought occurred to him later, after he was led into a room that looked more like a funeral service than a meeting. Before becoming a doctor, things like meetings had been really important to him; connecting with people had counted for something. Seeing people die every day and never knowing when you'd get to sleep or eat had sort of warped his mind some. After dreaming of Chenille again, and not in a way he'd be willing to recount to anyone, Sergio figured he'd better return her quilt once and for all. Since she wasn't taking his calls or returning his emails, a face-to-face visit seemed in order. That is, until he walked into that quiet, sad room. He probably should have been quiet too, but it was a little late for regrets.

"What died in here?" he whispered to no one in particular as he moved the shopping bag in his arms from one hand to the other. "It looks like a hospital waiting room. Bad news?"

"You could say that. I hope you get a better outcome than the rest of us." Mr.

Salvador, the older gentleman who'd put Sergio on the meeting agenda during his last fateful visit to the building, pushed out his smooth chin. The way the man moved stabbed Sergio with a memory of his own father, who'd worn the same neat clothes, who had the same streetwise elegance.

The pall of silence that filled the room drew his thoughts back to the present. For all his battles with life and death, whatever had died in this room was beyond Sergio's abilities as a physician. Of that, he was certain.

He cleared his throat as Mr. Salvador walked around him and out of the room, leaving his wife and Chenille's other friends behind. The others followed like a trail of tired insects, who'd found food but not had the strength to carry it home. Sergio smiled at Lily Chau as she tottered out last, holding her belly and giving him a wink. Whatever that was supposed to mean, he needed it. Not only was he about to be alone with Chenille, but it appeared that he'd chosen to come at a very, very bad time.

Her hands were trembling as she turned to him, waving her finger in the air. "I—I have something for you. Some quilt squares. I think they're in my office. Wait right here . . ."

He grabbed her by the waist and pulled her close, knowing instantly that this embrace was different than the way he'd held Megan the last time he'd seen her. This comfort was different than what he'd tried to offer then. Chenille was stiff at first, trying not to look at him. That only made him smile. He bit his lip to keep from chuckling out loud. She was stubborn as ever. Even when it made no sense. They had that in common.

Sergio tried to soften her, to make her rigid limbs rest against him, but they would not. Chenille would not. She looked up at him with large, wet eyes and said two puzzling words. "I can't."

He blew out a breath. What did that mean? What couldn't she do? Love him? Be with him? He'd already gotten that hint, though when they were together, when they were alone . . . His heart refused to accept it. Perhaps underneath her tense muscles there was the same knowing, the same feeling that they were good for each other, that they could make it. Maybe it made Chenille afraid. It sure scared Sergio. Blood and guts didn't bother him at all, but the look in Chenille's eyes made him question everything he knew.

Well, almost everything. Like a kid in Sunday school, there was one thing he knew for sure: Jesus loved him. He still sang the song every morning. It was corny, but it worked. He released Chenille's body and dug inside the bag he'd brought, pulling out the quilt with the purple daisies, a simple thing that had both comforted him and tortured him in recent weeks.

At the sight of it, Chenille couldn't help but smile. That was a good start. Sergio unfolded the blanket and gave it a quick upward jerk at one end, the way his mother always had done before making up the beds. There was no bed in the room, but the floor looked pretty clean. In fact, the carpet looked downright plush. He knelt down and spread out the quilt, then gave it a pat and waved Chenille over. To his surprise, she came.

He took off his jacket and balled it up into a pillow. As Chenille stretched out across the biggest of the quilt's flowers, Sergio gently shoved his coat under her head. He sat back on his heels, watching as she closed her eyes and made a deep sighing sound, a sigh of satisfaction.

Why did that sound just rip right through him? "That's how I feel about it too. That's why I brought it back. I can't say that I won't miss it."

I can't say that I don't miss you.

She pushed up, leaned on one elbow. Three curls fell forward over her left eye. Sergio bit his lip, fighting the urge to touch one of those curls, to push them away and kiss her on the eyelids, the way he did in his dreams, like the amen to a special prayer. That's what Chenille made him think of, the end of a prayer, the selah to a psalm. He pushed forward onto all fours and then onto his belly with his head resting on his elbows. Whatever she was going to say, he wanted to hear every word of it.

"I quit," she said with a weak smile. "I've never quit anything. My mother wouldn't let me. Not even Girl Scouts when I sold the least cookies. Not band when I realized too late that my mouth was not created for the flute. Not college when it got too hard and I ran out of brains and money. Not marriage. Not anything. Today, though, I quit the company that Lyle cashed in his retirement for. I quit my dream."

Sergio could be impulsive at times, but his mother had always said that he was a good listener. He'd had to be. "Just let people talk," she'd always said. "They usually know the answer. They just have to hear themselves say it." In school, in work, and even in his limited experience with love, the advice had held true. He hoped it would work today as well. He tossed Chenille's words around in his head instead of adding his own commentary, injecting his own experience. Instead, he inched closer and took one of her hands.

She didn't pull away. "I quit and they didn't say a word. What does that mean?"

He waited a few seconds and then shrugged. Maybe he'd have to break his mother's listening rules after all. "That means that they love you. That they need you. That you mean a lot more to this company than you realize. They can't think of this place without you."

The words came easily and they were all true. He didn't know Chenille's friends very well, but he knew how they felt.

The day when his father had come back for the last time to get his brother Blue and leave him behind, the same feeling had flooded Sergio's mind, had driven him into weeks of silence. Then finally, when watching his mother struggle to go to work in a blizzard, Sergio realized that things would go on without his father, without his brother. That he had to go on too.

He only wished he'd realized it sooner, before his mother had gone through so much, before he'd gone through so much. Bipolar disorder was a common diagnosis now. His mother managed well with a few pills and a good breakfast. Sometimes he wondered why they couldn't have helped her sooner. He had to let it go. Since meeting Chenille, he no longer had room for it all.

He ran his thumb over the back of her hand. She seemed impressed at the sight of him. "I see you took my advice on the nutrition. You look great."

She looked great too, although brown eyeliner had smudged into the creases below her eye, the places where he'd first seen her sadness. That bothered Sergio, the way sadness so easily settled onto Chenille's face, the way it seemed to know just where to go. He wanted to take some of that away, to make her happy again, if only for a little while. The wobbly, unsteady smiles she offered him every few seconds were a great start.

"I never knew apricots tasted so good. I've always loved sweet potatoes but never thought to buy any. They taste almost as good as your kisses."

A giggle escaped Chenille's mouth despite the hand she threw up to keep it captive. It was Sergio's turn for a satisfied sigh. He loved the sound of Chenille's laughter and knew he'd do anything he could to keep hearing it. Well, almost anything. He sat up on his knees again and pulled her toward him. This time she relaxed against him. Her hair tickled his nose. It was a glorious sensation.

"Don't worry about leaving your job here. You didn't quit. Not really. This place will always be a part of you. Your friends will always be in your life. Think of it as a transition. I know you prayed about it. If you're sure God is in this, then go for it just the way you did when you started the company. I'm sure people thought you were a little out there then too."

The hair against his face moved up and down, but she didn't say anything else.

So much for easy listening.

He held her as he had in the hospital waiting room. "Just trust and obey. That's all you can do. God will show the way, if we let him." He pulled his hands away. Had he said we? As in the two of them? "I meant you—that God will show you—"

She was laughing again, making that wonderful sound. Sergio tried to reach up and grab it with his mind, to tuck it inside his head to listen to later, like a favorite song. Before he could, Chenille turned. Her hands were on his face. Her lips on his cheek. "I don't know why you're always where I need you, when I need you, but I'm glad. Thankful. I wish I had something to give you, some way to—"

Before she could say something that would kill the little hope he had that one day she could feel for him what he was feeling now, Sergio pulled her head to his chest. "You've already given me more than you know."

She almost ignored the email. Reading her husband's journal from beyond the grave had been like discovering a treasure at first, but now, it seemed the opposite as she read each old entry, experiencing the loss all over again. It was like she was losing everything.

But after the third email from Raya asking whether or not she'd read today's entry, Chenille figured she might as well take a look. None of the partners had said much to her since her announcement the day before except that they'd like for her to stay on until the end of the year on a part-time basis at least.

The firm's lawyer was working through the buyout, and Ariatta Enterprises had made good on what had seemed an impossible sum a few years ago but would now simply help keep the wheels of expansion and transition moving.

The employees who'd made the snide remarks during the last staff meeting had just left Chenille's office after expressing again their regret for their comments. The word must have gotten out that she was leaving. Or at least there was some kind of concern. Though she accepted their apologies, she tried to reassure them too.

Now that she was alone in the office without much to do, Chenille had continued reading her husband's old blog, where he'd kept a journal of the last months of his life and evidently some future times in her life. Most of the posts were encouragement, prayers, and medical information for cancer patients. Until this past year, she'd never been able to make it through all the posts. It was too painful. Now it was the comments, so many that the pages were archived, that warmed her heart. People still came by, all this time later, leaving tributes and stories of their own. Until a few weeks ago, though, there'd never been a new post. Now there was a second.

Raya sent Chenille a personal message on the computer instead of coming to her office door. She wrote back, saying that she saw it and that she was okay.

She didn't even settle herself before clicking the link this time. What was the point? It was going to level her anyway. How could it not?

Hey guys, it's me again. I don't know if anybody still hangs out here, but if you do, thank you. I'm sure my wife appreciates it (hey, Red!). It's really my wife that I'm going to be talking to from now on here, so if things get mushy, just overlook it, okay? I am dead, after all. Cut me some slack.

And if my being dead is uncomfortable for you (or if you're worried that it's uncomfortable for me) don't be afraid. I'm in heaven now. I get excited just thinking about it. The only bummer is that my wife can't be with me when I play my first game of catch with our son.

Chenille looked away from the monitor. Even beyond the grave, Lyle knew how to put everything in perspective. Everything was black and white to him, heaven or hell, good or bad, God's will or not. Things had blurred for her, bleeding on top of one another into a gray blob of questions. But Lyle wasn't that way. Lyle could see the blessing in just seeing his son at all, even born dead. Lyle could see the blessing in his own death and reunion with their child. He could see God's hand in everything—while Chenille sat confused wondering what she'd done to deserve it all.

She forced herself to turn back to the computer screen and read the rest of the impossible words written there.

My wife is probably gagging right now. She thinks
I overspiritualize things. She's probably right. I
do think in the eternal pretty much, except when it
comes to her. I'm pretty much human then. Which makes
it all the more difficult to do what I'm about to do,
since I doubt she paid my last post any attention.

I'm releasing my redheaded beauty from pining away
for me. It's nice to know that somebody loves you
enough to stay home and cry into a bag of Cheetos
for the rest of her life. Really it does. And it's
so tempting to let her do it. But then I think of
how she felt against me at night, how she prayed
for me when she thought I was sleeping, how her
laughter sounded against my chest, or how good a
mother she was, I can't do it. When I think about
those things, I know that I can't keep her. I know
that she belongs to God and not me. She vowed
until death do us part, and though I know we'll be
together forever, I also know that it's time for
her to move on.

So will you pray for my wife, everybody? Don't fix
her up on any dates just yet—she's funny about that
type of stuff and I'm still alive as I write this
and don't want to think quite that far ahead today.
(Yeah, I lost some nerve since the last post. Maybe
it's just the new medicine.) Just pray. I'm pretty
sure God's got the matchmaking taken care of.

Thanks,

Lyle

PS This is a little weird, huh? I thought it'd be
fun to do this, but some of you may not agree. My

wife had nothing to do with this. It was totally my
morbid plan. Chenille, I'll love you forever.

Chenille forced herself to breathe as she scanned down
the full length of the page. There was already one comment
from an anonymous user.

Lyle,

It is a little strange commenting to a dead man,
but I felt like I had to say something. I really
wish I'd have gotten to know you better in life,
but you're funnier dead than most people are
alive. More honest too. You might have released
your wife, but I don't think another man on earth
has a chance with her. You were, and are, the
best.

Chenille smiled, even though she felt like her heart was
tearing in two. If Lyle was the best for her, if he was still the
best, where did that leave her and Sergio? She wasn't sure,
but she hoped there was room. She was almost scared to
know for sure. As scared as she'd been when Sergio had put
his hands on her face a few days earlier, when he'd called
her house last night.

They'd talked about dinner soon, but they both knew it
probably wouldn't happen. As she clicked on the link to Lyle's
post, her surety wavered. She was trying to stand up these
days, not lean on her friends or other people, but to lean on
God. Every time she tried, God seemed to show up clothed
in Sergio Loyola's skin.

She shook her head a little, forcing Sergio's kisses from
her mind as Lyle's entry filled her thoughts. Something that
he'd written about a new treatment . . .

Chenille felt her head bang the desk, felt the hot, wet tears rush over her face. She remembered it now, the day of that post, of the new treatment that had made him feel better, even for a short while. They'd fought that day. Not real fighting, just tense, silly words. He'd wanted his computer. Chenille thought he needed sleep.

She'd had a big meeting about something with somebody. She couldn't even remember now. There was always a meeting. Always something. And she'd been crazy enough to try to juggle it all, to try to keep the company alive while Lyle died a little more each day. And now, with him gone, she wanted no more of it. Resigning was definitely the right thing to do. It was just the wrong time to do it.

Why didn't I leave then? Why didn't I stay with him?

She didn't have the answers. Lyle hadn't wanted her to step down from the company to take care of him. Though he wasn't really into fashion, like Nigel or Doug, the firm was as much his as it was hers. He'd nurtured her dream when no one else would even consider it. He'd watched the company grow, sharing his wisdom, giving generously of his time, money, and prayers. And though it hadn't been often that she left him alone, in the end it'd been the firm that Chenille had chosen. The firm that no longer needed her. No longer understood her. That no longer made sense.

There'd always been more to it than money at the beginning. When you don't have any money, it doesn't matter much. A thousand or a million sound a lot alike when you don't have it. But then came Reebok and contracts, bright lights and even brighter-eyed employees. People who needed their paychecks to feed their families. Partners depending on her to make the right decisions. Somewhere in the middle of it all, the magic had been lost for Chenille. She had bills to pay too, so many that sometimes she made paper buildings out of them. Still, the work had to mean something. It had to be real. Each of her friends had taught her that.

She could see now that things were best this way, without her at the helm. Each of the others was doing something he or she believed in. Something they were passionate about. The only things that really got Chenille going these days were baby quilts and the maternity clothes she made for Lily when she got a chance. Lyle had said once that Chenille had a gift for helping others find their gifts, but that she struggled sometimes to find her own. At the time, she'd thought it an odd comment since she was leading the company and things were growing well. Now, she understood.

When you lose all you have, surviving isn't enough. And that's just what Chenille had been doing for the past two years, holding on to the company with a white-knuckled grip, determined to save something. Now she sat up and wiped her face, holding both her hands face up in her lap, releasing everything she'd fought to keep. Her heart beat faster at the thought of leaving, the way it had every night since she turned in her resignation.

As Raya entered her office, Chenille could see the questions in her friend's eyes too. *What will you do?* her gaze seemed to ask.

"I don't know what comes next," Chenille said, rolling her office chair closer to the desk. "I just don't know."

Raya looked around the office. "What are you talking about? I didn't say anything."

"You didn't have to." Chenille paused, then smiled at her friend. "Thanks for the heads-up about the blog post. It was hard to read, but I'm glad he left it. It just confirms my decision to leave."

Raya sat down in the chair opposite the desk. "I have to say that your resignation floored me. It took us all by surprise.

At first, I thought you were just trying to get back at me for what I said at the pizza place. Flex told me to pray about it. I am. I still don't really get it, but I trust you. I trust God."

Chenille picked up a pen and turned it over a few times, tip, then end. "Thank you. I'm in the same boat with you, clueless about everything except one thing, that I really need to leave. And soon."

Her friend gave a reluctant nod. "But what will you do?"

Chenille laughed a little, low in her throat. "I answered that when you walked in. I just don't know."

9

"You both look amazing." Sergio knew as the words left his lips that they probably weren't the right choice. Sometimes his honesty got the best of him, along with his nerves. These were the last two women he wanted to be alone with right now.

Megan, who seemed to have blossomed in both body and soul, answered first. "It's you who looks amazing, Serg. It's been so long since I've seen you out of a pair of jeans."

Chenille made a choking sound on the virgin daiquiri she'd ordered before Megan arrived.

"Don't worry, I didn't see him without the jeans on. I meant wearing something else." Megan put a hand to her head. "I'm shutting up now."

He hoped that Megan was kidding about shutting up. Silence was the last thing he wanted now. He and Chenille had been waiting twenty minutes for Megan to arrive, and in that time, they'd probably shared twenty words. He still wasn't even sure what he was doing here, but the lunch was free and the scenery, both around the restaurant and at the table, was quite pleasant. The conversation, however, left a lot to be desired.

"It's okay, Megan. You did get me there for a minute, but it was funny more than anything. I have to remember that you two were engaged and probably know each other a lot better than I know either of you." Chenille set her frozen drink aside and sipped her water instead. "Too sweet," she whispered, giving a quick explanation as the waitress appeared to take their orders.

Sergio gave the waitress a quick smile as he handed her the menus and then jumped back to the topic of discussion. He felt compelled to give an explanation of his own. "Megan and I do know each other, but not as well as you might think. She's never seen me out of jeans. Besides my mother, no woman has."

Way to go, Doc. Very impressive.

Megan lifted her glass and then held it in the air as though thinking something through. "Okay, a lot of things are making sense now. A lot of things."

Chenille fanned herself with a menu. There were tears in her eyes. Sergio wasn't sure if they were from laughing or crying, but he didn't like the sight of them either way. Or the condescending tone in Megan's voice. He knew already that he'd be leaving the restaurant a few pegs lower than he'd come in. Why'd he have to say all that? He'd been with Megan for over a year without telling her that he'd never been with a woman. His celibacy vow had been enough to make her think he was nuts. He hadn't wanted to add anything else to it.

His appetizer arrived, a shrimp cocktail. He thanked the waitress, but didn't eat any. His appetite seemed to have fled the room with his common sense. "Well, this is a great restaurant and it's good to see both of you, but I'm afraid I have to be going," Sergio said, wishing he'd made his exit before Megan had even arrived. Seeing her so pregnant and radiant made him angry, jealous, and happy all at the same time. Seeing Chenille just made him crazy. Putting both of them together just made him tired.

Chenille grabbed his wrist. Megan's too. "I'll make it quick. Just give me a minute. I just wanted to ask both of you to pray for me. I'm leaving the firm—"

"What?" Megan looked shocked. "Are you serious?"

Sergio only smiled. He was proud of Chenille for doing what she thought was right and hoped that whatever she chose to do next would bring her happiness. It would have been a lot nicer if they could have talked more about it alone, but being here now counted for something. Maybe she considered him as some kind of friend to kiss every once in a while. It was a nice benefit, but he wasn't sure he liked it without some other things attached. The friendship part meant a lot, considering the friends she had already.

Megan's mouth hung open for a second. Sergio was grateful it wasn't full of salad. She rested a hand on her stomach. "What did Raya say? I know you two are so tight. She's going to miss you. Jean too. I have to say, coming there for fittings and stuff, I got a little jealous. You all seemed to be so close."

Chenille straightened in her chair. "We were—are. We are close. We always will be. Maybe just not physically close like we've been for the past few years. I'm not sure exactly what I'm going to do, but I know that it has to mean something to me personally. I invited both of you here today because I wanted to hear more about the projects you each work with."

Sergio leaned back in his chair a little. So much for being

Chenille's friend. She was looking for a new project, something else to pour her life into. While he would have loved to have her as a full-time volunteer in the nursery and as a part of the Pajamas for Preemies program, he didn't know how he felt about auditioning against Megan for her interests. Chenille had been coming to the hospital all this time; didn't she know what the hospital had to offer?

What you really mean is, doesn't she know what you *have to offer?*

By the time Sergio realized that he was thinking of his own pride rather than what was best for the babies, Megan was already going full speed ahead with her pitch.

"Bloodlines is a nonprofit organization designed to assist HIV-positive pregnant women and children with resources to help them navigate the pregnancy, birth, and the first year of an infant's life. We provide resources for medical services and child care for HIV-positive mothers and children as well as more basic needs like maternity clothes, diapers, and infant clothing. I'd actually come prepared today to ask your firm to consider doing a maternity line and giving some of your proceeds to Bloodlines. We'd love to have you in any capacity though. Really. And by the way, both of you, my mom passed away since I saw you last."

Both Chenille and Sergio expressed their condolences, but Megan didn't leave room for pity. She just thanked them and went back to the focus of the meeting. Her mother had been ill for so long that it seemed to her a fact as simple as her own pregnancy. People lived. They died too. She was definitely alive.

Megan's face, as well as her words, were on fire. The shame and hurt that Sergio had seen on her face a few weeks ago was gone. Advocating for other mothers had definitely done something for her outside as well. Her hair was braided again today, this time in two long braids with a part down the middle. She'd come into the restaurant wearing a pair of jeans and a sweater, with a leather messenger bag across her body. Since it was his off day, Sergio had opted for a pair of slacks and a nice shirt. There were never any real off days, though. He intended to stop by the hospital to check on a few things after leaving here, which couldn't happen soon enough.

Chenille was bent over a notepad, taking notes on what Megan had said. When Megan had mentioned a line of maternity clothes, Chenille's pen had moved like crazy. She finally stopped and looked over at Sergio.

He leaned forward, looking past Chenille toward Megan. "Well, that act is hard to follow. Megan, your foundation sounds amazing, and I look forward to talking with you to see if there are any ways the hospital can partner with you as well. Even though your mother is gone, I know she's proud of you. I'm proud of you too."

"Thank you. Mom is proud of you too. She really liked you a lot."

This was getting too weird, like old home week, only at the wrong home. Best to be polite, though. "And I liked her."

He sat back, focusing on Chenille now. As a waitress delivered his salmon, he lifted a fork and used it as a microphone. "As for you, I'd love to rattle off the list of all the things we do at Pajamas for Preemies, but I think you know what we do. We give blankets and pajamas to preterm babies. We let their parents and families focus on getting through the stress of having a sick child instead of trying to figure out where to get clothes small enough to fit them. You've been a welcome addition to the nursery and the blanket donation program for a long time before I came on board. We'd love to see you stay and even consider expanding into a full-time volunteer."

Chenille didn't take any notes this time. She just listened

to Sergio's words, watched his movements. He would have paid a high price to know what she was thinking. He would have paid just as much to keep her out of his head.

She reached for his hand. "Thank you for all you do. It's been an honor to donate the blankets to the nursery and to be able to bless families who come through there. What you do is very important too."

At the moment, all Sergio could think was that Chenille's touch on his skin was very important. He thanked her, and the three of them shared a quick prayer and a quick meal. Though he'd planned to be the first to leave, it was Chenille who was called away on an urgent business matter, leaving Sergio and Megan alone.

She motioned for him to move closer as soon as Chenille cleared the door. He shook his head but took the seat next to her, wondering what she'd have to say about their strange lunch with Chenille. What she said, however, had nothing to do with Chenille at all.

"It's a good thing for you I've changed, Sergio," she said, squeezing his arm just above the elbow.

He looked at her full lips and bright eyes and tried not to think about what she was trying to say. Either way, she was right. Megan had changed a lot, and it was a very nice change at that. Sergio, however, had not changed. He was still a man. Through and through.

"You look good. Sounds like you're doing good too. I guess that's good for all of us." *I sound ridiculous.* He stood, knowing that it was truly time to go, off day or no off day. Being so close to Megan and Chenille had his mind shooting off in too many directions. His heart too.

Megan struggled to stand. Sergio pushed her chair back. The slight movement seemed to remind Megan of something, perhaps their many dates when he'd run to get in front of her to open a door or pull out a chair. "Thank you," she said, accepting her bag as Sergio bent down and handed it to her. "That used to drive me a little nuts, the way you insisted on opening the door for me all the time and always pulling out my chair. I liked it well enough some of the time, but everywhere we went seemed a little excessive. Now, I miss it very much." Without warning, she leaned over and gave him a kiss.

What was up with women kissing him lately? Sergio wasn't sure, but he wasn't complaining. Why did it seem strange, though, as if he were somehow cheating on Chenille? She wouldn't give him the time of day lately, except for this bogus meeting, whatever that had been about. She talked to him like he was some corporate client. Like she didn't know him at all.

To be honest, he missed Megan too. This lunch confirmed it. He'd relaxed totally when she appeared. He'd thought it was just out of habit because he knew her better, but now, kissing her again, he just wasn't sure. About anything. They pulled back at the same time, then laughed about it.

Megan sighed a little. "I wouldn't trade my baby for anything now, even though it's a lot harder than I thought it would be. Than anything for me ever has been. My one regret in all of this, though, is that things turned out the way they did between us. Whoever ends up as your wife will be a lucky, no, blessed, woman."

Sergio felt his heart twist into knots. Who would be his wife? He'd been naïve enough to think it might have been Chenille after some weird, sad moment in a waiting room. Now he knew that Chenille was sad most of the time and probably wouldn't be ready to even consider a relationship for a long time. And even then, there was no guarantee she would want him. Maybe the answer to Sergio's prayers had been in front of him all along. It had just taken some hard times to rip off some of the wrapping paper from Megan so that he could recognize who and what she really was.

Who she really could be.

As they left the restaurant, he took Megan's hand in his and pressed it to her belly. He stooped a little and spoke in an even voice. "Hi, baby. How are you? It's me, Serg. Just hanging with your mom today. I can't wait to meet you, and I pray that you'll be an amazing person, that you'll change the world for Jesus . . . just like your mommy."

He straightened up and stepped right in front of Megan. Her lips were close enough for a kiss, but he thought better of it. Instead, he gave her a hug and slipped one of his cards into her pocket. The one with his cell number on it. "It doesn't have to be this hard. I'm here for you. Call me when you need me."

Chenille was too excited to eat, but that didn't stop her friends from piling her plate with turkey and dressing and all the other goodies loading down the Thanksgiving buffet table. As jittery as she was, they must not have trusted her to make her own plate. They handed it to her once most of the helpings were generously mounded on it.

Raya's grandmother almost ladled gravy right onto Chenille's notebook. "Now I know you didn't try to bring work into this Thanksgiving dinner."

Chenille took a napkin and cleaned off the page, trying to think of something to say. The truth would do. "This isn't work, Gram. I quit the firm. This is play."

As beautiful as ever, though a little more stooped than Chenille remembered last year, Raya's grandmother nodded in understanding. "Ah, midlife crisis. It comes with or without the man, you know. And much sooner than they all say. By the time people start buying sports cars and running off with the help, they've been going crazy for years."

Wasn't that the truth? She and Raya would both be thirty-three this year. A friend at church with nine children and always a smile to spare had congratulated Chenille on making it through what she called "the Jesus years." Chenille had listened in wonder as the woman described how Jesus's life had twisted and turned during his last few years on earth. Now at the end of the year, Chenille had to agree. It'd been a long, hard year but a good one too. Some things had definitely been nailed to the cross; other things were in the process, she thought, as she scanned the room for somewhere to sit.

With so many people coming to eat at Gram's, there was always a main dinner table for moms with kids, and the adults scattered around at card tables and TV trays. Chenille found herself looking for a quiet corner. When she did sit down, she nibbled at the delicious food for a few seconds before going back to her notebook. Since her meeting with Megan and Sergio, her mind had been exploding with ideas. It was as if she was starting all over again, like it was in the beginning. There were no "ideal customers" or profit and loss statements working against her. Just dreams.

One idea in particular, the image of Sergio at the restaurant looking so handsome, smelling so good . . . And what he'd said, about no one besides his mother seeing him out of his jeans. That had stayed on her mind for days. He seemed so bold when she'd met him. So confident. Though he'd explained during one of their conversations that he'd become a Christian in high school, it hadn't occurred to her that he'd been a virgin. Virgins didn't walk like that, did they?

Of course they did. She ought to know. Lyle hadn't been with anyone before her either. Though they'd grown up in the same faith, Chenille hadn't been able to offer the same gift of purity on her wedding night. She'd regretted it until Lyle reminded her that there were always new things to feel bad about so she might as well let that one go. And she had. Pretty much.

Some of that regret, some of the pain, hung around, though, fueling Chenille to succeed, to give. She and Lyle had never really talked about her dark time in college when she'd walked away from the Lord. He hadn't wanted to know about the things she'd done, the men she'd been with. Chenille really hadn't talked to anybody much about those times except Raya. Until her lunch with Sergio and Megan, Chenille hadn't thought much about those times at all. Now the memories came as she paused from scribbling new dreams in her notebook. An accusing voice telling her that she'd be better off never to love again. Did she want to go back through all of that ancient history?

"I hope that's a decision about coming back to the hospital that you're writing down. Or at least a note to me declaring your undying love."

Chenille stayed hunched over her notebook, but she knew from the voice, from the smell of figs and peppermints overlapping the gravy and cranberries, that it was Sergio. As he sat down, Chenille looked around the room for her friends. They were obviously responsible for this. She saw Lily first, clapping herself silly. No wonder none of her friends had insisted that she sit with their families. She wasn't sure how, but she'd make them pay.

"Just some ideas that won't leave me alone." She closed the notebook and marked her place with a pen. In the back of her mind, she wondered if her meeting with Megan and Sergio had really been about her business plans or just her personal plans for her future. She'd really had some questions for the two of them, some things that she'd needed, wanted, to know. Something had stopped her from asking.

Sergio nodded a little. "I know how that is. Ideas that won't leave you alone, I mean. I hope yours work out better than mine." He took a bite of sweet potato pie and looked amazed at it, staring for a few seconds before taking another bite.

Chenille tried not to laugh. She'd had the same reaction as a kid trying Gram's food for the first time. It tasted too good to be real. "I hope you brought a better appetite today than you had at the restaurant the last time I saw you. It all tastes like that."

He took a bite of ham. "I see that." He got quiet then, but Chenille wasn't sure if it was because he was occupied with the food or because she'd mentioned their lunch. Though she'd felt bad about having to leave, she'd sort of felt like the odd person out once Megan arrived. And she hadn't liked it. With Sergio's change in tone when Megan joined them, she wondered if the two of them weren't headed toward getting back together. If so, she'd been the one to help them light the spark again.

Nice going.

Quiet settled in on their table as it had at the restaurant. Somebody's baby started wailing a few tables over. Sergio jerked to attention, then went back to his plate. He bit into each item with expressions of amazement and surprise.

Chenille's words were a surprise too. Ones she hadn't planned on. "So, do you think you and Megan will get back together? You both seemed very comfortable with one another when we got together."

That got the guy's attention. "Wow, you jump right into the light dinner conversation, don't you?"

She tugged at her earring, wanting to slide under the table.

"It's none of my business, really. Forget it." She focused on her own plate now, digging into a forkful of green beans almondine. It was even better than last year's, if that were possible.

He pressed his lips together as if savoring a flavor, then put down his fork. "It's okay. I don't mind talking about it. I don't know what the future holds for Megan and me. It seems like we're comfortable with each other now, but it really wasn't that way when we were dating. Even when we were engaged. Getting pregnant did something to Megan. She's opening up to me. Before, things between us were kind of like . . ."

Chenille swallowed her food in time to finish the sentence for him. "Kind of the way things are between us?"

Someone turned on some calypso music in a back bedroom. The strains filled Raya's grandmother's small apartment like a fog. Sergio tapped his foot immediately. "Yeah. Like things are between us. I guess it's like this music, like doing a dance. Each person has to be into it at the same time or somebody's toes are bound to get stepped on."

She got the message loud and clear. Though she hadn't known Sergio long, she'd hurt him. Pushed him away. She'd been doing the same to her friends lately, trying to work through everything by herself. Trying to dance alone. Now she was tired of it. Watching as Raya and Flex pushed their table aside and started to dance, Chenille picked a spot on the floor with her eyes.

Sergio grabbed her hand as she reached for his. Chenille stood slowly, letting the excitement settle into her toes. "One thing, though. I don't know how to dance like that." She pointed to Raya and Flex, moving together as one fluid body, from hips to arms and back again.

Sergio lifted his shoulders almost to his ears. "So what? I

don't know how to do it either. At worst, we'll both fall down. At best, we'll learn it together."

Chenille smiled to herself as he led her to the corner of the living room. It was the best logic she'd heard in a long time.

10

"All right, Ginger Rogers. Spill it." Raya had a letter opener in her hand and tried to look villainous.

That only made Chenille laugh harder. "About what? Sergio or the other stuff?" She ran a hand across her notebook as she said it, just to be cautious. It was almost December now. The Advent traditions that her friends practiced every year were something she'd never quite made it all the way through. She and Lyle had talked about making one of those felt calendars for their Anthony. After they lost him, they never brought it up again. She opened her notebook and scribbled down a note.

Celebrate. Make felt calendar. Bake cookies with silver sugar balls.

Her friend made a dive for the notebook. She missed. "That raggedy spiral book is driving me crazy. I thought I was bad with my sketchpad. You're dancing with guys and wearing a new perfume. Dressing all colorful. I hate to see you leave us, but if it's going to set you off like this, maybe it's a good thing."

Chenille threw her head back and stared at the ceiling. Was she different? Yes, she felt different. A lot different. She lowered her eyes, locked stares with Raya. "Look, I don't know what, if anything, will happen with the guy. I may never be ready for that. I guess it's something that I think he smells good and I kissed somebody. I'm still mad at Lyle for knowing that I'd need that again, that I'd want that. I thought I'd be above it, that I'd just want Jesus, not man-love. But maybe I'm not above it. Maybe I'm just a woman who needs a kiss now and then." She blinked, thinking she might start crying, but she didn't. Words that might have stabbed her heart six months ago felt good today. Strong.

"Man-love? You are so funny. Even when you're trying to be serious."

Chenille had always been the one to tease the others about their expressions when they'd met someone. *Man-face*, she'd called it. Her friends had been kind enough not to identify it, but she was sure she'd worn the look a few times now herself.

Raya lifted a box from Chenille's desk and set it on the floor. It was one of the last boxes she'd packed up from her office, which had more fabric scraps and craft supplies than anything. Lily's office was full of her graceful rock projects and funky music CDs. Raya's office was like a cross between Toys"R"Us and fashion week. Jean and Nigel had a sleek, architectural space. Chenille's office had always been pretty much bare. Just the essentials: computer, file cabinets, a good chair, lots of pens, a phone. The stuff to get the job done. She'd given up on office plants after killing so many. Her only decorations had been a few pictures of company milestones and the Garments of Praise logo on the back wall. Raya had insisted on the logo once they got new offices. Said the white walls gave her a headache. Chenille understood again, remembered the power of color, the shades of her dreams.

Raya tried to slip the notebook off the table. Chenille caught her wrist. "Don't. Please. I know that if it was turned around, I wouldn't give up until I knew, but don't be me. Be you. I have something growing in me again. Not a baby, but something alive. I like how it feels. Can you understand?"

Her friend tried to smile but ended up with a lopsided smirk instead. Her voice broke up a little as she spoke. "I think I understand, but I'm scared. It's like I'm losing Lyle all over again. Like I'm losing you. I'm glad you've got this guy and your notebook and all that. I'm sorry I freaked about the money. I'm sorry if that had something to do with you stepping down. But more than anything, just don't slip away from me. I'm getting too old to try to grow new friends. It takes a long time, and like yours, my thumb is less than green." She picked up the remains of Chenille's last office plant from beneath the desk. They both laughed at that.

Chenille opened her arms to her friend. Opened her heart to her words. Sergio had said something at Thanksgiving about being open. About being real. Maybe it was time to open the tattered pages of her notebook, to share the scattered dreams growing in her mind. She hugged Raya harder. "I have a dream."

"So did Martin Luther King Jr. What are you talking about, girl? Speak plain. You know I have kids now. I can't grasp subtleties. You have to lay the thing out." Raya wiggled up from Chenille's grip to get some much-needed air.

"Well, I'm going to—"

There was a knock at the door. Lily and Jean coming to check on something that Chenille couldn't quite make out. They'd probably made it up on the way down the hall. She knew what they'd come to check on. Her. And she was glad of it.

Lord, I've been with these women every day for so long. How will I make it without them?

No answers came to heart. No solutions to her soul. Yet, when she held her arms open to them, her friends—the women who'd worked with her, mourned with her, laughed with her—Chenille felt an easy assurance. Everything would be okay. "Group hug, people. I was just about to tell Raya some of my ideas."

"The secret notebook? Now? Oh, I want to hear," Jean said, taking a chair off the stack piled in a corner waiting to be moved somewhere else in the building. She took down another for Lily. "Raya, I thought you would have done your spy girl thing by now and cracked the case on that, but this works too."

Lily shook her head. "You all are so nosy. Why can't she have something to herself?"

Raya shrugged. "Besides the fact that it's impossible around here, why not? As for the spy thing, I tried already. I think she sleeps with that thing." She sat down in the chair Jean had set out for her and folded her arms. "Let's hear it, babe."

Chenille's confidence of a few minutes earlier seemed shaky at best. So many things? How best to explain?

Just say it.

That was one approach. "I'm going to make things for mothers. And babies. Maternity clothes, quilts. Everything."

"Yeah!" Lily tried to stand up and give Chenille another hug, but she didn't quite make it to vertical. She bobbed back down into the chair. Jean gave her a "be careful" glare. Lily nodded but waved at Chenille with excitement. "This is great. So, so great. Too bad you didn't get the idea earlier. Do you think anything will be ready before I deliver? Will you do hospital robes? Gowns? Last time, when I lost the baby, the clothes were horrible. I was itchy and cold."

Fighting the urge to grab her notebook to get the details, Chenille reassured her friend the best she could from memory. "Yes, there'll be a whole line for the hospital stay. A prepacked layette for mother and baby that can be pulled on wheels. All soft, comfortable things. Pretty but functional. Oh, and proceeds from each line will go to different charities like Megan's Bloodlines foundation. A certain number of blankets would be donated to hospital nurseries throughout the country. Families who lose babies will be able to give blankets in the children's names with something about their child on the tag."

Raya, who'd been silent until now, gave a thumbs-up of her own. "I have to give it to you on this one. I don't know how you do it, but your ideas always hit more than the market. They hit the heart. This is really needed. Being pregnant this last time was really hard for me, and that was with a husband, you all, church folks, Gram . . . Every little bit of love helps."

All eyes went to Jean then, especially Chenille's. She hadn't realized how much the approval of her friends meant to her. They were all smart women, godly women, praying women. What they said, what they thought, usually predicted fairly accurately how things would go. So far, she had two good pieces of feedback, but the way Jean was tucking one of her pumps under the chair and bringing it out again had Chenille a little worried. Very worried, if she was honest.

She pulled down a chair of her own and tried to get a read on Jean's impression of her ideas. "So . . . I know it's been awhile since you had a baby, but you know more about this business than any of us. What do you think? Will it work? Is it a good idea?"

Jean swallowed hard and spoke in a dry, quiet voice. "It's

a good idea, Chenille, but that's not enough. Good ideas are a dime a dozen. It's the people that make it work. You've got to have the right people. You may get the right people for your project in a few years. Probably about the same time we find a CEO that can guide us where God is leading. We both will have lost time. Momentum. Destiny. And for what? To go out and rebuild what you already have?"

"It's not the same thing." Chenille hadn't been prepared to defend herself or her decisions. She definitely wasn't prepared for the sting of Jean's words across her face. And her mind.

Her friend and partner stood and smoothed her knit suit. "It is the same thing, Chenille. It's clothes. It's families. It's Jesus. It's what we do here. It's what you'll do there. Why? Because it's who you are. This is the same reason I get sick of all our marketing meetings about the brand and logo and all that mess. We"—she pointed at each woman around the room—"are the brand. Chenille is the visionary. She sees in her heart what we see with our hands. Now we're all walking blind."

Chenille didn't defend herself this time. She didn't say anything at all. Raya started to say something, but Chenille shook her head. Her aching head. It'd been like this before, at the beginning of Garments of Praise. She'd had Lyle then. He'd protected her from confusion, helped her point her eyes straight ahead.

She picked up her notebook and flipped through the pages, past the page of company names and logos, past the pieces of the business plan, the marketing program. It had been diamonds in her eyes a few hours ago; now it all looked cheap and sharp, like glass in her hands.

All three of her friends were still in the room, even Jean, who she'd hoped would walk out and slam the door. It would have been the right punctuation to her little speech, though far from her style. Jean said all that cutting up and running out was for the movies, that if you were going to say hard things to people, you'd better be able to stand there and go through the hard times with them too. She was true to her word, both now and for all the years that Chenille had known her. And what had she been to Jean? To all of them? Some flighty widow having a midlife crisis? She hoped not.

"I'm sorry. I know that each of you gave up something to be part of this company. That it cost you to stay. I know that Raya could be making gowns right now, that each of you have surrendered parts of your dreams to make my dreams come true . . ."

Raya and Lily shook their heads, but it was Jean who spoke before them, who took Chenille's hands in hers. "We didn't surrender to you, honey. We surrendered to God. We love you, really we do. But it's bigger than you. Bigger than all of us. So if you're hearing the Lord on this and you're sure that you're sure that you're sure this is what you should do, then go for it. It is a good idea. It's going to touch a lot of people. Probably even make a lot of money. In the end, though, only you know if it's some place to run or God's will for your life. Ask me how I know. For me, this place started out as one and became the other."

Chenille turned away from all of them, unable to face her friends or their questions any longer. She felt like she'd spent her life studying for a test, only to realize too late that she knew none of the answers.

She ended up at Megan's. How Chenille got there, she wasn't exactly sure, but it'd be nice to spend some time with someone who didn't know her quite so well. It was a short trip uptown to Megan's small apartment. Well, small outside anyway. Inside, it seemed as big as the world.

"Come on in," Megan said as she opened the door. "I made us some lattes. Do you like gingerbread? If not, I have pumpkin spice. I should have asked. I've never been a big Christmas person, but this year I'm all into it. Must be the baby."

Chenille paused for a moment, taking in the room. It seemed to be one polished surface, from counters to floors. Even the walls were tiled. A crooked mosaic of the Black Madonna hung behind the coat rack. "I love gingerbread. Any kind of bread actually. Did you make that? The picture, I mean?" Chenille asked.

"Oh, that? Yes. I took a class. It didn't come out as well as I liked, and it'll probably fall off the wall in the middle of the night and scare me half to death, but I tried it there and that seemed to be where it should go, if you know what I mean. Some things just have a place they should be and you get scared to move it. Or maybe you don't. I do, though."

Chenille understood. She understood perfectly. In her life, the thing she was afraid to move was herself. "No, I get it. I do. Your place is nice. Very colorful, yet peaceful."

There was really no other way to describe the mauves and beiges, the blues and browns. Chenille probably wouldn't have chosen any of the colors, but they looked good together. And the candles. There were candles everywhere. Along the floor at the base of the walls. Along the mantel, the bar where Megan was stirring their mugs. The living room was like a sunken bathtub with no water. She took a seat on one of the bamboo chairs at the counter and accepted one of the mugs. She took a sip. "Delicious."

That made Megan smile. "Glad you like it. All of it. The house and the latte. It's how I feel when I come to your offices. When I'm around you and Raya. The others. It's like you all fit together. There's a power that comes from you when you're together. It's a little intimidating. I can admit that now. It's still intimidating with just you by yourself. I'm both happy and surprised that you even came. I didn't really think you would."

Chenille blew across the rim of her mug, buying time, wondering whether or not to run back to the subway station. Raya had said that she didn't have time to grow a new friend. That wasn't necessarily true. Megan was already acting like she'd been part of the crew for years. Intimidation. Doubt. Competition. All the makings of an honest friendship.

Not.

Best to nip all this in the bud. "Look, Megan. Forget all that power and intimidation business, okay? You have power too. God's power. I see it all over you. I see it and wonder if I still have what I had when I first came to Jesus, when nothing was too much to ask, nothing too much to give up. So forget about who you think I am, what you think I have. I need what you need—Jesus, good friends, and gingerbread."

Megan nodded and lifted her cup. As she did, the satin ribbon holding back her hair, more curly than straight today, almost fell into her drink. She saved it just in time. "Thank you. For saying that. I know I need to see myself like God sees me. It's just hard. I've messed up so much stuff. And I know it." She looked down at her stomach. "This baby is one thing that I really want to get right."

Chenille reached out and touched Megan's hand. Perhaps this is what she'd come for—to listen and not to be heard.

God knows my girls have listened to me enough. I owe big-time.

And so Chenille took Megan's hand and led her across the shiny floors. Sat next to her on the glossy leather couch. And listened.

It went slow at first, the way it is when riding a bike for

125

the first time or walking in a new pair of shoes. Wobbly here and there. Tight in places you don't expect. The identity of the baby's father was one of those places.

"It's not a big deal. I don't mind you knowing. It's not like a lot of people know, but he's not trying to hide it. I'm not either. You remember Darryl, the guy Raya was going to marry before I—"

"Complicated things?" Chenille rubbed her hands together as though warming herself at a fire. She wished she really was doing that. She felt cold inside. Stupid. That wasn't the right word. She waited for Megan to respond, hoping that she'd still continue and not shut down. In the beginning like this, it was easy for things to just go quiet and to never get around to getting together again. To see someone on the street and wave, wondering why you never really became friends. As weird as it felt to consider it, Chenille didn't want that to happen. She wanted Megan to be her friend.

"Exactly. I complicated things. That's just what I did. Well, anyway. Even though I did want to hurt Raya, I really did like Darryl. I even convinced myself that I was doing her a favor. I knew that he wasn't like her no matter how many church services he attended to make it seem that way. I knew that he would probably hurt her, break her down the way I did the men who came my way. I thought I'd do everybody a favor and hurt him first."

Chenille pulled a fringed afghan from the back of the couch, noting the stitches. Only one person she knew pulled their yarn through and made that kind of knot. Gram.

Megan tossed the rest of the afghan onto Chenille's lap. "Raya's grandmother made that for me. Can you believe that? I cried when it arrived the other day. She sent a note saying that God takes care of babies and fools and even helps old women to forgive. I keep that card in my nightstand. I want to

126

remember how good it is for people when you forgive them. I know it wasn't easy for her after all the mess my mother and I did to their family."

Chenille sat still. Other people might have downplayed what had happened to make Megan feel better, but that wasn't going to help anyone either. Even listening to the details of how Megan had gone after Raya's fiancé was hard to hear. She had to commend Megan for her honesty, though. Chenille sometimes had trouble giving her own testimony when it came to the hard parts like this. "Raya's grandmother is amazing. I remember the first time I heard someone call her. We were on the train, I think. I was just a kid, but it gave me chills. We still all want to be like Gram when we grow up."

Megan went on telling the story of how she'd struggled with trying to live for God and not knowing quite how. She talked about Darryl, a new Christian himself, who'd become a good friend. He'd advised Megan to build up her relationship with God before trying to marry Sergio or anyone else.

"When he talked to me about it, I realized that he saw in Sergio and I what I saw with him and Raya—two people that didn't match up. Darryl knew that I was going to end up hurting Sergio, that I wasn't ready to be celibate no matter how much I tried to fake it. At the time, he was right. Sergio was celibate, so I was too. Or at least I tried to be. It wasn't for God, though.

"I realized that I had just been focused on getting a husband and not who I was marrying or even if I was supposed to be getting married at all. I just wanted somebody to love me, even if it was just for a while. My mother still talked on the phone with her ex-husbands. Sent them Christmas cards. Fought over me. It wasn't true love or anything, but I figured it was something."

Chenille sighed then, but not loud enough for Megan to hear. She'd known true love, only now there weren't any lunches or Christmas cards. No kids to see Lyle's eyes in. True love hurt too.

She kept her thoughts to herself. This wasn't about her. Or about Lyle. This was about listening. Hearing too. Chenille was trying to do better about practicing both of those gifts.

"Anyway, I'm not proud of it, but I guess I just kept coming around Darryl, and things got out of hand. He was trying to pray with me and talk to me. Sometimes he wouldn't even open the door. He was really trying to do right, to obey God. But you know me . . ."

Chenille rubbed Megan's shoulder. "I do know you. Or at least I'm trying to get to know you. That was the old Megan. That isn't who you are now."

Megan agreed. "I know. It's just hard to think about. I remember back in college, when Raya and I were roommates. I'd done something to her, stole a guy probably. I remember Raya looking at me with pity in her eyes. It made me so mad. She told me that she was just thinking of how hard it was going to be for me when I finally got it, when I finally realized how much I'd hurt people. How much I'd hurt God. She was right."

Something warm rushed through Chenille, pricking her skin. Raya had been wise, even back then. Even with everything she'd been through with Megan, with her father, Raya had always been able to look at things through God's eyes. Lyle had done the same. Chenille wished she could say that she always took the sky view as well. It would have been a lie.

Megan got quiet for a while. The phone rang a few times, but she didn't get up.

"Do you want me to get that?" Chenille reached behind the couch for the portable phone.

128

"No. Don't. It's just Darryl. I'm supposed to start Bradley classes tonight to prepare for the birth. He wants to come."

Chenille looked around the room, trying to figure out if she was missing something. "So let him come. It's his baby too."

The phone rang again, only this time in Megan's messenger bag on the floor. She sat still. "He doesn't really want to come. He just wants to do the right thing. To make good and not be a deadbeat dad. I don't need somebody to be with me out of obligation. I had that all my life with my parents. I want someone to be with me because they want to be, because they love me."

Chenille pushed the afghan back in place at the top of the leather sectional, trying to hear and understand now that she'd listened. It didn't all make sense exactly, but she could sort of understand. Sort of. It still seemed silly to turn away what probably belonged with you anyway.

Where had she heard that before? Jean. In the office. Maybe hearing was overrated. Maybe listening was enough.

There was a knock at the door before she could decide.

Megan looked startled. She stared at the phone. "Was that the door? What time is it?" She fumbled for her phone. "I'm sorry. My coach was supposed to meet me at the class, not here. Hold on."

Chenille gathered her things, hoping it was Darryl, that he'd been calling while on his way. Even though they'd both hurt her friend, Chenille wanted the two of them and their baby to have a fresh start. A new chance. "I'll let myself out."

"No, wait. I—"

It was too late. The door was open and Sergio was standing in front of it with a smile and a bunch of roses. Yellow roses and a stuffed baseball bat. His eyes were closed and he was singing. "Take me out to the ball game . . ."

There was something in Sergio's expression, in his smile, that made Chenille think of Lyle on the night she'd told him she was pregnant. Lyle, wearing that hallelujah shirt. Megan was right. Sometimes things just belonged together. Right now, she didn't belong here.

His eyes were open. His hands on her shoulder. "Chenille? Wait. Listen. It's not what you think . . ."

It all blurred behind Chenille as she grabbed her coat and purse and pushed past Sergio and out the door. His words trailed behind her, muted by someone ringing a Salvation Army bell on the street below. Megan was saying something too. Chenille took the steps two at a time, with Sergio pounding down the staircase behind her.

"Chenille! Please. Wait a minute!" Sergio had nearly caught up to her but was separated by a rush of passersby who'd come between them.

She didn't wait. She couldn't. Not any longer. She had to get home, to call her lawyer, to see if it was too late to change her mind about leaving the firm. Too late to go back to the only family she had left.

11

Sergio had gone through medical school and residency without throwing up once. He worried that Megan's labor class was about to break his perfect record as the instructor flipped through yet another shot of her own labor and delivery. She said that she'd used her own photos so that she didn't have to worry about getting anyone's permission, but it seemed a little too intimate for Sergio, like taking a class with a talking cadaver. He pressed into Megan's back a little more, applying counterpressure as per the teacher's directions.

Megan reached up and put her hands on his. "Let's get out of here."

Sergio felt bad then. Had he been that obvious? "No, I'm fine. Just got a lot on my mind."

Another photo flashed on the screen. *Ugh. This lady should take her show on the road.*

Megan covered her mouth to stifle her laughter, but it was loud enough to draw angry stares from the intent couples around them. Sergio helped Megan to her feet. "Maybe we should go," he said.

131

She was already walking ahead of him, ignoring the teacher's scolding. "I'll be back soon. With my real coach. My friend here isn't quite up to standing in today."

There were more curious glances, this time from everyone in the room. Sergio felt like the worst guy in the world. Good thing he'd tugged off his badge before leaving work. They really would have had words for him. He had words too, but not for anyone here. Not even Megan. He had things to say to Chenille. Things that he needed to say regardless of how she might respond.

He waited for Megan to wind her scarf around her face and opened the door for her. "Hey, I really wanted to do this for you. I'm really sorry that I'm not into it today. I know that you don't want to bother the baby's dad. I'll do better next time. But—"

"Stop it, okay?" She stepped outside and Sergio followed. A light snow sprinkled the tops of their heads. Megan let out a fog of breath into the cold air. "Just find her and make it right. I used to do stuff like this on purpose, try and hurt people. I don't want that. Not ever again. I'm going to call Darryl tonight and talk too. Chenille is a lucky woman."

Sergio stared out into the white, now coming down harder and going to grey slush on the curb. Lucky? He doubted that Chenille thought of herself that way. He couldn't quite figure what she was thinking at all. He only knew that he wanted to get to her. Needed to talk to her. "Thanks for understanding," Sergio said, his phone already in his hand.

He punched the numbers as he had several times on the way to the birthing class. The result was the same. No answer and another corny message from him.

She's going to think I'm a stalker or something.

"It's me again. Last time. I'm trying not to be a pest, but I really need to talk to you. To be with you. In fact, I'd like to know if you'd consider spending Christmas Eve with me. I know you probably have plans with your friends. I'd just like to see more of you. And them. Thanksgiving was great—"

Beep. What a mess. At work he could dictate a whole patient visit in that amount of time. One thought of Chenille and those red curls, the pout of her lips when she was about to laugh . . . and he was rambling like a kid.

Oh well.

He punched a few more keys to save her number to speed dial. He even assigned her a number.

One.

It took awhile, but he found her. Though Sergio had tried to give Chenille a little space, considered calling her tomorrow, he just couldn't wait. Being a doctor had taught him a lot about tomorrow. It was a slippery thing, sometimes getting away before a man could grab it. Today was here, in his hands, in a velvet box wrapped in a red bow.

He knocked on the office door. It was late and everyone else had gone home. If he hadn't met up with Raya Dunham on her way out, he might not have gotten in himself. "Mind if I come in?"

Chenille's head jerked up. She gave him a surprised look, a look that had something else in it too. Fear. Determination. "I do mind." She went on with what she was doing, measuring a length of red felt from a bolt of fabric, tracing something that looked like stockings onto a piece of cardboard she'd ripped off the side of a box.

It's going to be a long night.

Sergio dropped to one knee and steadied the fabric so that she could get a straight cut. She tried to ignore him, but he could see her jaw loosen up a little, her shoulders slope down. He wanted to turn it on full blast, to give her the gift he'd hopped three trains to find, to tell her the things he'd been waiting what seemed like forever to say. But he didn't. He just watched as she made the cut, careful to hold the felt taut. There might not be tomorrow, but he didn't want to rush and blow it either. At least he'd found her. He was here. That was something. "What are you making?"

"An Advent calendar. That's what it's supposed to be anyway. It's looking more and more like a kindergarten art project." She made the last cut and lifted the fabric in the air, then folded it in half.

Sergio got up. His heart was beating fast. He'd watched the nurses make a few Advent calendars at the hospital. It didn't look too hard. Not as hard as Chenille was making it look, with her face all serious like that. She hadn't given his little silver gift bag a second look. Or at least not that he'd seen. He turned to her desk where there was a stack of Christmas CDs. He grabbed the top one like a little kid. "Johnny Mathis? You've got to be kidding me. My dad loved this one. Can I play it?"

The eagerness in his voice must have put a crack in Chenille's armor because she turned to keep him from seeing her quick smile. She didn't turn quick enough though. He saw it and started grinning himself. She waved a hand his way. "Go ahead."

She didn't have to tell him twice. Within seconds "White Christmas" was crooning out of the CD player, and he was attacking her stocking pattern with the scissors.

Chenille stared with her mouth open as though he were cutting up her best gown. He shrugged it off. "Hey, no self-respecting elf would wear those stockings. A fellow needs toe room. Trust me on this."

The wall crumbled then as she laughed long and loud,

taking a swipe at her red eyes once she was done. Sergio restrained himself from running over and taking one knee again, saying things that wouldn't make sense to anyone but the two of them. He managed to hold back the motion. He didn't quite shut down the words. "You're cute after a good cry, you know that? I guess I'll just have to keep you laughing."

Chenille leaned forward like a ballerina doing floor exercises, this time battling a dowel rod that she'd spray painted gold. She really had been getting crafty tonight. It was Sergio's turn to laugh, as he held up the now pointy-toed stocking. "I'm going to be afraid to make you mad now, you know. Especially around holidays. I'd hate to come home one night to find a giant Easter Bunny in the living room."

All of a sudden the room looked bright. Too bright, like he'd been zapped by a stupid tazer. Had he said "come home one night"? He should definitely stick to the cutting. "I didn't mean . . . well, I did mean it, but not yet. See, I know that—"

Chenille dissolved in a heap of laughter. The length of felt twined around her neck. The dowel rod leaned against her head. She held out a hand to him, calling him the way he had that first night under the blanket. She'd been teary-eyed and beautiful then too.

She didn't have to tell him twice. Sergio was on the floor before he knew it, holding Chenille against him. He wiped her tears with the back of his sleeves then kissed her eyelids, one at a time. "I love you." There, he'd said it. "It doesn't make any sense. I didn't plan it. All I know is that when I saw you, when you kissed me, I knew that I'd been missing you all of my life."

He swallowed hard as she moved both hands up his shoulders and around his neck. "That's not how things usually happen with me. I make plans. Usually long ones. Everything takes forever, and when it happens I know just what to expect. I didn't expect you, but I'm so glad you came. And I'm so proud of your new business. Megan told me a little about it, and I don't know which I've been thinking about more today, you or your idea." He kissed her temple. "You, of course. But it really is a good idea. I mean it. Do you have a name yet? A logo?"

Just when he thought that things were going well, that they were getting somewhere, Chenille started to cry. And not just a few tears either, but the for-real kind of crying. Boo hoo and all. He held her tighter, refusing to let go even though she was trying to turn away, to move away from him. "That wasn't the reaction I was looking for, but hey, this is what we do. Sad hugging. It's growing on me."

Chenille tipped her head upward, cupped Sergio's face in her hands. She gave him a look of such gratitude, such thankfulness, that he didn't know whether to be happy or worried. It was the kind of look you give someone before you dump them or vote them off your reality show. He didn't think he could be dumped yet, since despite declaring his undying love, they were never really together. And yet he felt his brow starting to furrow. With women, one could never quite be sure. Well, some guys could probably be sure. Just not Sergio.

He placed his hands on top of hers, trying to both break and keep the moment. He looked around for his stocking pattern, but it was too far away. The gift was closer. He took a deep breath and hoped it was the right time. "I got you something," he said, sitting back on his knees and offering Chenille the bag.

She almost snatched it away, then apologized. That made Sergio loosen up a little. Whether it was the gift or the fact that it was from him, it was a much better response than a downpour of tears. Though right now, he was willing to work with those too. "It's okay. Just something early for Christmas. I wasn't sure if you'd like it, but now that I've seen all the felt and cardboard, I feel pretty good about it. Nothing like a little decoration to spruce things up."

Chenille eased the black velvet box out of the bag. She looked excited, but afraid too. Confused. That made Sergio smile. He'd had the clerk at the store search long and hard to find the right box for his gift. This was the right one, big enough to totally fill Chenille's palm, tall enough for her fingertips to rest on.

You did good with this one, Doc.

Still, as his excitement grew, Chenille's seemed to fade.

"Thank you," she said, standing quickly and putting the box on the corner of her desk. "I'll save it for Christmas."

Sergio tried to jump up right behind her, but his right leg was asleep. He ignored the tingles and ground his heel into the carpet. On his feet, he grabbed for her hand. "No, you should open it now. It's not really the kind of gift you want to leave laying around until Christmas morning. That would kind of take the fun out—"

Little Miss Advent Calendar turned on Sergio like a wildcat, swatting his hand away. "Fun? Don't you see that I'm not fun? That you shouldn't love me or bring me gifts? I guess you don't see. You almost married Megan. Well, I'm not her. I'm going to put it out there for you—don't love me, okay? Love God, love your work, love your life, but don't love me. I can't love you back. There's just no more room left."

He kept his stance for a second before reaching for his jacket, to gather what was left of himself and drag it home. It had taken a lot to come here tonight and say what he had to say, to put it all out there. This was one reality he hadn't counted on. Her telling him not to love her? When he got back to work, he'd have to ask somebody if there was a drug for whatever sickness he had with women. If so, he'd like a prescription, preferably the three-day routine.

No, you wouldn't. You love her still. Even now.

The truth of the thought made him yank his jacket sleeve over the corner of the table. The black velvet gift box fell fast and hit the bottom corner of the desk hard. Hard enough to flip the lid.

Chenille closed her eyes like the contents were radioactive. Sergio would have laughed if he didn't feel like his heart had just been ripped out. He picked up the gift and placed it in her hands anyway, watching as she peeked at the shiny ornament on a bed of silk.

She blinked furiously as if something had gotten into her eye, then whispered the word engraved on the outside of the tiny silver ball.

Wishes.

He swallowed hard at the sound of her voice, wondering if he'd ever hear it again. No point in thinking about that now. Just get out of here with some dignity. He avoided her fingers and tipped the top half of the ornament back so that she could see the words engraved inside.

Do come true.

"Wishes do come true. Oh . . . it's beautiful."

At least he'd gotten something right. "It's sterling silver. It'll keep forever. I figured you could put your logo in there or the name you pick for your company. Maybe even the dreams you have for what next Christmas will be like. Anyway, enjoy it, Mrs. Rizzo. And have a Merry Christmas if I don't see you again at the hospital. I'll tell them to put in an order for some blankets as soon as you set up shop."

She gave him a lingering look, like she wanted him to stay, like if he bent down close enough she'd give him a kiss. He turned away. She'd made her choice. Now he'd have to make his. By the time he made it through the winding halls and out into the snow, his mind was pretty much made up.

She hadn't meant to lie. At the time that Chenille told Sergio not to love her, that she couldn't love him, she thought she'd been telling the truth. She'd thought he was about to propose and she lost it, said things she didn't mean. Now, sitting in her living room cutting stocking shapes out of Lyle's hallelujah shirt, she knew she was wrong. It wasn't the shirt she was looking at anymore but the cardboard pattern, with its upturned toes. She could still see his smile, hear his laugh when he'd done it.

He scared me, Lord. I'm sorry. I didn't know what to do.

She still wasn't sure what to do. Maybe even though what she'd said to him hadn't been true, it'd been for the best. Sergio deserved a happy young wife who cooked meat loaf just right and had babies born breathing with glowing pink cheeks. He didn't need some kooky executive prone to fits of grief and craft obsessions. No, he didn't need that, but he sure seemed to have wanted it.

He sure seemed to have wanted her.

Reaching up to light one of the candles she'd pulled out from their dusty hiding places, Chenille stared in the mirror, baring her teeth, counting the faint freckles that peppered the bridge of her nose. Everything was pretty much there and functional, but none of it was anything that would make a doctor, much less a hot one, look her way. It had to be God then, which was even scarier.

She shrugged her shoulders. If she'd missed her blessing, so be it. It was done now. And as much as she felt hurt about it, Chenille felt relief too. She wouldn't have to try to get to know Sergio the way she'd known Lyle, to build the frame for a marriage to hang on. That was hard work, the framing. Work that took a long time. Years, in Lyle's case. Still, she couldn't help agreeing with one thing that Sergio had said, something that had bothered her since that night in the waiting room.

She hadn't had to try anything. Not to get to know him, not to feel comfortable with him. It was like he said—she'd known him a few minutes and felt like she'd always been missing him, like he'd been on a long trip and she'd been thinking about him every day. But she hadn't. She'd seen him plenty of times at the hospital, but until that night in the snow, he'd always made her think of Lyle more than anything. Chenille didn't think of herself as the love-at-first-sight type of woman. That was for Raya and Lily. And yet, here she was, knee deep in a love that made no sense, but hurt all the same.

The scents of the candles all over the living room joined together, infusing the room with the scent of vanilla and pomegranates. She had almost been afraid to light the curious blend of red and white candles, but now Chenille didn't know whether to rejoice or blow them out. They smelled like a wish, like her shiny Christmas ornament or her new idea. They smelled like the life she might have had if things were different.

If she were different.

But she wasn't different. She was sickeningly the same. Jean had been right about that. Everything she did went in the same direction, this new venture included. She'd thought she was helping everyone by stepping down, but maybe she'd had that wrong too. She'd left a message with the lawyers to see if it was too late for her to rethink her discussion, but no one ever returned her calls. If she wanted a discussion, she might have to take it into her own hands, with the people she should have talked it through with in the first place.

She picked up her cell and started dialing, ignoring the blinking message about her missed calls. Sergio's calls from before he'd stopped by. There was no time to think about that now. No way to control it or turn the clock back. Her business—if she still had one—was different, though. That was something she could work with. Work on. Work through.

And that was just what she needed to do. With the snow and the late hour, Chenille didn't want to get anyone out in the cold, but she did want to have a discussion and not at the office, either.

She checked online to see if any of her friends were logged in when she got no calls back. Everyone seemed to be on the Net, which meant either they were asleep and had forgotten to turn off their computers or they were in cyberspace. The latter turned out to be true.

ClothedinKindness: Hey, I know it's late but can any of you spare about 15 minutes for a conference call?

While waiting for what could either be a volley of quick replies or no reply at all, Chenille logged in to her conference call account and created a phone number and password.

She checked her box again. Everyone but Flex had responded, which probably meant he was sleeping, out of town, or putting the kids to bed while Raya caught up on work.

ClothedinKindness: Thanks. Here's the number and password. Identify yourself when you come in the room so I know you're there. You know how y'all do.

The one drawback to that kind of teleconferencing was that, on some calls, people didn't announce their presence when they entered a room to listen in. A lot of feelings had been hurt that way between all of them, so Chenille made sure they had all identified themselves before going ahead with what she wanted to say.

"I called you all here because what Jean said to me the other day and some of the things that have happened since have made me question my decision to leave the company. This is hard for me to admit because you all know I have little patience with double-minded people. God's teaching me a lesson in this. Everything isn't as cut-and-dried as I thought."

It was hard to say, but necessary. Nigel cut in first. "Jean, what did you say to that girl? Don't put guilt on her, babe. We don't know what God is doing. Everything doesn't always make sense. Not until a whole lot later."

Now she was really confused.

Jean was glad to clear things up. "Chenille, I meant you no harm. Sorry if I started you walking in circles, but I stand by what I said. If you told me you were going to retire to some mission or go back to college and teach kindergarten, well, I'd be hugging you and sending you off with confetti. You tell me you want to do maternity clothes, to bless families, and I tell you it's part of our mission statement, part of who we are as a business. So what are you doing over there?"

Raya wasn't saying much of anything, though Chenille could hear the light tap of keys and the occasional whispered scoldings to Raya's youngest children. As Nigel and Jean continued to speculate about what Chenille should do, Chenille heard Raya's oldest son Jay, whom they'd adopted after coaching his church basketball team, asking his mom to quote him the quadratic formula. The sound of the phrase made Chenille cringe. If she ever did have another baby, somebody else would get the math.

I can make a mean pair of jeans, though.

As family needs mounted and they completed their call, Chenille felt no more certain about her decision than she had before the conversation. Though she thought she'd wanted someone to tell her what to do, it really wasn't so appealing once she'd actually heard it. What she'd needed more than anything was just for someone to believe that she could make it on her own, to know that she was capable of doing it all again, building something from the ground up.

She took a deep sniff of the sweet, sharp fragrance filling the room and picked up the shiny ornament Sergio had given her. Only one person had been willing to believe in her, to trust that she could make happen whatever needed to happen for her to be successful. And she'd shut the door on that person, pushed him away.

Chenille set the ornament back on the mantel, wondering if its belly would ever be full of wishes, lined with dreams. She sat down in the recliner she'd bought Lyle and knew that the ornament would always be empty.

She knew that the one wish she hadn't known she wanted might never come true.

12

Chenille had turned in her resignation, but she went to work anyway. There really wasn't anywhere else to go, anything else to do. If for no other reason, she convinced herself, she had to go in and clean up her office after the Advent calendar disaster.

The receptionist didn't look surprised, but she didn't waste a lot of time greeting Chenille either. "Morning. Should I have someone brew you some tea?"

Chenille shook her head at the thought of someone else taking the time to brew her tea. Her heels clicked a little too loudly against the tiled part of the hall, drawing a few looks from the employees she passed.

"Is she back?" someone asked.

"I don't think she ever left," said another.

"You'd better pray they keep her around. She's the brains behind it all."

That last statement almost made Chenille trip and drop her briefcase. Brains? Not quite. More like the knees behind it all. Prayer and lots of it had been her forte. God had blessed the company again and again, starting with the blessing of sending her some of the best and brightest designers in the world. If there was anything smart about Chenille, it was that—knowing something good when she saw it.

At work anyway.

She paused in front of her closed office door. Had they locked her out? Had she left it that way? Hmmm . . . She turned the knob and it gave easily, opening up to a room almost bare of furniture but overflowing with fabric, spray paint, and craft supplies. Despite the clutter, the sight of it gave Chenille a warm feeling, a memory of her mother's sewing room.

The mess cleaned up easily, leaving behind a rather barren office. Desk, chair, phone. That was pretty much it. She'd brought her laptop along, and her files were still around somewhere. In Raya's office maybe? They might be waiting at her door when she got home.

She ran a hand around the back of her chair between the back and bottom cushion and tugged at the yellow tip she saw there. A Cheeto. That made her laugh a little. Lyle had once said that she was worse than a kid with a car seat. He was right.

It was quiet. Too quiet. By now, the phone usually would have been ringing off the hook with questions from the manufacturing plant, calls from wholesalers. Lawyers wanting to go over licensing.

Lawyers. Had they ever gotten her calls? There had been no messages from them. Maybe they just hadn't wanted to deal with her. Who could blame them? She didn't too much want to deal with herself.

But she had to.

The laptop plugged in easily and buzzed to life as Chenille

took out her now battered notebook and set it on the desk in front of her. She'd been so excited about these ideas when they were just hers, a secret held close to her heart. Now what seemed so clear had been muddied by questions of her motivations, doubts about her abilities. Maybe she should just go back to school and become a kindergarten teacher like Jean had mentioned. Designing for some big corporate house just wasn't something that interested her right now. Maybe ten years from now she'd think differently. On the other hand, maybe it'd be too late. Fashion was a strange, confusing business.

What really bothered her was the sense that she wouldn't shoot for a high-profile designing job because somewhere in her heart, she was still making room to be a wife. A mother. It was like paying a valet charge when you don't even own a car. She had to stop it, she knew, but she just didn't know how. But God knew how. That much she knew. She'd pray for his help in letting go of these unneeded sides of her. Maybe one day, when those parts of her were needed, she could pull them out and dust them off. For now though, she had to accept—no, embrace—the blessings of where she was. Where she might always be.

Someone rapped on the door.

Chenille stayed facing her computer instead of swiveling her chair. "I told you not to make me any tea. Thank you, though. I do appreciate it."

"I don't have any tea, just cookies."

The chair rotated quickly. It was Megan, holding a beautifully wrapped tin of shortbread. What had made her search for Chenille here? Maybe her new friend was already seeing right through her. "Hey. How are you? You just caught me. I'm actually officially gone. Just came in to tie up some loose ends."

146

It was true, in more ways than one.

She took a quick look at Megan. Darkness circled her eyes. Megan moved slowly toward the chair across from Chenille, but slumped into it immediately. "I just wanted to apologize. For everything. Mainly I wanted you to know that what happened at my house was an accident. A misunderstanding. Sergio was supposed to meet me at the class and not until hours after you and I got together. I guess he just figured that a pregnant woman running a foundation out of her living room really doesn't have anyplace to go."

"Don't worry about it. I didn't think anything bad of you. I know that you've changed. I wish you hadn't come way over here, though. You need to get some rest. I wish my couch was still in here—I'd force you to take a nap. Did you eat breakfast?"

Megan admitted that she hadn't eaten this morning, that she'd been too sick to eat. "I keep getting this heartburn every few minutes. It just won't go away."

Something in Chenille snapped to attention as she remembered another morning when she'd come to work without breakfast, complaining of the heartburn tumbling in her pregnant belly. By the time she'd realized the heartburn was really labor, it was too late. She stood up fast, almost knocking her laptop onto the floor. "Does your back hurt, Megan?"

Megan was half-dozing now, holding the cookie tin to her chest. "Oh, I guess it's hurting, but I don't know if it's any more than usual. Everybody says that the sickness ends in the first three months, but not for me. Stomach, back, head. Lately, it seems like my body is just one big squeeze."

That was all Chenille needed to hear. She pressed the buzzer. "Raya, I know I'm not supposed to be giving orders here, but I need a favor. Can I borrow your car? Megan needs to go to the hospital."

Though she'd fussed at first about going in to be checked, by the time they made it to the hospital, Megan was glad that Chenille had brought her.

"There is a pain in my back now. It was sharp, but it's just sort of an ache now."

Chenille nodded. She remembered that too. "Let's just get you to triage and see what they think. There may be something they can give you to stop it." She didn't say that there might be something to stop it if it was really labor. Chenille knew that it was. Megan knew it too.

Please, God, don't let me be too late. Don't let her lose this baby.

Chenille tried to be positive as the orderly wheeled Megan to the maternity ward. They'd insisted that she be taken in a wheelchair since they suspected preterm labor. Chenille remembered that too, being pushed in a wheelchair, only her memory was of coming home with a flat stomach and empty arms, of how slowly the man had pushed her, as though he were sad too.

She reached down and held Megan's hand. This guy was pushing pretty slowly too. "It'll probably be fine. They have medicine they can give you. You may have to go on bed rest, though. Stay off your feet. I've even read about mothers who had to stay upside down until delivery."

Both Megan and the hospital orderly looked at Chenille like she was crazy. She let Megan's hand go. Maybe she was a little crazy. She wasn't trying to be negative by any means. She'd actually been trying to cheer up Megan. Obviously she'd fallen short of her goal.

The guy sped up then, wheeling Megan toward triage without even slowing down for the bumps. His passenger moaned a little but seemed relieved to get away from Chenille. For the moment anyway.

"Are you all right?" It was Sergio, all arms and legs, bounding into the triage room. All eyes and heart. Just the person Chenille needed—wanted—to see.

Only he hadn't come to see her.

Unfortunately, she didn't realize that in time. "I'm okay, I guess. I was so scared, but we got her here. It was labor like I thought . . ."

Chenille's words faded as both Megan and Sergio turned and stared at her. "I'm sorry. I meant you too, of course," Sergio said.

He hadn't really, but was trying to be nice, as was his way. Chenille cleared her throat, hoping to drown out the embarrassment roaring in her ears. Her efforts were to no avail. She could hear it over and over again, like a siren in her head, *You are stupid, stupid, stupid!* "Sorry, you were talking to Megan, huh? I just jumped right in."

As usual.

That's what I loved about you, the way you always jumped right in. Keep jumping, Red. God will keep catching you.

It was Lyle again, though the voice was faint, just beyond a whisper. It was nice to know he was still there. That God was still there. That they both still held their arms open to catch her when she jumped off the deep end. Like now. Like before. Why hadn't she been able to take a real jump and let Sergio love her? Maybe then she would have been the one in his arms now instead of Megan.

She turned away from the two of them, telling herself to stop being jealous and crazy, to think of Megan and her baby and not herself. She knew where Megan was and what she needed. Sergio did too.

Chenille took a deep breath and looked around the room, a stark white with pictures of ducks on the walls. A stiff-looking teddy bear sat in a basket on a nearby counter. The entire wing had a bloody, needy smell about it, a scent Chenille remembered all too well. Still, Megan had managed to keep her baby inside, even if she thought Chenille was a bit crazy. Maybe she was crazy. She was definitely tired. Of that she was certain. It'd been a long night.

After hours of trying to stop Megan's labor, the doctor on call had requested that a shot be given to speed the growth of Megan's baby's lungs. They should prepare for a C-section and expect the baby to need lots of help to live. Megan was twenty-seven weeks, a week further along than Chenille had been. She knew it would take more than lots of help. It would take lots of prayers. Sweet nurses and fine doctors didn't hurt either.

Especially not the fine doctor who was touching her shoulder now. Chenille turned to look at him. At them, Sergio and Megan. Though Sergio touched Chenille's shoulder with one hand, his other hand was twined with Megan's.

He leaned over and kissed Chenille's cheek. "Thanks so much for bringing her in. She'd mentioned something to me a couple times about backaches, and I told her to maybe slow down a little at work and drink more water, but even I didn't take it as seriously as I should have." Sergio motioned to a strip of paper scrolling out of the machine monitoring Megan's contractions next to the hospital bed. They were only small hills now and quite far apart, but they were still there. "You probably saved the baby's life. Maybe Megan's too. Now I'm worried about you. Have you gotten any rest at all? Can I call someone to take you home?"

Chenille swallowed hard. She heard what Sergio was saying, but she was more focused on what he was doing. His kiss had been light against her face but weighed heavily against her heart. She pushed those thoughts away and tried to focus on what was best for her friends. Both of them. "I'll rest soon. I just wanted to get her here and make sure she makes it through the birth. They're talking about a C-section soon." She moved to the side of the bed opposite Sergio and took Megan's hand. "How are you, lady? Ready to be a mama?"

Megan managed a weak smile. "I'm tired, Chenille, but I don't know how you are even awake. Every time I open my eyes, Serg, she's talking to the doctors or nurses for me, recounting everything that's happened to the next nursing shift. She really did save the baby. I see that now. I didn't want to believe that something was wrong. I was even angry when she brought me, but without her . . ." Her words choked off in a sob, and Megan pulled away from Chenille and covered her face with her hand.

Megan didn't need to say what might have happened. They all knew, especially Chenille. Several times in the past twelve hours Chenille had wished she'd just sent Megan with an ambulance and called later to check on her. The memories, some of the same faces of the hospital staff, their questions . . . *Didn't you come through here too? How's your baby? Oh, that's right. I'm so sorry.* Just as many times, though, Chenille was glad she'd come, sure that God had ordained it. When they'd recommended a C-section and started prepping Megan for surgery, it was Chenille who'd noticed that the contractions had decreased in frequency and told the doctor. An hour later, they'd stopped altogether.

Now it would be a matter of Megan living day by day, trying to keep the baby in another hour, another minute. Chenille would do everything she could to help make that happen. She knew how precious every extra second was. Sensing that they needed some time alone, Chenille pulled the blanket up over Megan's shoulder and told her she'd be back soon. She walked to the door and turned out the light, bidding Sergio good-bye. Her voice cracked a little, but she hoped he hadn't noticed.

She caught a glimpse of his long legs moving away from the bed as she flicked off the light and stepped into the hall. He took Chenille's hand and halted her getaway. "Thanks. Again," Sergio said, whispering now. "I guess I was so taken with Megan's spiritual transformation that I didn't give her physical needs enough consideration. She needs a support system. Friends. Family. I don't know if she told you, but her mother passed away a few weeks ago and her father seems to feel more comfortable sending checks to her foundation than spending time with her. I thought Megan was kidding when we were dating and she said she didn't have any friends, but now I guess I see it was pretty much true. Thanks for being her friend." He hesitated, then added, "And mine."

Friend? Why did such a wonderful word sound so horrible all of a sudden? Chenille made a mental note to try never to use that word or this tone of voice when speaking to a man who cared for her. It ranked right up there with "You're like a sister to me . . ."

Stop it. The guy told you he loved you. You choked. Now he's with someone else.

Chenille tried to smile. She wasn't successful. "Thank you for being my, um, friend." Why did it hurt to even say that? Maybe she should have thought about that before, when she turned him away. All the resolve she'd had to tell him how she felt seemed to have melted away. Megan needed him now. Sergio and Megan had been engaged before. They had a history together. She was just some needy widow kissing people in the waiting room. She was just a friend.

If this new label hurt Sergio, he didn't seem to show it. Not the way he'd shown his disappointment that night at her office. She longed to see that look of love on his face now. Instead, he gave her a smile, a cute one that warmed Chenille's heart. His words, though, still cut her to the bone. How could she have ever said that she couldn't love him? It seemed impossible to her now that she'd convinced herself of that, even for a second. This love felt real, deep, like what she'd felt for Lyle. She swallowed hard at the thought of it. It couldn't be. That was impossible.

Nothing is impossible with God, Red. Nothing.

Sergio leaned down quickly, looking from one of Chenille's eyes to the other. He held her close. "What's wrong? Don't tell me that you're sick now. When did you eat last? It has been a long night. You should probably lie down. Go home—"

"Unh!" Megan gave a sharp grunt on the other side of the door. Both Sergio's and Chenille's heads snapped up. Their embrace dissolved instantly. Sergio pushed the door open and clicked on the light. Both their eyes widened as contractions peaked in red arcs across the paper scrolling out of the machine. With only nods and pointing, Sergio and Chenille agreed on a course of action. He'd deal with Megan, she'd get the nurses.

Chenille hit the call button and gave a quick explanation while Sergio talked to Megan in a calm, quiet voice. "Megan, relax. Take a deep breath. You're not alone. Chenille and I are here. God is here too."

13

Chenille wasn't their boss anymore and it wasn't her baby, but her friends came to the hospital anyway. And she was glad to see them.

"You didn't have to come," Chenille said, realizing while her words still hung in the air how much she missed them, how much she needed them. Relief washed over her as she watched Raya, Jean, and Lily enter the hospital waiting room where she'd been napping. At the sight of them, her mask of strength began to slip, the voice of authority she'd been using with the doctors and nurses broke with a sob. "You didn't have to come, but I'm so glad you did. This was hard."

She had talked to them off and on over the phone and passed off Raya's keys when Flex had come for the van. Each time, the subject centered on Megan and her condition. But now it was different. Their arms surrounded her. Jean's knit jacket crushed against Chenille's face as her friends pulled her close. She took a deep sniff of Jean's perfume and started to break down. The familiar smell, the warmth of all of them, the memories of other waiting rooms, other hard times, took Chenille from sobs to a good hard cry. They released her shoulders and left her to it.

Raya patted her back. "Go ahead. Let it out. This *is* hard. We're proud of you, though. You reached Megan in a way that none of us could. You let the Lord use you, even when it meant going through something yourself."

As usual, Raya summed things up well and put Chenille's focus back on God where it should have been all along. She watched as her friends spread out, putting down their belongings, kicking off their shoes. Taking over the same waiting room that she and Sergio had run to on another night when things got hard. A night when she'd been so blinded by grief that she'd kissed a man she barely knew. It scared her sometimes to think what could have happened from that. It scared her even more to think of what might *not* happen from it.

She didn't regret the kiss. Lyle had taught her that life was too short to dwell on regrets. Still, sitting here with her wonderful friends, it was hard not to regret accepting the new love she'd been offered. It was hard, but Chenille tried to forget it anyway. If she didn't, she'd go crazy, and she wasn't sure how much crazy she had left to go before she'd be, well, crazy. Not far, she thought.

"You look terrible, darling. I knew I should have put a cucumber in my purse. Come here. Someone give me a brush." Jean dumped Lily's purse onto the table, got a brush, and went to work on Chenille's curls.

"Be nice, Jean. Goodness." Lily replaced the contents of her purse and shook her head.

Laughter broke through Chenille's tears as her head jerked back and forth. Jean had a way of telling things just as they were without being offensive. "It's okay, Lil. She's right. We all know it. Brush your heart out, Mom." Chenille hadn't had a mother to care for her in a very long time. On days like these, they all borrowed Jean to be their mother-friend. She never minded it a bit.

Raya lay out across some empty seats. "What's with you and waiting rooms anyway?"

It was a little bittersweet, being in here, but Chenille had needed a nap and this was as far as she had made it. They'd given her a cot a few days ago, when Megan had started laboring again, but since she wasn't family, Chenille had to leave the room several times a day. There'd been some rough times, but the baby was still hanging on. Today marked twenty-eight weeks, giving the child a much better chance of survival, though there were still many risks. After today, she'd go home and get a good night's sleep. Decide what to do next, both about Megan and about herself. Chenille wiped her tears and collected herself, looking up at her friends with gratitude. She had to find a way to come back to them, to give to them again all they'd given.

"I love you, all of you. I may not act like it sometimes, but I do." She said the words slowly, almost tasting each syllable. "I'm sorry for all I've put you through in the past few years."

None of them said anything. In fact, they acted as if she hadn't said anything. A minute passed, and Raya got up and slid into the chair next to Chenille. She gave her a long, hard hug, the kind your mother gives you when you break up with your first boyfriend. An I-know-it's-bad-but-it'll-get-better hug. Chenille smiled. It was just what she needed.

She stood and retrieved a tote bag, shoving it onto Chenille's lap. There was a clean pair of jeans, sweater, and T-shirt inside, a pack of underwear, a toothbrush, a pocket-sized Bible that Chenille had given Jean a few years before, a picture of

Chenille and Lyle at church in a small frame . . . Everything she needed and more.

Though Jean had squeezed her breathless when they came in, she hung back a little now, not saying much of anything, but offering supportive smiles. Chenille frowned. What was up with that? Jean never spared anyone her opinion. "Jean? Why so quiet? Are you sick? Are you done attacking me with that hairbrush?"

That made Jean laugh. She slid over a little closer. Her salmon-colored leather skirt squeaked against the seats. "I'm not sick, but I'm not done with your hair either. Just giving you a break. I'm just thinking of how I treated Megan all that time we were working on her dress. She was a beast back then, I have to admit it, but still . . . And now, she has no mother. A baby and no mother. That is a hard place. I'm glad you came here with her."

Lily was quiet too, wringing her thin hands. She was probably thinking of her own mother, wondering how long Mrs. Chau would live after the birth of this baby. She dug into her own tote bag. "Oh, I forgot! I brought you some flowers." The bouquet in her hand, baby's breath and ice-cold green roses, fell forward and hit the floor. They looked like little cabbages or something. Lily could find the most unique things.

She tried to lean forward to get them, but Chenille lunged for them, holding up a hand as she went. "I've got it, Lily. I appreciate everybody coming, but you should have stayed in. It's bad outside. You need to rest or Doug will come home and beat us all up. We have to take care of you. Who is with your mom today, her friend Pinkie or the day nurse?"

"The day nurse. Pinkie doesn't get around so well lately. I take Mom over when I can. They talk on the phone every day, though. I love to listen to them. I know I probably should be at home, and I won't be able to stay long. I was listening to the two of them talk, and I thought about how long it will be before we're like that, not seeing each other anymore. I guess that's why I'm here."

Chenille sat quietly doing some wondering of her own. How much longer would it be until they were all down to only anniversaries and birthdays? Cheesy cards and unanswered emails? It pained her to even think of it.

I thought I was hearing you, Lord, but how will I ever survive without them?

Warmth flushed Jean's cheeks. She seemed to be over her remorse about Megan. From the flicker of her lashes, she was ready to start in on Chenille. Twenty Questions really wasn't what Chenille wanted to spend her time on right now, so she prayed she was wrong about that look on Jean's face.

She wasn't.

Jean's skirt squeaked again as she moved even closer. "I'm sorry about Megan, really I am, but I'm also worried about you. What's going on with you and the doctor now? Did you tell him you love him? I'm sure you have, but I don't know. You girls try to be so cute sometimes. I say just put it out there and get it over with. I know I'm one to talk, but—"

"I say let's change the subject, shall we?" Raya was out of her jacket now and wearing a black cat suit with thigh-high riding boots. Chenille shook her head slightly as her friend reached out and began kneading her shoulder blades. Who would have thought Catwoman was under that big pink jacket? That Raya was always full of surprises.

Jean, on the other hand, was pretty consistent. She could smell blood and, like any good ex-Army nurse, believed in cleaning out wounds thoroughly and immediately, even if it made someone scream. She gave Raya a stern but loving look. "Let's not change the subject. She can take it. She has to."

Chenille sighed. They were both right. She wanted to

change the subject, but she needed to face it too. "I didn't tell him that I loved him, Jean. In fact, I told him the opposite, that I didn't love him and that I probably never could."

Raya's hands stopped moving. Lily's frozen, silent smile turned into a round hollow look of confusion. Words started flying out of her almost faster than Chenille could comprehend. Almost, but not quite.

"You're kidding, right? Tell me you're kidding. Oh, Chenille. You quit your job. You kissed the guy. Was Jean right? Is this a midlife crisis or something? It's obvious that you care for him. You're driving us crazy. I'll be the one in here on bed rest again if you keep this up!"

Everyone but Chenille laughed at Lily's outburst. Chenille heard the truth in it, saw the lines etching her friend's face, the work veining her hands. Lily's husband Doug was gone to Nigeria for a short-term missionary trip, something he did several times a year. Lily should have been at home in bed. Chenille didn't want to be in this waiting room for another friend. "You're right, Lily. You're all right. I messed up. Freaked out. He said he loved me. He had a gift box in his hand that looked like a ring, and I—"

"A ring?" All three women just about shouted the word, making Chenille cover her ears and pray Sergio had gone home. With her luck, he was in the hall making a podcast out of this whole thing to put on the Internet. Whatever that was. After years of Lyle trying to explain blogging to her, she was just getting the hang of that.

Chenille shifted in her chair and considered going back to her nap. This was getting taxing. "It wasn't a ring, okay? It just looked like one. It was a black velvet box. It did look too big for a ring, but I wasn't sure, and well, I lost it. He was tracing Christmas stockings for me for the Advent calendar. It was too much. It was too much like something Lyle would have done."

159

There was a collective groan from Chenille's friends before she went on with the story, telling them about the ornament and how Sergio had supported her in her business ideas too. "He asked if I had a logo yet. A name. Can you believe that? He just encouraged me. No business plan. No profit and loss statement. He just believed in it. I don't know if I could have even had that discussion with—"

The three women glared at Chenille. There she was, comparing Sergio to Lyle again. Would she ever see a man as himself alone instead of in Lyle's shadow?

Raya looked off in the distance. "Did you? Get a logo, I mean." Raya was tapping her chin with her index finger now. Very scary.

Oh no. That look meant that Raya had some ideas of her own to add. Sergio was one thing to deal with. Once Raya got going, Chenille would be done for, with product cranking through the warehouses by spring. She wasn't ready for that yet, to hand her baby over and have everyone tell her how ugly it was. She'd been through that too many times before.

Chenille stood, thinking of something to say to still the tide of whatever was about to happen. Maybe she should go on home. They probably should too. It suddenly felt very, very late despite being three o'clock in the afternoon. In the end, though, she just answered Raya's question.

"I don't have a logo yet, but I do have some ideas. I'm confused about the whole thing now, I have to admit. Maybe I'll just go home and make some quilts and sell them on eBay." She'd meant it to be funny, but she got glares from her friends instead of laughter. That made Chenille angry too. Or was that just more confusion? She'd read so many grief books in the past year. Which phase of recovery was this? Denial probably, though she thought she'd navigated that stage long ago. All her emotions were starting to run together.

160

Raya picked up the bouquet of green roses and pressed them into Chenille's hands. "I guess we'll go now. Lily isn't looking so good. Get some rest. Can I give you a ride home? I know you're trying to be a good friend to Megan, but everyone has limits—"

"I agree." It was Sergio, standing in the door's entrance in his lab coat, looking as handsome as ever. "I didn't mean to eavesdrop, but you all were talking pretty loud. Take her home, ladies. Doctor's orders." He gave a quick wave and stepped back. His eyes lingered on Chenille before he put his head down and went on his way.

Chenille's heart pounded. She wanted to jump up and leave her friends, to run down the hall after him. But she didn't run after him. She just sat there, wondering how she'd gotten to this place. A month ago, she'd been fine. On top of things. She hadn't had a code blue—her friends' term for a "significant mental health event"—in months, almost a year. Now she saw a swirl of sky coming at her again, a mess.

Raya was already taking out her keys. "You heard the man. You coming?"

Why not? She definitely had to get out of here. "Sure. Take me home. I'll come back tomorrow," Chenille said.

Chenille went along with them, thinking that Raya was wrong about her. Chenille knew she had limits. She saw them all the time . . . as she passed them by. It was all of them that she worried about. "What brought you guys up here anyway? You know you could have just called."

Jean looped arms with her. "We came because it's the anniversary of Lyle's death and you had such a hard time last year. I can see that looking after Megan was a good thing for you in that regard. You haven't mentioned it once."

Chenille closed her eyes but forced her feet forward.

She'd forgotten.

It was still there.

In the box where she'd left it over a year ago, resting on a pillow of satin, was Chenille's wedding band. It'd taken months not to feel the weight of it, not to run her thumb down her finger in search of it, but eventually, she'd gotten used to her new hands. Her new life.

Or at least she'd thought so, before a handsome, thoughtful man said he loved her. Now she felt like the balloon letters she'd had to work so hard to combat in first grade, soaring above the margins, crossing all the lines. She felt confused at the hospital, but now, with time to think about it, time to slip on her wedding ring one more time and realize that it would never again fit, she really wasn't confused. Lyle had been right. He'd said that someday the hurt would move over, leave some room. She hadn't believed him then. She hadn't wanted to. But now, with another anniversary of his death, she knew the best gift she could give him was to live.

A week had gone by now and she hadn't shed any more tears. Not for Lyle, not for Megan, not for herself. Perhaps they'd dried up or she'd run out after the past few weeks of crying. Chenille wasn't sure and at this point she didn't really care. She'd gone to Jean and Nigel's anniversary party and even sent out Christmas cards. Her Advent calendar was complete. Each day when she peeled back the felt squares to reveal the day's date, she ran her hands along the stockings Sergio had traced for her. She hadn't seen him for a while, though he called every few days to update her on Megan's progress. The bun was still in the oven, and everyone was hoping she could make it to thirty-two weeks at least. She was on a constant IV drip of magnesium sulfate now, which had made Chenille feel hot and sick for the few hours she'd been on it before her son came anyway.

She felt for Megan, but she felt for Sergio too. And not just as a friend. Chenille knew for sure now that she had feelings for—no, loved—Sergio. She just didn't understand how. Hadn't Lyle taken all her love with him? Evidently not.

Sure, guys had been looking a lot better in the past year, and sometimes she had to remind herself when someone held open a door not to lean in to them, not to thread her fingers through theirs out of habit. She always caught herself before doing something foolish. Until lately, anyway.

Widow. It'd been her identity, her new name for so long now it seemed. A new box to check, something to say to telemarketers who wanted to speak to her husband. "Widow," she would whisper and go back to her knitting-quilting-cutting with abandon. A nurse at the hospital had offered to teach Chenille to weave on a loom and even sell her the loom if she liked it, but Chenille had declined the lessons. Another hobby wasn't what she needed.

She needed Jesus. Now more than ever.

With a cup of pumpkin chai tea she'd bought after hanging out with Megan and some cranberry biscotti on the table, Chenille curled up in the living room with her Bible in her hand. Well, both hands. She stared at the book for a few seconds, wondering where to read. When Lyle was alive, she'd never had that problem. The two of them were always on some Bible reading plan or doing some study book. Now, she sat in church sometimes and had to flip to the table of contents to remember where the books were. She flipped to that page now, shopping for some food for her soul.

"What is happening to me? I don't even know what to do, where to begin."

Good. I will show you. I am the Beginning and the End.

163

She took a deep breath and waited then for something to be shown to her, for something to come to mind. Nothing. She scanned through the table of contents starting with the Old Testament. It had been her favorite before. "Jeremiah? Too sad. Psalms? Maybe, but I always read that. Romans? Too deep. What about. . . ."

She flipped to the middle of the Bible and opened in Psalms. She grabbed the right section of pages and opened that to the halfway point too, landing in Philippians. It was a trick she'd learned during her Foundations of Christianity class many years ago. She almost laughed remembering how zealous she'd been then. How obnoxious. Now she was just glad to find her page. Any page. Philippians. This one would do just fine.

She bit a cookie and read the first few verses. And then a few more. By the end of the first chapter, her chai was cold and her biscotti a mess of crumbles across her mouth. It wasn't the first time she'd read this book of the Bible. In fact, she and Lyle had memorized it years before. She still had that inductive write-in-the-margin Bible somewhere to prove it. She'd been faithful to the daily study, digging out themes and marking the key words. Lyle had discovered something in that study that he said changed him forever—joy. It was all over the book, he said, a call to rejoice in all things. At the time, Chenille had agreed.

Today she saw something else, the desire of a dying man to bring peace to the people he loved while he still could. A letter before going to the grave. Paul gave practical commands in the book, things that had to be said from afar because Paul couldn't be there in person. It was the other part of the book that Chenille saw now, the desire to get things in order for the day when Paul would be absent from the body as well.

Her fingers were all over the pages now, the way they'd been on her wedding ring when she got home from the hospital the week before. This time, though, there was a perfect fit. The words slipped into all the right places. She went on to chapter 2, sitting up straight as she went, stopping when two verses took her breath.

Therefore, my dear friends, as you have always obeyed—not only in my presence, but now much more in my absence—continue to work out your salvation with fear and trembling, for it is God who works in you to will and to act according to his good purpose.

Though the other verses had marched along through her mind in good order, allowing her to pick up speed, these words would not comply. Instead, they came to Chenille like speed bumps, making her slow down and hear them. In Lyle's voice, no less. She had obeyed God in Lyle's presence. She had worked out her salvation with fear and trembling. Now she was just trembling and afraid.

She wrapped her arms around herself as her husband came to her heart, the healthy Lyle, with muscles and olive skin, breath smelling of Fruity Pebbles. Her morning man.

He will rebuild. Let him finish what he started. I was just the foundation. You are just the stone. The pot. Don't be afraid, Red. Not for me. Rejoice. Christ has risen. And so have I. Rejoice and fall in love . . .

The phone rang and whisked Lyle away from her mind, jerked him out of her heart. She sat dazed for a second, scrambling to catch the Bible before it fell out of her lap. She was setting it aside when she heard the voice on the machine.

"Hey. It's Serg. I know we've talked about Megan lately, but before the New Year kicks in, I wanted to talk to you about us, our friendship, I mean. I'm sorry for not saying more to you at the hospital last week. I'm glad your friends were there for you. They take really good care of you. I guess I just wish that it was me that you came to, that I was the one taking care of you. I still love—"

The machine beeped, cutting off the words, but it didn't matter. Chenille was already looking for her shoes and a purse big enough to hold her Bible.

She'd gotten the message. Loud and clear. She'd been given another chance.

14

"Machine cut you off?"

Sergio turned slowly from where he'd been banging his head against the wall in Megan's hospital room. He'd stopped when it occurred to him that he'd woken her up despite her drugged stupor and that someone might come and drag him down to the pysch ward. He definitely hadn't considered that Megan may have heard the whole conversation in the first place.

He slid down the wall into the chair next to Megan's bed, which was now tilted up at the end so that no pressure would be put on the baby and start labor again. He laced his fingers on the top of his head and sighed. "Yeah. The machine cut me off. I shouldn't have called. I shouldn't have said any of that. I don't know why I keep doing this. I need to just let it go."

Megan was resting on her side, her hair a tangle of black curls against the pillow. She gave Sergio a weak smile. "You should have called. You should have said what you did. It hurts to love people, but you have to.

If you stop, then you stop knowing how to love, and then when the right person comes along, somebody you really care about, you won't know what to do to keep them. To make things work." She gave him a pained look, one so sad that Sergio looked over at the machine monitoring Megan for contractions. Nothing.

They kept looking at each other like that for a long time, first because Megan wouldn't turn away and then because Sergio couldn't. She was trying to say something to him, trying to help him out. He got that. He heard where she was coming from. But there was something else too. She poked her hand out of the bed rail and took his. A tear rolled across her nose and onto the sheet.

Sergio pulled his chair closer to the bed. He raked his fingers through her hair. He'd be glad when she didn't have to lie upside down like this anymore. It had to be uncomfortable. A baby was more than worth it, though. Love was worth it. It had to be. "What's wrong? Why are you crying? Don't worry about me, okay? I'll be fine. I always am."

Megan shook her head a little, as much as she could in such an uncomfortable position. "It's not you I'm crying for, Serg. Not really. I know you'll be okay. I'm crying for myself. I wish I could go back to a year ago and have had the courage that you just had on the phone. I wish I'd been strong enough to call you the way you just did with Chenille."

His hand stopped moving through Megan's hair. Something in his chest tightened. What was she trying to say? He wasn't sure if he wanted to know. "Things just didn't go right for us. You can't blame yourself. There was the faith thing, and I know you always thought I was kind of square. Not exactly your kind of guy. I got that. I'm just glad we can still be friends. That I can be here for you now."

She pulled her hand away, crossed her arms over her eyes

so he wouldn't see her tears. He could see her shaking her left leg under the sheet, something she'd done a lot at the end, before they called off their engagement. He took a sharp breath, remembering when they'd made that decision. It had been a relief at first, but afterward, he'd really missed Megan, her diva ways and all.

What had really surprised him was his mother's reaction. She'd cried. She'd made it clear that she hadn't liked Megan, but Megan had tried hard to make his mother happy. From the beginning, Sergio had felt that they were just too much alike. His mother was a Christian now; she was older, sick, and she wanted to see him married before she was gone. It was important. She said that Megan had good in her, that she'd just never had enough good women around her to bring it out. Seeing how much a difference Chenille's friends made in her life, Sergio wondered if his mother wasn't right. He wondered if he didn't need some good men around him too.

Megan was crying harder now, turning away from Sergio, pulling the covers up over her head. He got up and bent over the bed rail, tried to turn her around. "What is it? You can't be getting upset like this. It's not good for you or for the baby. Tell me. What's wrong?"

It took awhile for her to turn back to him. She'd told him the day before that having her head lower than her feet made her dizzy most of the time. Maybe that's why she was acting this way. The magnesium sulfate in the IV made people a little strange sometimes. All warm and weird inside, they said. It did a great job of keeping the contractions away, though. He took her hand again and kissed the top of it. "It's probably just the medicine, okay? It can make you feel funny."

He knew the words he was saying were true, but what he couldn't figure was why he felt weird too. He wasn't on the medicine.

"It's not the drug," she said. "It's me. It's you. I love you, Sergio. I have for a long time. I just didn't think I could be good enough, to be perfect like you are. I didn't want to disappoint you the way I disappoint everyone else."

Sergio grabbed the bed rail with his free hand. He grabbed and squeezed as hard as he could. He only stopped because it started to creak. He tried to understand what Megan was saying, to make room for it among the tangled feelings he already had for Chenille, for his mother, his little brother whom he'd lost years ago . . . Too long. Somehow, the words found a place, somehow they shot right to his heart. He stared up at the ceiling.

Lord, what am I supposed to do with this? What?

He was speaking to Megan before an answer came. "Why didn't you tell me? Why did you push me away? Why—why did you go and get pregnant by some guy?" He wanted to bang his fist on the rail the way he'd banged his head on the wall, but this wasn't the place for that. He'd have to hold that in until he got back to the punching bag at the gym. Were all women crazy? Was Chenille lying to him too? Right now, with Megan squeezing his hand, looking out at him like this, he wasn't sure if he wanted to know.

She loved him. She needed him. Just like his mother had when her mental illness had driven away first his father and then his younger brother. Sergio had stayed because his mother needed him, but would that be enough with Megan? Would he stay with her too? Did she even want him to? Though she said she loved him, she was different now, stronger.

It sure seemed like Megan needed him from the look in her eyes. She wasn't crying anymore. She was serious. "I'm so sorry. I wish that I could go back, that I could be like Chenille and Raya, be the kind of woman you need. The kind of woman you want. A good woman. Maybe this baby will help me be that woman. Maybe God will—"

Sergio covered her mouth with his, smothering Megan's doubts, kissing away her fears. He didn't know what it meant or where it would take them, but for a moment, a second, he wanted Megan to know that she was good, that she deserved to be loved, that she was acceptable to God—and to him—just as she was. He did it for himself too, to remind himself that somebody wanted him, that somebody cared about him. That somebody needed him.

And as much as he hated to admit it, it felt good.

So good that when Chenille walked into the room, he didn't even hear her.

As she peeked around the curtain in Megan's hospital room, Chenille made a mental note to extend the time for callers to leave a message on her answering machine. She'd been so sure that Sergio was trying to tell her that he loved her during his last message. Now she was just as sure that she'd either been totally off the mark or love had a very short life span. As she watched Sergio bent over Megan's bed, kissing her like some urban Prince Charming, even Chenille had to admit it was a picture-perfect scene. Once again, a scene that she didn't belong in.

She moved back one foot at a time, hands out at her sides like a tightrope walker. There were a lot of things trying to go through her mind, but she forced them all back, asking them to wait so that she could focus on getting out of the room.

One step. Two steps. Three steps. They weren't kissing anymore she didn't think, but Sergio's head was still far over the bed. She couldn't see Megan at all because of the way the bed was leaning. Chenille was glad for that. She didn't want either of them to see the look that must have been on her face. She wasn't crying, though, and she didn't intend to. Not here.

Four steps. Five steps. Six . . .

"There you are! Get some rest?" A nurse that Chenille knew from the NICU bounded into the room, giving Chenille her best smile.

"Not really," Chenille said as she slipped past her. "I'm headed home now. Be back later."

She tried not to look back, not to see Sergio's face, but as she turned sideways to get out of the door, she got a glimpse of him. He looked a little sad, the way he had when she'd seen him last week. The way she sometimes looked when she faced the mirror in the morning. He looked shocked at first and stood quickly to his feet. Then, as if he'd remembered something, he gave her a smile, though it seemed halfhearted. She paused to listen for his footsteps behind her.

Sergio did leave Megan's room and come into the hall, but he didn't run her down and beg her forgiveness. He didn't say anything at all, just a wave and another sad smile before turning the other direction and heading toward the nurses' station.

Chenille stood in the hall, trying to force herself to move, trying not to cry.

Sergio is at work. Megan's trying to save her baby. What am I doing here, Lord?

What you're supposed to do: FOLLOW ME.

She pinched her eyes shut. Following Jesus was all she wanted to do, even if it took her to places she didn't want to be. Even it meant seeing things she didn't want to see. Even if it meant letting Sergio go.

His knuckles were bleeding, but Sergio didn't care. He punched the bag again. And again. And again.

"Hey! Slow down, partner. Let's have a look at that hand. Where are your gloves?" It was Flex Dunham, one of Chenille's friends. He knew Megan too. Great. Just what Sergio didn't need. He'd come to this new gym on a free trial because his usual one was packed out with all the people starting early on their New Year's resolutions. He'd thought it might be nice not to have to talk to anybody. Now this.

"Sorry. Just working off some steam. I forgot my gloves at home." He looked away as Flex checked his fingers.

"Right, well, you're going to have to stop for a minute so we can clean things up. No blood allowed. Are you a member? We have someone who can look at that." Flex's eyes were narrowing, like he was trying to figure something out. "Wait. You're the doctor, aren't you? Chenille's doctor?"

That made Sergio smile in spite of himself, but the smile faded quickly. Maybe it was best if he just didn't think of Chenille at all. Maybe he should just be practical and forget about that whole thing. Marry Megan and have a family. "Actually, I'm more like Megan's doctor. Chenille and I are friends, though. Raya is your wife, right? And Lyle was your best friend?"

Flex stopped cleaning the punching bag at the mention of Lyle's name. He was really thinking now. "Yes, Lyle was my friend. Did Chenille tell you that? Or did you know him?" He looked a little suspicious now, as though he had something to defend. He needn't have worried. Sergio wasn't going to infringe on that either.

Someone from the desk came and offered Sergio a first-aid kit, and he set about cleaning his fingers and re-taping his hand. "Chenille didn't tell me you were best friends. Lyle did. I only met him once, but I emailed him quite a bit. I still read his blog now. He was an amazing guy."

Nodding, Flex sat down on the bench. "He really was. I could probably go my whole life and not meet another person like him. Or at least that's how it seems sometimes. I guess I'd forgotten how hard it is for a guy to make a really good friend. Most people seemed phony to me, even guys I've known all my life. I pretty much kept to myself. With him it was different." He stopped short as though he'd caught himself before diving off the side of a cliff. With a fresh towel, he wiped off the cleaning solution from the punching bag. He waved for someone to bring Sergio a pair of boxing gloves.

"Sorry," he said. "I didn't mean to go on like that. Thanks for coming to Heavenly Bodies. Talk to me on the way out about a membership. We'll work out a deal. Any friend of Chenille and Lyle's is a friend of mine."

Before he knew what he was doing, Sergio's hand shot out and grabbed Flex by the shoulder. "I don't know if Lyle would have considered me a friend necessarily. I don't know that Chenille would think of me as a friend right now either. I need a friend, though. Badly. And as weird as it may sound, I'm thinking all of a sudden that maybe God sent me here to meet you. To talk to you. You know Megan too, right? Megan Ariatta?"

Flex took a deep breath and waved off the person heading over with the boxing gloves. "Hold on to the gloves, please." He told Sergio to follow him and bring the first-aid kit too.

Sergio complied, wondering what training with Flex would be like as he struggled to keep up with his pace down a back hall. "Where are we going?" he asked, scrambling for breath.

"To my office so that we can pray," Flex said. "I remember exactly who you are now. I figure you're in a mess that only

God can fix. I'm no Lyle, but I can offer you what he gave me—honesty and prayer. I have a feeling that maybe God sent you here too, but I'm still probably going to regret this."

Sergio didn't say anything. He wanted to reassure Flex that he wouldn't regret talking to him, praying with him, but he couldn't make that assurance. Not anymore. Sometimes obeying God didn't make things easier. Sometimes things got a lot worse before they got better. His life had been proof of that. Though people looked at him and saw a successful doctor now, all Sergio saw sometimes was the struggle to take care of his mother, to try to do right and stick by her. Maybe his brother had been the smart one after all, going with Dad and looking out for himself. Sergio had never mastered that. He probably never would.

Inside Flex's office, time seemed to stop. There wasn't much in there: photos of his wife and kids, a handsome older couple that had to have been his parents, a teen boy playing basketball, Chenille, Lyle, and their other friends. There was a chalkboard with phone numbers and the costs of different kinds of flowers. The rates were good. Sergio made a mental note of the names of the shops. A treadmill and a basic weight set were in one corner. A couch and a Bible in another. A small refrigerator, a desk, and a chair. Nothing fancy. And yet there was peace.

Sergio pressed a bandage across his knuckles and set the first-aid kit down on the desk. He'd spent a lot of time praying in his life, but most of that time had been spent alone. His brother and father were gone, his mother caught up in her own suffering. God had healed his mother's mind, saved her soul, and helped him become a doctor like she'd asked. Now there was just one last thing she wanted—for him to marry Megan. He'd made the mistake of talking to her about it, telling her what had happened at the hospital. She'd been overjoyed. She remembered Chenille from when Megan had shown her dress the first time. She held nothing against "the lady," as his mother called Chenille, but she thought he'd spent enough of his life living with a sad woman. Now he needed a happy family. Babies. A simple life.

Sergio was so deep in his thoughts that he hadn't realized he'd started telling his story to Flex, talking to him as though he'd known him all his life. Sergio blinked to clear his head and apologized, but Flex told him to go over to the couch and talk all he wanted. They'd pray when he was ready.

And that's just what he did. Sergio stretched out on the couch while Flex jogged quietly on the treadmill, asking questions every now and then as he crisscrossed from past to present, talking about his family, about Lyle, about Megan, about Chenille . . . When he got to the part about kissing Megan and Chenille seeing the whole thing, Flex stopped the treadmill and shook his head.

"Okay, my friend. I've heard enough. It's time to pray before I try to come up with my own harebrained solution and I get us all beat up by the ladies." He got off the treadmill, went to the couch, and knelt down. Sergio slid off the couch and onto his knees, trying to remember if he'd prayed with a guy since he and his brother were kids.

He hadn't.

Christmas came and went. Chenille packed up her Advent calendar, her grief, and even her crush on Sergio, and greeted the new year. That's all it seemed to be now, a crush. Some schoolgirl infatuation that could never be anything more. Her friends disagreed, but she was through discussing it with them. She was through discussing it with herself. These days she only brought it up with God. He didn't have much to say on the subject, so Chenille abandoned it as well.

There were other things on her mind now, like getting back to work. No one had said anything, but she knew that her friends and many of the Garments of Praise retail accounts were wondering if her stepping down as the firm's head was a permanent decision. No one seemed to think so, and now she wasn't sure herself. One thing was certain: she had some things to sort through. Packing away her holiday decorations and sending more of Lyle's things out to charity had been helpful in starting to clear her mind as well.

She needed something else now though. She considered making another quilt for the hospital, but even that didn't seem right. It was a new year. She needed a new thing, a new start. Or maybe a new start on an old thing? It came to her all at once. She ran to Lyle's old laptop and accessed the Internet. She searched her email archives for the link to the web journal that Lyle had set up for her. She'd only posted in it a few times before deciding it wasn't for her. Her life had been about holding in her emotions then, trying to see Lyle through to the end, about finishing well. Was her blog still there? Chenille was amazed to find the email saved on her server.

She found the link and clicked it. It took her to her login page. She typed in the password she used for everything, HisRed1. It worked. There it was—*Snips and Snags: A Designer's Life*. She'd meant it as a joke at the time. Now it seemed a very apt title. Except for the designer part. She hadn't designed anything in over a month. She missed it.

Chenille stared a long time at the screen before selecting "Start a new post." A black box stared back at her, waiting to be filled with words. She hesitated for a moment, then giggled a little and began to type away. Who would ever read it anyway? She needed this.

It's been a long time since I wrote anything here.
I'm not even sure I'm the same person who wrote
here before. Lyle is dead and I am not. It's an
impossible truth that I wake up with every day.
At first, it was like waking up every morning and
realizing my lungs had been stolen. Or my heart.
For months, I couldn't catch my breath in the
mornings, couldn't stop my thoughts at night.

I don't believe in ghosts or anything, but he is
here with me. Less now than before. It's like he's
letting me go a little. Well, a lot. That scares
me.

I scare me.

Though I still miss him terribly and always will,
I think I have finally forgiven Lyle for leaving
me and God for taking him. I can't believe I'm
even writing that, but it's true. I'm almost
to the point of forgiving myself for feeling
somehow responsible. Why hadn't I cooked him
more vegetables, prayed more, been more . . . ?
The questions don't assault me so much anymore.
It's the watery, infinite answer that haunts me,
the knowing that for some things there will be
no answer in this life. No explanation. Only the
aching sound of a widow's scream echoing back into
her own ears. The valley of the shadow of death is
a deep place. Sound carries very well there.

Without knowing it, I seemed to have climbed up
to "see" level, where I can see God again, hear
Him. Only now I'm not so sure if I like what He's
saying, that though I may never get over losing
Lyle, I will get around it. I will love again.

178

Though I know that is what Lyle wanted, it makes me
feel like a traitor. Like a wimp. My grandmother
loved one man, the best man on her block. And when
he died, she met the suitors at the door with a
smile and a curt nod. She'd turned down all of
their proposals before she married her husband—why
would she go backwards now? She lived out her life
caring for people, praying for people, sewing for
people, never knowing the love of a man again.

I thought I was that strong. I hoped I was.

I'm not.

Lyle tried to tell me that, but I wanted to be
better, to be like him. To be like Jesus. I'm not
Jesus, though, and I'm not Lyle. There's something
left in the corner of me that aches to be held, to
be kissed, to be ushered into rooms on the arm of a
husband. There's something in me still left to work
with, to love with.

And that terrifies me.

It terrifies me that love might be about more than
being safe, that it can be a kiss on the mouth of a
man you don't know very well, that sometimes it's
just where you find it, just when you need it. It
isn't always forever with marriage and babies and
names on the mailbox downstairs. Sometimes it's
just for a few weeks, a few days, but it's love all
the same. Just enough love to remind me that I'm
not the one who died, no matter how much I wish it
was me.

Just enough.

Chenille paused for a moment before posting the blog,

surprised and even shocked at some of the things that she'd written, but knowing it was all real, all true. As the new post appeared on screen, she exhaled slowly, thankful that no one else would read it. Writing her thoughts down had cleared many of the thoughts clouding her mind, even answered questions she hadn't known her heart was asking.

Was the love she'd felt for Sergio real?

Yes.

Was it over?

Probably.

Did it still count for something?

Maybe.

Though her husband and baby son died, the love Chenille felt for them still meant something, still counted. Her love for Sergio was real too, even if it had come too late. It had taught her that she still had room, still had time to be a woman, not just a widow. If for nothing else, she loved Sergio for just that. Now she had to set about loving herself.

She opened the other files on her computer next, new files with business ideas and lists of pros and cons for each. These were the files she would have shown to Lyle for his input and prayers. Reading through them now, she didn't find anything that would have garnered his approval. The ideas were all viable, smart, and marketable, but Lyle was always about ministry. He believed that ministry was the best marketing tool and that God would take care of Chenille's business if Chenille took care of God's business.

He'd been right about that. Her firm had been nothing more than a drafty warehouse with a ragtag bundle of inexperienced or burned-out designers. She'd chosen uniforms, of all things to begin with, too practical for the likes of Raya's skill with evening gowns and sportswear. And yet her friend had come and humbled herself, given herself to the job. Even when an old roommate who'd wrecked her wedding asked Raya to design a million-dollar wedding dress, Raya had set her hurt aside for the good of the company.

Chenille's company.

Although she'd signed the resignation papers, Chenille was still the major stockholder in Garments of Praise. She just wasn't acting like it. Jean, who could have worked for any designer in the world, chose Chenille's firm as a place to hide, a place to heal. She had taught them all so much about elegance and about obedience too. Jean's husband Nigel had left a promising career at Reebok and possibilities of his own house in the future to become Chenille's right-hand man. Lyle had died soon after Nigel agreed to take the position. Chenille had often wondered if that had been the thing that kept him hanging on through all the pain, trying to be sure that Garments of Praise would survive.

It had started out as her dream but quickly became theirs. The children they clothed, the charities they gave to, had all come through Lyle and his prayers. He agonized with her over each detail of the business. Prayed with her (and without her) for the employees, accounts, orders, revenues . . . Lyle never would have advised her to leave Garments of Praise. He was about stability. Legacy. She was the one who jumped first and looked later.

I never would have left the business, Red, but I never could have started it either. Go in peace or stay in love. It's okay either way.

Chenille wrapped her arms around her shoulders, trying to drink the bit of Lyle that whispered to her. He was gone though as quickly as he had come, receding back into her memory, pulling back into her mind. The words were true. Lyle's practicality had served a purpose, keeping her from spinning off into a million different directions.

Like she was doing now.

181

He was always the one looking out five years, seeing beyond the edge of her spitfire ideas. Even in his sickness, he'd helped her plan to get the company where it was now. Her company. But it wasn't hers anymore. She owned the biggest share, but her friends all owned it together. It was no longer her vision to carry alone. It was theirs too.

Chenille pressed the heels of her hands to her eyes. In the technicolor blackness behind her hands, she saw a robe in her mind's eye. The mother's robe for her layette. She reached for a sketchpad and began to swoop and dash off a fashionable, comfortable shape. Maybe Lily wouldn't have to be itchy and hot after all.

A smile settled across Chenille's lips as the truth came to her. She let out a breath and relaxed her shoulders as everything came clear.

Whether she stayed or left, her heart and hands would always be affiliated with Garments of Praise in some way. Maybe not as the CEO, maybe not as the boss, or even partner, but always as a friend. She couldn't leave them. Maybe it had been a premature midlife crisis, a hot flash, power surge—whatever Jean wanted to call it—but trying to leave Garments of Praise altogether had definitely been a mistake. The question was, how could it be undone? There'd been papers signed, stocks sold . . .

She shrugged it all away and headed to the kitchen. She was thinking too hard, making things too complicated. She'd worry about her position later, if she even needed a position at all. Right now she just wanted to make some blondie brownies and take them in to the office as a surprise. Right now, she just wanted to be a good friend.

The brownies came together quickly, but someone buzzed at the downstairs door just as she put them into the oven. They buzzed again but didn't say anything. That probably meant Raya's hands were full with the baby and Lily was out of breath. She hoped Lily would have stayed home to rest, but she knew better. Chenille shook her head. Just when she was trying to be nice, her friends go and beat her to it. She hit the button and rambled into the microphone. "I was just making some brownies for you ladies. Come on up. Lily, if you're down there, go home, all right? Your husband called me to check on you, and I told him you're going a little—"

"It's me, Chenille. Sergio."

She wiped her hands on the apron tied loosely around her waist and looked around the flour-dusted kitchen. There was no use even trying to clean it up. Or cover up her feelings either. Things were what they were. "Come on up. I hope you're hungry."

15

Sergio ate three brownies and drank two glasses of milk before he said much of anything. He was stalling, Chenille knew, but it still did her good to see him enjoy the brownies. She'd make another batch for the girls as soon as he left, Lord willing she was still in the mood. The look on Sergio's face troubled her.

"Is it Megan? Did something happen to the baby?" She bit into a brownie herself and closed her eyes. It was her best batch in a very long time.

He brushed the crumbs from his mouth and cleared his throat. "Megan's fine. The baby's doing well. They did the surgery today. This morning."

Chenille snatched off her apron and dropped the brownie onto the plate. "Why didn't you call? I would have come." She turned in circles, trying to gather her thoughts. Where were her keys? They weren't on the hook next to the stove . . .

"I know that you would have come. That's why I didn't call. Megan asked me not to. She's thankful for everything you've done for her, but we both realize that you've

184

probably done enough. We didn't want to put you through all the waiting and worrying again. So far the baby is okay. She's a fighter, like Erica was. Very cute."

"I'll bet." *We.* That was hard to hear. Everything he'd just said was about *them.* Didn't it confirm what she'd known when she'd seen them kiss? It didn't matter now. She needed to get over there, to see that baby. She'd have to deal with her own issues later. Chenille was in the hall closet now, getting her coat and trying to remember the bus and train schedule and deciding which would be fastest. She was still thinking it through and looking for her keys when Sergio stood and said the words that stopped her in her tracks.

"I asked her to marry me. Megan, I mean. She accepted. I didn't want you to hear it from anyone else. I see now that it was really ridiculous for me to think there could be anything between you and me. You barely know me. Megan and I don't have the best track record, but she loves me and she needs me."

He was right, on both counts. Chenille surprised herself by appearing happy for them—as soon as she remembered how to breathe again. "Congratulations. I hope that the two of you are very happy together." She wanted to say more, to tell him that he wasn't crazy for loving her, that she'd been crazy for not loving him back, but she didn't say any of that. Now wasn't the time for it. Marriage meant something, something forever. Chenille wouldn't stand in the way of forever. She might have to put a hurting on this whole pan of brownies when he left, but she wasn't going to hurt him. Or Megan either, though Chenille was starting to understand some of how Raya must have felt about her. Saved or not, Megan still seemed to end up in the middle of things.

Sergio walked toward her and held out his hand. He seemed tense, even subdued. "Thank you for understanding. I think this is the right thing, the best thing for everyone. My mother is really happy. Megan is too. I'm glad you're happy for us too."

But are you happy, Sergio?

What about Sergio's happiness? Didn't that count for anything? Chenille knew better than most people about sacrifice and the costs that God sometimes required, but she wasn't sure this was one of those times. As she shook his hand, it took everything within her not to ask Sergio if he truly loved Megan. Instead, Chenille focused on the chocolate berry cream she'd have when he left. This wasn't her business anymore. Maybe it never was.

Just remember that the love with him was real. That it was enough.

She opened her big mouth anyway. "You said that she loves you and she's happy and your mother is happy. Do you love Megan, Sergio? Are you happy?"

He reached out and touched Chenille's cheek. "Happy? I'm not sure what that means anymore. I'm not sure if that's even the goal. I feel blessed. Blessed to have you to care about whether or not I'm happy. I hope I can make Megan happy."

"I think you've already made her the happiest woman alive." Chenille reached over and grabbed a brownie before she said something else that she'd regret later.

Some things are even beyond chocolate. It was difficult for Chenille to admit, but true all the same. She cooked up every chocolate chip, chocolate bar, or bit of cocoa powder in her kitchen and ended up packing it all away in the refrigerator. Two days later, when the snowstorm subsided that had begun not long after Sergio left her apartment, Chenille pulled out her goodies and headed for Garments of Praise. Chenille was glad to get out of the house. The news of Megan and Sergio's upcoming wedding was still a shock, but she couldn't focus on it any longer. She wondered if Sergio really thought she'd taken it as well as it had appeared. She hoped not. Knowing Megan, they might ask her to be part of the wedding or something. That would truly be a disaster.

Don't be like that. She's your friend now. Act like it.

When she got to Garments of Praise, her treats and her appearance were a hit. Everyone from the receptionist to the janitor stopped by Raya's office to say how much they missed Chenille and to ask if she was coming back. She only smiled and hugged them all, not wanting to make promises that couldn't be kept. When all the cookies, brownies, and triple layer cake were gone, the office cleared out, leaving her alone with Raya.

Her friend shut the door and locked it before opening both arms to Chenille.

Chenille dissolved into a heap of tears she hadn't known she had left. "How did you know?" she said through her sniffles.

Raya laughed. "How could I not know? You baked enough chocolate for a small nation. Whatever happened is either really big or really bad."

"It's both. Sergio and Megan are getting married." There. She'd said it out loud.

Her friend got a startled look on her face. She reached over for a white chocolate chip and cranberry cookie, the sweetest thing in the bunch besides magic coconut bars. "Okay, I have to sit down. I really want to believe that Megan has changed. I know God is able. But still, I just don't know. And I can't believe that Flex didn't say anything."

Chenille reached for a magic coconut bar, but her stomach

growled in protest. She'd eaten three in the middle of the night and was still paying for it. "Flex? What does he have to do with any of this?"

Raya squeezed her eyes shut. "These things are sweet! But they are so good. Anyway, Flex and Sergio have been praying together at the gym a few times a week."

Now Chenille was mad and she didn't know why. Had Flex told Sergio to do this? No, that wasn't how he and Lyle did things. She and Raya did the let-me-tell-you-what-I-think-and-then-pray thing. Flex, on the other hand, was pretty much about taking everything to the Lord. Still, Chenille felt angry that no one had told her. "Why didn't you tell me?"

Raya gulped from the water bottle on her desk. "Tell you what? That Flex is praying with the guy? It's really none of my business. Or yours."

"So why are you telling me now?" Yep. She was definitely mad, though she wasn't sure why. Was it because Sergio was becoming friends with one of her friends? Maybe. He had Megan and his mother. Couldn't he take the two of them and be done with it? Flex and Raya belonged to her.

No, Red. They belong to God. So do you.

Dead men can be so annoying.

Raya threw up her hands. "You got me there. I guess it's still none of our business. I'm under the influence of chocolate and extreme distress. I have no answers this time, only questions. Are you going to fight for him? How do you really feel about this?"

Chenille shook her head. "Nope. No duels to the death or anything. Just be prepared for more baked goods. She had the baby too, by the way. A girl. I didn't get a name from him. Guys. They forget the birth details."

"So he proposed because she had the baby? Wow. He really is an amazing guy. Most guys would run from their own

188

kids, let alone someone else's. I've got to sit down. This cookie is making me dizzy. I was doing so good with that no-sugar thing, and now I'm inhaling it. You've killed about five of my resolutions already, and it's not even lunchtime."

They both laughed. Chenille brushed the remaining crumbs off Raya's lap. "You could use a few calories, Catwoman. Flex will burn it off you anyway."

"Ain't that the truth? That's what I'm worried about. I think he likes me bigger, if you can believe that. As much as he's a workout freak, when I'm pregnant and get a little meat on me, he's all over me."

Chenille rolled her eyes. "Um, Raya. He's all over you anytime. You two are sickening. In a good way, of course." Most of the time, anyway. Sometimes they were just plain sickening.

Raya shrugged. "Well, I guess. Gram says that people think that Flex and I are the perfect couple. We're not. We brought a lot of baggage into our marriage. Add two small children and a teenager into the mix and there's a lot of issues to deal with. I'm thankful that God checks baggage. I guess he knows what to do with Megan too. As much as I worried about her still being single, I didn't necessarily want her to snag your man."

So much for the stomach. That called for a coconut bar. Chenille shoved a bite into her mouth. She felt dizzy too. Oh well. As she sifted through Raya's words, an understanding dawned on her. She stopped chewing. "Wait a minute. What do you mean, you being worried about Megan still being single? You've been worried about Megan all this time? You shouldn't. Flex loves you like crazy."

Raya answered a knock at the door and signed some invoices. She went to her computer and logged in some disbursement forms. Forms that would have gone to Chenille a month ago. What had she done to her friend?

She twisted around in her chair to face Chenille. "I know that Flex loves me. I love him too. I know he'll be relieved when Darryl gets married too. I'm just being real. It's crazy out here."

Darryl, the guy whom Raya had almost married—before she found him kissing Megan at the rehearsal dinner. His wasn't a name Chenille heard mentioned often from Raya or Flex. Until lately, Megan had been someone they all avoided as well. Now it was like they were all back where they started four years ago, when the firm got started. It'd seemed like a century.

The mention of Darryl turned back the clock quickly. The fact that he just happened to be the father of Megan's baby didn't make things any less complicated. Now Sergio would inherit Darryl to worry about. What a mess. Darryl had straightened up and made another shot for Raya after "the incident," but Flex put a stop to that, and fast. Darryl had lain low for a couple of years trying to grow in his faith and seemed to have done well with that until he hooked up with Megan and got her pregnant. Chenille wondered what his reaction would be to all of this. "Have you talked to Darryl lately? What does he think about this whole thing with Sergio? I know he was trying to come to labor classes with Megan at one point, and she didn't want him to."

Raya reached out her hand for another cookie, but she stopped in midair. Maybe she'd realized the limitations of chocolate too. "Wait, are you telling me that Darryl is Megan's baby's father?"

Chenille nodded. "I thought you knew." From the look on Raya's face, she definitely had not known anything about this part of the story. "Now see, I know I'm glad I'm saved and married. That is just too much drama for me to even comment on, but you know I'm going to have to, right? I just have to think of something to say. You messed me up with that one."

She wasn't the only one messed up. Chenille was messed up by everything, including standing in Raya's office watching as she ran the business she'd foolishly left behind. Raya held up a finger to take a call, which Chenille quickly identified as Reebok.

Her friend mocked up a few dress forms as several people spoke on the line, presenting strategies for the fall sportswear collection. At one point, Raya paused over the mannequin in front of her, trying to decide where to gather the fabric on a blouse. Chenille started pinning before she realized what she was doing.

Raya gave her a crazy look and shooed her away before concluding the call a few minutes later. Knowing how much Raya disliked people messing with her designs, at least until she was sure where things were going, Chenille closed one eye and waited for an outburst. She got one, but it wasn't about what she expected.

Her friend waved a pair of shears back and forth. "Now I was going to hold my peace on this one because Lord knows that none of these folks are any of my business anymore, but Megan went too far on this one. Darryl was really walking strong with the Lord. She had to take her fast tail and go and visit him. I should have known that wasn't going to work out—"

"Wait? You knew about all this? That was almost a year ago. You'd just had the baby, right? What were you doing talking to Darryl?" Red lights flashed everywhere in Chenille's mind. No wonder Flex would be glad when Darryl got married off. Her pastor always said that sex joined people together in ways we can't imagine. Darryl had talked Raya into losing her virtue not long before their engagement. Her friend wasn't

191

answering and Chenille didn't like that either. "I'm going to ask again, what were you doing talking to Darryl?"

Raya turned away. "Nothing, that's what. I haven't talked to him since either. I wasn't in a good place with God at the time. Darryl was. He asked about being friends with me and Flex. He even wanted me to put Flex on the phone. I didn't think that any of it was a good idea. He mentioned Megan coming to visit to attend his church, and I freaked out. She was supposed to stay with his pastor, but still, I just know how she can be, even when she doesn't mean it. How any of us can be."

Chenille was stunned. What was that supposed to mean? She was too afraid to ask. She'd always seen Flex and Raya as this perfect couple. Their love had looked beautiful next to what she shared with Lyle, but since she'd been alone, being with them could sometimes be like trying to stare at the sun. Too bright. Now her friend seemed to be saying that even their marriage had its dark places. That forced Chenille to remember that her own marriage hadn't been perfect either, no matter how much she tried to remember it that way. "So Flex doesn't know that you talked to him? And that was it, just that once?"

Raya turned away from her. "Flex knows. He took over talking with Darryl after that. Anyway, I didn't want to get in the middle of the Megan thing, so I left it alone. Figured I have my own husband to worry about. I prayed for Darryl, but I see now that I didn't pray hard enough. I guess that's why he left California and came to New York, to try to be with Megan. He never said. He must have been ashamed to tell us what happened."

That made sense. When Chenille had first become a Christian, she'd had little compassion for Christians who fell into sin. They'd made a choice and would have to deal with the consequences. Now that she was older and had been walking with the Lord longer, she knew that fellowship and accountability was often the only hedge between even the most upright person and a horrible mistake. Both Megan and Darryl had lacked something she was blessed enough to have several of—good friends.

"It's not your fault, Raya. It's not Flex's fault either. I know you want to help, but I think it was wise for both of you to keep some distance from Darryl and Megan, considering what happened."

Raya didn't agree. "You know what, Chenille? Jesus doesn't think that way. I hurt him all the time. I betray him. Peter cursed and denied Christ, but he became an apostle. Lyle's death really rocked Flex in a lot of ways. I do hope he and Sergio can become friends. It'd probably be good for both of them. On the other hand, I've got to be a better friend to Flex too. And to God. Raising the kids and taking care of other people is all we can focus on a lot of the time."

Chenille hung her head under the weight of the words "other people." She was "other people." Her friends' marriage had been strained and she hadn't even noticed. Lyle would have noticed, would have been praying about it for weeks before she even brought it up. But she wasn't Lyle. She was the needy friend who'd been sapping their time and energy the past few years. Megan and Darryl were new Christians. Chenille should have been able to stand on her feet, even to minister to them. It's what Lyle would have done.

Forgive me, Lord. For everything.

She sighed, coming to terms with just how different she and Lyle really had been. He'd made her better. She'd made him braver. That's the wonderful thing about marriage—you become part of the other person. She hoped for Sergio's sake that he got the good part of Megan. It'd be a shame to see him change for the worse.

As she thought about that, Chenille laughed at the irony of it.

Raya lifted her head from where it'd been cradled in her hand and gave her friend a funny look. "As crazy as all this is, you're laughing. What is it? All that chocolate made you lose it, huh?"

Chenille held her side. "No. I was just thinking that Megan is going to have herself a wedding after all. I guess we'll actually be making a dress for her to earn all that money her father gave us."

Raya covered her eyes with the back of her hand. "Oh goodness. Don't remind me. I'm starting to think that you left this place just in time. Sure we can't offer you an internship, Ms. Rizzo? We could use your help about now. If I recall, you were the last one working on Megan's wedding dress. What happens now that she's talking marriage again? For all that her daddy paid us, I just can't go there."

Chenille rolled her head to one side, thinking through what Raya had said. "I hope you're kidding. As much as I'd like to say that I could do it, I don't think I can. Maybe I could assist someone else? I don't know. But that other part . . ." Her friend had meant it as a joke, of course, but it actually sounded interesting. An internship? Now that was a thought. She had been the last one working on Megan's dress and probably the person at the firm closest to her. "I may take you up on that internship thing. You pray about it and I will too."

Raya threw up her hands and squealed with joy. "I was only half kidding, but I didn't think you'd even consider it. Are you serious about praying about it? I hope so. Everyone will be so happy to know that you're even thinking about coming back in any capacity." Raya's face brightened.

Chenille smiled to conceal her doubt. Lots of people around the company thought she should have stepped down a long time ago, even soon after Lyle died. They were probably right about her emotional state, but she no longer cared about falling short of the standard people had come to expect from her before. She was different now. Her life was different. "I knew you were kidding. That's what makes it such a great idea. I've been taking life seriously for a long time, even before Lyle got sick. I'm not sure if I ever want to do that again. The cost is too high."

16

"So you told her?"

Flex's voice grated against Sergio's ears worse than the sound of his own grunting as he pushed the barbell up over his chest. He could hear the accusation in his new friend's tone, hear the real question behind his words. *So you hurt her?* Why did Flex act like Sergio was the only one who'd done any hurting, like Chenille even wanted him in the first place? "I told her. She took it well."

A little too well.

Not that he'd expected her to toss the brownies across the room or anything. If she had, he probably would have dived for the pan. He was still nibbling off the extras he'd stashed in his pocket. He wondered now if it was the brownies themselves or the fact that Chenille had baked them that made them taste so good.

You're getting married. That's over.

"So it's over between the two of you?" Flex asked again, as if reading Sergio's mind. He was leaning over Sergio to spot him in case he couldn't lift the weight, but his hands were on his hips as his friend pushed out the last two repetitions and rested the bar back in its slot on the stand.

Offended now, Sergio sat up and wiped his face off with a white towel with Heavenly Bodies imprinted on it. Flex owned the gym, but he didn't train many people personally anymore. He spent as much time on the road as spokesperson for the sportswear line of Garments of Praise as he did managing his gym. The fact that Flex was working with him one-on-one had drawn everyone's respect and attention at the gym. But right now, Sergio was thinking this whole prayer-partner-buddy thing was overrated. "Look, I said it's over, okay? Whether I proposed to Megan or not, it was still over between me and Chenille. She ended it before it began. I just put the corpse in the ground, that's all."

"Uh-huh," Flex said, waving Sergio to the side door. They walked down the hall together to Flex's office, where he had two treadmills set side by side for a grueling thirty-minute run of hills and intervals. "I ain't buying it. Not for a minute. But I'm not going to argue with you today. We're not that cool yet. So it's on to the dreadmill for now, Dr. Loyola."

Sergio froze. "I hate it when you do that. You know I don't like to be called doctor. I'm just Sergio. I'm your friend. Or at least I'm trying to be. You're not making it easy. I know I'm not Lyle, but I'm here." Sergio was more out of breath by the end of his words than he had been during their entire workout. He hadn't meant to say that. Not yet anyway. Flex was right—they weren't cool enough yet for that. He could tell by the pain that flashed through Flex's eyes. He looked like a lion about to roar.

He laughed instead. "Maybe we're going to be tight after all, bro. You got me on that one for sure." He slapped Sergio across the back as they entered his office. The stark yet plush room in leather and granite always had a stray teddy bear or basketball nearby.

Flex clicked on the light inside. "I'll try not to call you doctor, okay? In the meantime, you need to tell me why there are blondie crumbs all over my office. Chenille's blondies? I'd know them anywhere. And no, I'm not questioning you about your diet."

Sergio stared at the floor. Just like Hansel and Gretel, he had sure enough left a trail of crumbs as he'd munched his way into the gym this morning. He rarely got days off and definitely didn't take time to eat right or exercise, even though he made a living saving other people's lives. But since he was going to be a father and a husband, he'd decided to do better, starting with working out with Flex whenever his schedule would allow. Now he wondered if he hadn't made a mistake in opening himself up to yet another person, and Chenille's friend at that. He laughed in spite of himself.

"Man, it looks like I was leaving a trail to get back home, doesn't it?"

"Maybe you were." Flex pulled his leg behind him in a runner's stretch. He wasn't laughing.

Praise music filled the room as Flex hit a switch and climbed onto the treadmill next to the door. "Let's go, man. Run it out. We'll talk later."

With a nod, Sergio took his position, pressing the correct program button and thankful that the routine came with a warm-up. Right now, running on this treadmill was the last thing he wanted to do. He wanted to run back to the hospital and check on Megan and the baby. Maybe even call Chenille—

A banging sound cut through music and the door flung open. A tall, angry guy bounded in, heading straight for Flex on the treadmill. "Where's the doctor?" he screamed over the song.

Flex turned toward Sergio and shook his head. "Serg, I think he's here to see you. This is Darryl, the father of Megan's baby."

Sergio had seen people slip off the backs of treadmills, but he never thought it would happen to him. Yet, when Darryl's eyes fixed on him, both men froze, and it wasn't until he was half off the machine that Sergio realized what was happening.

"Watch out, man! Are you okay?" Flex reached out for him with a quick hand.

"I'm fine." Sergio righted himself and brushed his friend's hand away before circling the machine to meet more than eyes with Darryl. "Nice to meet you, Darryl. It's a little late, but better late than never."

Darryl clenched his jaw. And his fist. "Late? Never? You've got a lot of nerve, Doctor. Is it every day that you go around proposing to your patients—"

Flex, who'd slowed to a walk, held up a finger. "She's not his patient now. The baby is, but—"

The other two men looked at Flex as if he'd lost his mind, pretty much the same way they'd been looking at each other. He took the hint and punched up his speed again, signaling his exit to the conversation.

"What he said," Sergio spat out in a terse voice, wondering why he wanted to laugh all of a sudden.

A near-smile formed on Darryl's mouth. "Man, are you laughing at me? This is for real. I've got a daughter and no-body called me. That's not right. And now you're trying to take her mother from me too?" The flash of humor faded quickly as pain clouded Darryl's eyes.

Flex's treadmill came to a stop. He walked in front of Sergio and faced Darryl, taking him by the shoulders. "Nobody is trying to take your baby, D. Nobody. Serg is a good man. You are too. You know you messed up, though. Let God work this out." He shot a wary glance at Sergio. "To be honest, I'm not so sure that this wedding is God's solution either, but I can't say it isn't." He looked back at Darryl. "Neither can you."

Sweat rolled down Sergio's forehead and burned his eyes. He wiped at it with his sleeve, praying for something to say. How could Flex be here consoling Darryl, the same guy who had taken Raya's virtue and then kissed another woman at his own wedding rehearsal?

The same way you're engaged to the woman he was kissing. You're no better than Darryl, and Megan is no worse than him.

The thought hit Sergio like a brick. He had always seen things through the filter of Megan's presence, knowing her better than Raya or Flex. Getting to know them now, he could see just how much Megan had hurt them—although if Raya had married Darryl, she wouldn't have ended up with Flex in the first place. He took a deep breath. Flex was right. God would work this out. He'd have to.

As Flex stepped away from Darryl's stooped head and slumped shoulders, Sergio stepped into his place. "You know what, man? I apologize. I let Megan handle all this with you, but I should have made sure that you were there. I thought that you didn't want to be there, that you didn't care. Now that I see that I was wrong—"

"What? Now that you know that I want my baby, you can stop treating Megan like some charity case and make her stand up and work things out with me? Is that it? I don't think so. I think you like being the hero. Well, she ended up with me because things wouldn't work out between the two of you. How do you think it's going to work now? Just because she had a baby?"

Darryl raised his head and gave Sergio a look that chilled his bones—the look of a wounded animal.

Sergio reached for the towel hanging from the treadmill beside him and then for his duffel bag and keys. He waved to Flex. "Thanks for the workout, man. I'll call you. I need to go before I do something I'll regret."

Like asking Megan to marry me? Too late for that.

He gritted his teeth together as if ripping the thought to shreds. It was time for him to get married. He knew Megan well. She was flawed, but he was too. At least there wouldn't be any surprises. Maybe it wasn't some passionate love from a TV movie, but they'd get there. They'd have to.

"Darryl, I'll ask Megan to call you." He dug into his bag for a card. "Here's the number to the Neonatal Intensive Care Unit where the baby is. Call anytime for updates. Just tell them you're Brianna's father—"

Darryl gripped Sergio's arm like a blood pressure cuff at full compression. "Wait. Brianna? Is that her name?"

This was so awkward. Why had Megan put him in this situation? What kind of way was this to learn the name of your own child? And the firstborn, at that. "Yes, that's her name. Brianna Renee Ariatta." The name lady had thought it was a lot of syllables, but it sounded like music to Sergio. Brianna looked like music too, like a sweet little love song. The problem now was going to be dealing with the man who'd written it.

Darryl dissolved in a heap in one of Flex's office chairs. He was nodding to himself and mumbling. "Okay. Okay. I get that. I get that. At least she gave me that."

Sergio looked at Flex with what he was sure must have been a puzzled look, as confused as he was feeling. "What's he talking about?" It wasn't as if Megan had named the baby Darrylicia or something.

Thank God.

Flex was running easy now, the way only someone who logged a lot of miles could. "Brianna was his sister. Raised him up when his mother died. She never had any kids of her own. He always told Raya that if they had daughters, he'd want the first one to be named Brianna. I think Renee was part of Megan's mother's name."

Sergio clutched his keys until they dug into his palm. Yes, Renee had been Megan's mother's middle name. He'd met the woman a few times at the AIDS hospice center in California before she had died. She'd become a Christian during her illness, but seeing Megan always made her cry for one reason or another. And apologize. She was always very apologetic.

Still, he was disturbed that Megan had used Darryl's sister's name without saying anything about it. He was even more disturbed that Flex could recount what some joker had told his wife when the two were dating. "Man, how do you know what he told Raya when they were together? That doesn't even have anything to do with you."

Flex increased his incline, but his breathing never faltered. He laughed into his fist. "When are you supposed to be getting married again? 'Cause I'm going to have to school you in some things, brother. You might have to know a whole lot of things you don't want to know in order to be a good husband to your wife. You're going to have to carry all the baggage that other men left behind in her life, starting with her daddy. And yes, even folks like our friend Darryl here."

Darryl, who'd been silent since learning his daughter's name, looked at Flex with a mock scowl. "Man, let it go, all right? I get it. I get it. All this is payback for all the jacked-up things I've done. I got saved, but there's still payback. There always is."

Flex turned off the treadmill and bowed his head. Then he bit his lip.

Sergio didn't like the looks of his expression as he got off the machine and stepped toward Darryl. Sergio tried to make it around Darryl's chair and out the door, but he didn't quite clear the chair before his quiet, calm friend turned into a tornado and snatched Darryl up out of the chair.

"You're not getting what you deserve, D. None of us do. That's what the blood is for. We deserve hell, everyone of us. God knows the both of us do. But having a baby in less-than-perfect circumstances is not your punishment. It's your blessing. Nothing but the blood of Jesus could repay what you did to my wife and what you almost did to me. Don't think I don't know where those little phone calls last year were heading. You don't have the sense to know, but I do. Now get out of my gym and go to the hospital and handle your business. And don't ever barge into my office again. Understood?" He released the knot of Darryl's shirt that had been in his hands and walked out of the office.

Sergio was right behind him. He'd have to remember never to get Flex mad. That man could move a little too quick to be played with. His wisdom was nothing to be dismissed either. He'd dropped some serious knowledge in the midst of the baby-daddy drama today, wisdom that Sergio was going to have to go home and ponder.

He moved quickly past Darryl, who was still trying to smooth his shirt back into shape. A lost cause.

"Wait, Doc."

He'd almost made it. "Yeah?" It was all he could think of to say. After all that had gone on this morning, Sergio's mind was reeling.

Darryl pulled a bracelet wadded in tissue paper out of his jean pocket and shoved it into Sergio's hands. "Take this. Give it to Megan and tell her—no, ask her, if she'd please put it on Brianna for me. Tell her that I'll be up there today to see her too. I'm not going to come at you again about this wedding thing, but I'm not going to stop praying either. If it's over between me and Megan, then God is going to have to make that clear to me."

Wasn't planning to marry another man pretty clear? What did the guy want, a legal decision? Sergio clutched the paper and the small piece of jewelry inside. Baby bracelets. Lots of people were fond of those. He didn't want to tell Darryl that it probably wouldn't fit since Brianna was a preemie. No use in ruining the guy's day. "I'll give it to her." He took a deep breath thinking how much Darryl reminded him of his brother Blue and the night that had separated them so many years before. Neither the memory nor the reality gave him a good feeling. What had he gotten himself into?

Things were slowly changing at Garments of Praise. Chenille's formerly bright blue office was now a muted chocolate brown. The creative hour, when employees were free to pursue any artistic endeavor of their choice, had been cut from daily to once a week. Her barely audible praise music had been drowned out by streams of jazz and reggae pouring out of offices and into the hall.

As Chenille filed through the halls waving hello on the first afternoon of her internship, she wondered how much longer she'd be able to recognize the place at the rate things were changing. And then she reached Raya's office, still bright pink with feather boa doorknob covers, more like a college dorm room than an office. Inside, she could hear a baby crying and Jay, Raya's older son, crooning a lullaby with the voice of an angel. It was the most beautiful tune she'd heard that day, despite her new iPod addiction.

Some things never changed, and Chenille was glad about

that. She pushed through the door with a relieved sigh, opening her arms to Jay as though it were her own son she was seeing for the first time in far too long. "Jay! How are you, sweetie?"

She gasped as he answered in a voice much deeper than when he'd talked to her last. Even deeper than Flex's. And was that a full beard on his face? She covered her mouth with one hand as he leaned down to hug her.

Her reaction made him laugh out loud. "You're so funny, Aunt Chenille. Hold on, let me pick up little sis. She's pouting because I hugged you."

Looking Jay up and down, Chenille could hardly believe that this was the same boy whose picture she'd held up in a staff meeting four years ago. He'd been orphaned by AIDS and was living with an elderly aunt and headed in the wrong direction. He'd been in her Sunday school class at New Man Fellowship, and she'd been ashamed of herself when she got the picture for not having known his situation. She'd wanted to try to adopt him herself or at least take care of his needs, but Lyle advised her to still share his picture and story at the staff meeting. "You think you know that boy, but God knows him. He knows what he needs too. Let's talk to his aunt and see what she thinks, but I have a feeling that this boy needs something you and I don't have."

And Lyle had been right. Flex and Raya had what Jay needed, only they had to realize they needed each other first. Jay had played a big part in making that happen. In trying to be good mentors to Jay, they had both learned how much they had in common, namely, a lot of love for one boy with a great smile. Tears threatened as Chenille looked at that same smile now, watching as he held his baby sister, who'd grown like a weed since Chenille had seen her last.

"Jay, I'm just amazed. Look how handsome you are. I

mean, I see you at the front door at church and at all the activities, but I guess I thought it was the suit. It's not. You have really grown into a wonderful young man. Have I told you that? I know I've been so wrapped up in myself that—"

"Shhh." He kissed her on the cheek. "You don't need to tell me anything. I know that you love me. I know that you're proud of me. I also know that you had a big loss. It isn't easy. If anybody knows that, I do. Go easy on yourself." He held his sister's tiny fingers in the air with his. "Isn't that right, baby girl? Go easy . . ."

Chenille pressed her eyes shut for a second. She'd always thought that when Raya and Flex adopted Jay, everything in his life had automatically changed for the better, that everything was all right. She realized now, having lost Lyle, that although he loved Raya and Flex and they'd been good to him, he still loved his parents and his aunt too. Though many people called their mother's friends *auntie*, she knew that Jay meant it. She, Raya, Flex, Lily, and Jean and their husbands really were his family. They were hers too.

"Go easy, huh? I'll try to remember that. By the way, what are you doing out of school, Mr. Senior? And where's your mother?"

Jay rocked back and forth with the baby, peeking over her little shoulder to see if she was sleeping. She was. In fact, Chenille thought she heard the little girl snoring, if that was possible. Jay nodded to confirm it. "You should hear her at night. She gets it from Daddy. He purrs like an engine when he's moving, but when he sleeps, he sounds like a bulldozer. I'm out today for teacher planning day. I usually hang out with Dad at the gym or on the road, but Mom said you were going to be coming in today for your first day as an intern, and I wasn't about to miss that for the world. I'm sort of an intern now too. I come by here most every afternoon, for a few minutes at least."

"Great. You can show me the ropes." Chenille kicked off her pumps and shoved them under Raya's desk. She'd been so happy to see Jay that she was still in her coat with her bag over her shoulder. She slipped the bag off her arm now. Jay offered to take it, but she would rather that he concentrated on holding the baby. He was a pro at it by now with Raya having two little ones, but still . . . He was a teenager. And a boy, at that. "You still haven't told me where your mom is."

Jay lowered the baby back into her portable crib in the corner. "It's Tuesday, Aunt Nilly. They're in staff meeting, It's in the afternoons now," he whispered so as not to wake the infant.

Chenille walked over to the overstuffed chair that Raya kept in her office for nursing the babies. She curled up in it, thankful for the tight fit. Staff meeting. In the afternoon now. Of course that's where Raya would be. It's where she would have been too if she hadn't lost her mind and given up on everything. The last staff meeting she could remember was the one where Sergio had come and talked about them making quilts and baby clothes for the NICU. He'd been so happy to see her that day. What she wouldn't do to see that look on his face again.

Quit it.

It pained her too that Jay had called her Aunt Nilly, his little brother Ray's name for her. Ray just couldn't get Chenille to come out of his mouth in one bite. One afternoon he'd toddled into her office and pointed to a box of cookies on her desk. Chenille had run her finger under the words and read "vanilla wafers" off the box just like Raya had instructed her. *Don't baby talk to my kids. Read to them. Explain.*

His little eyes had gotten round and wide. "Nilly wapers?" he'd said in an amazed voice.

"Yes." Chenille had nodded, waving as he headed back for Raya's office. Later that evening, Raya had called her, cracking up. "Aunt Nilly has her own cookies!" he'd exclaimed proudly at dinner, producing the soggy proof from his pocket. It was a joke between them all and a bittersweet memory of what types of funny stories she'd never share with her own son. And yet, God was good.

"Sleeping on the job already? Now what kind of intern do we have here, Jay? I think I might have to put you in charge of training this one." It was Raya's voice. She must have come into the office without Chenille noticing. It wouldn't have taken much for that to happen. She was definitely in her own world.

She swung her legs around and jumped out of the chair, giving Raya a tight hug. "I love you, you know that? I mean really."

Raya kissed her hair and hugged her back, just as snugly. "I do know that, Silly Nilly. Now let me go before you pop a button."

Chenille looked at her friend, a vision in a winter white cashmere sweater and a gold suede skirt that buttoned up to a high, slim waist. She looked queenly as always, just not as colorful. "That reminds me of . . ."

"Jean," Raya said, leaning over her desk and flipping through her rolodex. "You know y'all shop for me like you're shopping for yourselves. I like this, though. I don't have to be bright every day."

Chenille smiled. Raya was pink no matter what color she had on. Only when she was with Darryl and wearing a three-foot-long wig and a deluge of sheath dresses to please him had Raya looked the color of the clothes she was wearing. Her friend's love for God and her husband's love for her kept her bold and beautiful. The hairstyle she was sporting, a platinum blonde afro with gold highlights, was just another example. "I see you went back to your goldi-fro. It looks even better than last time. Isn't it cold, though? That wind out there almost knocked me down this morning."

Raya ran a hand over her head. "Flex kept looking at a picture of me with that hair and commenting on how good I'd looked with it. When he said it the fifth time, I made an appointment. Funny how I cut it in the first place because I'd been wearing all those crazy weaves to please Darryl. Now it's different. I know Flex thinks I'm beautiful all the time. That, plus trying to remind all those little heifers at the gym that I'm still me, even with all my kids in tow, makes me want to look nice for him."

She had Chenille there. Not that she'd looked like a slug all the time or anything. She and Lyle just hadn't been as high maintenance as Raya and Flex. A haircut meant "Are you busy tonight?" She chuckled at the thought of it. She'd once put lipstick on at home and Lyle had given her the eye and asked her if she was trying to seduce him. It was the little things like that now, the talking and the laughter, that she missed most. Not just Lyle, but having someone around. She missed that too.

"Whoa. You ladies are getting way over my head. Especially you, Mom. Next thing I know, you'll be talking about feminine products on sale or something." His long legs squeezed past Raya's desk. He held up his cell phone. "I'm going down to the bakery on the corner and help them with the bread. It's herbed focaccia day, I think."

Raya's face tightened a little. "You're going back to the bakery again? Don't you think you need to be sticking around here and learning something about this business? Or going over to the gym with your dad? Stop bothering that man over there. He has enough to worry about without you in there, all legs and hands, covered with flour."

In the way only an eighteen-year-old boy on the brink of manhood can, Jay looked at his mother and batted his eyelashes. He had on his coat and hat before saying a word. "I am going back to the bakery again, Mom, unless you're forbidding me to do so. In which case, I'll sit here and be bored to death and then go in the back and try to choke myself on a bolt of polyester. It's too cold to get the bus all the way to the gym, and I'd rather smell bread than sweat right now. Oh yeah, I'm also not bothering the man. I'm teaching him."

It was Chenille's turn to give Jay a funny look. "You teaching him? Who? The baker? Why, that's impossible. You're a kid. That man has been to culinary school. He's been making bread for years."

Raya, however, did not seem surprised. Though Jay wasn't her biological child, he was hers, and they were the same in many ways just as if she had birthed him. When she and Chenille were teens sweltering in the Brooklyn summer heat, Raya would come to the Garment District with her notebook, explaining to seamstresses how to make some sketch that her grandmother had torn out of her dream book and passed around. Some people were trained how to do things and became very successful at it. Other people were born knowing it, born feeling it. For Raya, "it" was clothes. For Jay, "it" was food. She had the grocery bill to prove it.

"Chenille, that boy is a bread-baking fool. There's no telling what he's down there showing that poor man. You should see my kitchen on the weekends. It looks like some kind of chemistry lab, only with flour."

Jay started laughing again as he wound his scarf around his neck and pushed his gloves down between his fingers.

"But do it be good though? That's all I'm asking. Have I ever fixed you something nasty? Ever?"

Raya put a hand on her hip and waved Jay on. "Go on, boy. We all know you can cook. I think it's the only reason you're good in math now. Go on, but don't blow up the man's place like you do my kitchen with yeast exploding out of bowls and mess. And listen to him too. You don't know everything."

He bent low and tipped his skull cap. "Yes, Mother. Shall I bring you ladies a sample of our creations?"

"Yes!" Chenille half shouted the words. The baby began to cry in the corner. "I'm sorry," she said, running for the crib.

Raya made it there in one stride, swooped the baby up with one hand, and patted Chenille's elbow with the other. "I've got her. It's time for her to eat." She sat on the floor and rested against an exercise ball, nudging up her sweater.

Jay kicked his foot up on a chair to tie his boots. "I know I'm going now. If you think her snoring was something, wait until you hear that baby eat. When she gets teeth, we might have to move—"

"Leave my baby alone!" Raya said playfully as Jay checked his phone for the time and headed out.

He gave Chenille a final quick hug and then took her hand, leaving something smooth and cold in her palm. "It's a turquoise. Aunt Lily got me into the whole rocks-and-minerals thing for a minute, so now I pick things up here and there. Dad and I were out West for a shoot he was on, and they had this place where you could pay five dollars and mine your own gemstones. I didn't think that was real, but Aunt Lil says it is. I was going to give it to her, but when I was praying this morning, you came to my mind. I guess you do like blue."

Chenille turned the stone over and over in her hands. Jay had given Lily a green jade stone a few years ago. She'd always admired it. "I do like blue, young man. I've been blue too, for a long time. Whenever I look at this, I'll remember that I'm coming out of the blue and that God has something for me. My great-grandmother was Indian too, by the way, so it's perfect. I've been meaning to go and visit some distant relatives on the reservation in South Dakota."

Jay's face grew serious, his eyes intense. "You should go. Family is important. Any family. We've got this here. It's not going anywhere. Besides, Garments of Praise will go with you. Think about it."

She did think about it. Even after Jay was gone and Raya was back at her computer typing away, she was still standing there with that rock in her hand, thinking about it. One conclusion that she came to very quickly was that Jay was going to make some woman a heck of a husband. He was to rocks what his father was to flowers, a genius at choosing the right one for the right person.

That's God, Red, doing the choosing. He has other perfect gifts for you too.

She blew out a breath and slipped the stone into her purse, not sure whether she'd enlist Lily to cut the stone down to size or Jean to make jewelry out of it. Probably both of them once Lily had the baby. She was due on Valentine's Day, but none of them thought she'd make it except her.

"Need to check your email?" Raya got up from the computer and offered Chenille the chair. "I've got some invoices to sign off on. Nigel delegated a certain part of the purchase orders to each of us. A little different than how you did it all."

Smart guy. That had really started to pile up before she left. The thought of checking email was almost a joke now. With all her backlog from work finally cleared out and forwarded to all the right people, she realized that outside of work, she'd really had no life at all. These days she got more spam in her box than anything. Every now and again, there would be something important, or even interesting. Not often, though. "Sure, why not? It's not like I'll have any mail, but hey . . ."

Raya laughed and positioned herself at the end of the desk to burp the baby before setting in on her paperwork. How she could nurse and type was beyond Chenille's understanding, but Raya had it down to a science. Right now, Chenille was having a hard time even remembering her own password. After three tries, she got in and sat amazed. There was an email—and not just any email, but a message indicating a comment on her blog. She pressed the button and tried not to panic.

She turned to Raya. "Did you read my blog?"

Her friend shook her head. "Nope. Didn't know you still had one. Send me the link—"

Chenille tuned her out as the email opened and she clicked a link of her own to find an anonymous comment.

```
I don't know you, but I feel like I do. Or at least
I want to. I wish I had known your husband too. I
think somewhere along the line, I stopped believing
in love, but now I think I can. Maybe for a minute
or two, I have loved you. Like you wrote about. It
feels real all the same, but I know that's crazy.
Goodness, now I sound like a stalker. Please write
more and write often. I won't comment again if I'm
scaring you, but I need to hear more from you. You
have really helped me.

Sincerely,

A new friend

PS I'd love to meet you sometime.
```

Chenille dropped her hands into her lap and stared at the screen. She didn't know whether to call the police or leave a comment setting up a date. So she did neither. She just thanked God that he had used her words somehow and that the person had sent her back more love than she'd ever sent out. Still, it was creepy.

17

Interns worked just as hard as chief executive officers, Chenille soon learned. They just didn't work as long. In her new spare time, Chenille spent time with Lily decorating her nursery and traveling the halls of the company she founded, watching as it morphed from her baby into a full-grown publicly traded company grounded in the ideas of many smart and hardworking people. Her internship wasn't a bad gig at all, especially with Jay bringing her free bread for lunch every day. That boy sure was something.

Her Internet friend was turning out to be something too. She blogged in her online journal most every day now, trying at first to forget that he might be there reading her thoughts. The words couldn't be cautious, censored. There was enough of that in real life. She had to be able to live with the lights off for a few moments each day, to scribble down her thoughts about life, about love. About everything. And that's just what she did, write from her heart, ignoring her invisible reader. For the most part anyway. Sometimes, like today, she left him a *PS* at the end of her post.

Today is Irish beer bread day. The bakery down the street from my job-that's-not-a-job is warming up for St. Patrick's Day, even though it's still February. I'm not mad at them, that's for sure. The stuff smells like my father's beard and tastes like his kisses. I saved some for one of the Irish cops I once knew around my place. It brought tears to his eyes and made him ramble about his mother, who he seemed to think I'd resurrected and put to work in some kitchen downtown. When I told him that a young black boy from Brooklyn had made the bread, he only nodded. "When he makes his first commercial, tell him to call me. I'll be in it and smile real big. That was good," he said, holding the last bits of crust to his face before springing one of my curls.

I'm tired of these curls all of a sudden, by the way, but that's a whole nother post. I woke up the other day just tired of everything. My nose scrunched up when I looked in the mirror like when I smell milk that's out of date. I'm not sure what that means exactly, except maybe it's time to do something new.

Or something old in a new way. I'm starting to think that's all anything new ever is anyway. We really just keep building on what we know and snipping off pieces of other things we want to know, people we wish we knew. I digress. It's all about the bread. And the boy who made it, of course. He makes me wonder about my boy and what he might have been, what he might have been made for. But then, I wonder, what if he was just made for me and for Lyle and for God? What if his death mattered more than

his life could have? I don't know and if I'm honest
I don't care to think about it. Maybe if I was a
theologian and not a widow, it'd be easier.

But it isn't easier. I'm getting lonelier by
the day. Valentine's Day is coming and for the
first time in a long time, I think I'll actually
notice. I went to see my other friend's baby. She's
beautiful. I saw HIM too. He was as beautiful as
the baby. Forget it. I'll start all over again.

Out of the blue,

Chenille

PS Hello, friend. To answer your last comment,
no, you can't call me. Don't start that again. My
friends are already considering calling the police.
It does seem like I know you, though.

And she meant that. They shared more in their exchanges
in the comments of her blog than she'd shared with a lot of
people in a long time. Some of it was cryptic, of course, with
names and things omitted, but somehow she got the gist of
it. He did too. Except for the "no meeting" part. He didn't
seem to get that at all.

Out of the blue, huh? I like that. I like you too.
I know it seems weird and you think we'll end up on
Dateline or something, but I really want to meet
you. Somewhere public. Bring your friends. You
don't even have to talk to me if you don't want to.
Just blow me a kiss or something. I think I know
the answer, so shoot me a prayer instead. Kind of
going through it over here. You made my day.

217

And he'd made Chenille's day. Again. At least until the phone rang.

"Hey." The voice landed softly upon Chenille's ear, but heavy on her heart.

"Sergio? Is that you?"

"Yes," he answered just as quietly as before. His voice held weariness, the kind of tired that made you choose your words carefully and speak deliberately, knowing you don't have the strength to repeat yourself. "It's me. Got a minute?"

Her heart pounded in spite of her efforts to stay calm. "Sure, I can talk. Is it the baby? Is she all right? I can come up if you'd like—"

"No. It's not the baby. It's me. Me and Megan. See, I was just wondering how you know if it's going to really work out, if it's going to be the real thing."

One indication is that you don't have to wonder. "You don't know. You can't. That's what love is. Even when you know everything you think you could know about a person, there's still a stranger, a secret self inside of there that only God knows. Sometimes we don't even know it ourselves. My best advice would be to find out as much as you can know about God and about yourself and then go from there. If you at least know who you are, you'll be way ahead of the game."

There was a long pause on the other side of the phone. "That was deep, Aunt Nilly." His tiredness gave way to laughter, and without even closing her eyes, Chenille could see in her mind that his naturally arched eyebrows were easing back into place. He probably had on those ratty jeans too. She should have thrown them out while she had the chance. Oh well. Megan would certainly take care of that. She'd have to.

"Aunt Nilly? I can see you've been hanging out with Flex and his crew."

"You know it."

"Please don't call me that." Her voice sounded more force-ful than she'd intended. Powerful. She was getting a lot of those kinds of surprises these days.

"I'm sorry. I didn't mean anything by it. I'm not even sure why I called. I'm just worn out, been on for three shifts, going on four. You kept coming to mind. Oh, I know . . ."

Chenille held her breath . . . and the back of the chair in front of her. "What?"

He took a deep sniff. Probably snoring on his feet. "I, um, was supposed to ask what you're doing for Valentine's Day. Megan's having some dinner thing. I don't know the de-tails, but it should be pretty simple. Maybe even dinner in the nursery here if I can't get off and Brianna hasn't gone home. Anyway, I know you probably have plans with your friends—"

"Not really." She swallowed hard and fought an urge to scratch at the backs of her knees, a horrible feeling she'd get when taking standardized tests as a child. One teacher had made Chenille bend over to make sure she wasn't hoarding answers in her sock tops. Those were the days. This test was much harder to pass. Could she really sit through a Valentine's Day dinner with Sergio and Megan? And even if she could, why would she want to?

Somewhere public. Bring your friends . . . Just blow me a kiss . . .

What sounded like a relieved sigh blew into the phone. "Okay, so do you want to come or should I tell Megan that you want to spend some time alone, seeing as it's Valentine's Day and you'll probably have Lyle on your mind and every-thing."

The chair that had steadied Chenille's grip now looked like a good place to sit down. She eased into the kitchen chair and stretched out her legs onto the chair next to her. What did Jean call hot flashes? Power surges? Well, Chenille wasn't menopausal, but it definitely seemed as though a switch had been flipped. She'd played the part of the brooding widow for far too long.

"Actually, I think I would like to spend Valentine's Day with you and Megan. Just let her know that there will be two of us for dinner."

The doctor's tired voice perked up. "Okay, thanks. It probably will be only you and Megan for dinner. And the baby of course, not that she can eat anything." He laughed nervously.

Chenille didn't join him. "No, that's not what I meant. I'll be coming with someone else. A friend. Provided he can make it, that is. I'll have to talk to him to be sure, but we've been talking about getting together anyway, so this should be a good time. Should I tell him to meet me at the hospital?"

"I guess. Megan will call you. I've got to go."

I'll bet you do.

"Well, thanks for the invitation." She meant that sincerely. Without this opportunity, she probably never would have taken a chance on meeting her online friend in person. She'd still have a ways to go in getting her girlfriends on board. If she told them, that is . . . Images of her body in the morgue with no identification quickly squashed that thought. She had to stop watching *CSI* before bed. Tonight she wouldn't. Tonight she'd curl up with the Song of Solomon and one of Lyle's sweaters that she'd just discovered a few days before. Tonight she'd dream of the way things had been and maybe even the way things could be.

When Chenille's friends heard about her plan, they turned her dream into a nightmare. They'd all been watching too many forensic crime shows from the way they raved on and on.

"It's a hospital, for goodness' sake. One of the biggest in America. And we'll be dining with one of the staff members. What exactly is the guy going to do to me?"

"Track you like a deer and follow you home and then . . ." Raya shook her head, unable to finish Chenille off with her sentence. "You know the rest."

The sad thing was, Chenille did know. Unlike Lily, who'd met Doug the first time as she strolled home in the dark going to the subway, Chenille had been used to traveling with Lyle and then with the confines that Lyle's illness brought. There was always someone with her from the church or another friend. Only her trips to the hospital had been late and alone. For some reason, she'd felt safe going there, even though in reality it had been one of the most dangerous places she'd ever been. She'd lost everything there. Twice. And then found it all again on the lips of a stranger who wasn't a stranger anymore.

She needed to put some distance between her and Sergio, both for her own sanity and for the good of his upcoming marriage. And Sergio would marry Megan, no matter how wishy-washy he sounded. Like Lyle, he was one of those kinds of men who were made to be married and wouldn't wait around forever for it. Guys did the rebound marriage thing too. Not that she'd been something to rebound from, really. It wasn't as if they'd had some relationship with dates and all the pleasantries. It was just a right-now love, the kind you see on TV and scoff at, but when it shows up, it seems like it's always been there, like it will always be there.

Only it won't. And that was why Chenille had to go to this

dinner, even if her friends did think that she was risking her life. And they definitely did think that. The conversation got so heated, in fact, that it took Lily going into labor to stop it. Her husband wasn't too happy about that part, but he was pleased as punch about his bouncing baby boy. Of course, that meant more trips to the hospital and possibly running into Sergio, but Chenille didn't care. She couldn't stay away if she wanted to. Stephen, as someone had finally named the baby after days of calling him "Little Doug," was a gift to them all.

Nigel came too, changing diapers and looking up baby facts on the Internet from his laptop. He was a grandfather and his friend was having his first child. It was hilarious to listen to them looking up all the things necessary to keep the baby clean and happy.

"There's a wipe warmer here, Doug. That sounds good. It's pretty chilly still." Nigel had his laptop on his knees in the corner of Lily's room, typing furiously.

Doug tapped his chin. "Sounds good, but check the consumer reviews. Half the stuff I've bought is broken already."

Lily punched the pillow and gave Chenille a "men, you gotta love them" look. "Honey, everything is breaking because you won't read the directions to anything." She was wearing one of the robes that Chenille had made for her. She vowed to stay in one of them for the next month to keep the well-wishers away.

Both men protested that they just didn't make things like they used to. And on it went with two fashion moguls acting like fresh new dads. Lily didn't scold them much since the pregnancy and delivery had really worn her down. She'd had a miscarriage the year before, and her mom was now under around-the-clock care. "It was all worth it," she said over and over. "Every bit of it. I may need like a year off, though. I may need physical therapy. That was one big baby."

And he was. Almost nine pounds. Chenille felt uncomfortable just thinking about it. The great thing was that now she had time to spend at the hospital with Lily, carting the baby back and forth. She was there so much that she almost forgot about her friend on the computer.

Almost.

She'd asked for a private email to send him an invitation to, and he created one for her to send the mail to, calling himself ValentineGuy now. She'd told him all the details she knew, but that was before the Mod Squad stormed into her apartment telling her to squash the whole thing. Then came Stephen and, well, now she wasn't sure what to do. Or at least she hadn't been sure. And then she saw Sergio, lingering in the hall as she pushed Stephen back to the nursery to get his vitals taken at the end of the shift. Even though Lily was still dog tired, she wanted the baby with her in the room despite the nurses' advice to get her rest. She'd sleep, she said, just with him. Chenille and Doug took shifts making sure Stephen checked in each shift for an hour or so and then went back to his mama.

Tonight Sergio was just a pit stop along their way. A very handsome pit stop. Although he'd sounded uncertain on the phone about his relationship with Megan, something in his life was suiting him well. It was still bitterly cold, and Chenille was pale as ever, but he looked as tan and toned as someone coming off a vacation in Hawaii.

Maybe bronzer would be a good investment. Just for winter anyway.

"He's beautiful," Sergio said. "I watched you with him earlier. He looks good on you. You're a natural mother."

Was he trying to kill her or what? "I don't know about all that, but I love being Aunt Nilly." She held up a finger in reminder. "To the kiddies only, of course. You should see Lily and

223

Doug with him. They just break down crying and start kissing like crazy. They're a mess in there. A beautiful mess."

He opened his mouth to say something, then closed it again.

Stephen started to stir. Chenille wanted to know what Sergio had started to say, but she decided it didn't matter. They'd both made their choices. There was no sense in flirting like school kids. It would only get someone hurt, most likely her. "Well, stop by and see Lily when you get the chance. I've been peeping in on Brianna now and then. She's growing bigger by the day. Talk to you later."

She started down the hall. So did Sergio, in the other direction. Just as she'd gathered herself and prepared to turn the next corner, he appeared again, jogging behind her. She noticed that his shoes were new, and so were his jeans. They were Flex's favorite brand too. French. Someone was definitely out to get her. At least she couldn't smell him from here . . .

He closed in. So much for the not-smelling thing. Chenille tried not to breathe too deeply and thanked God she was close to the nursery door.

"I just wanted to know if you were still coming. To dinner, I mean. I got it worked out, and we can have one of the labor suites to ourselves."

Chenille made a face. Having a dinner in a labor suite didn't sound very romantic to her. She wasn't sure what her friend would think either. She'd probably be too nervous to notice. She hadn't dated in forever. There had always been Lyle, it seemed.

"I know how it sounds, but they're really nice. Like a living room. Seven o'clock. Room 413. Just sniff for the candles."

She'd arrived at the door, and the nurse was taking Stephen from her before Chenille really processed everything that Sergio had said. He was gone before she thought to say that she wasn't sure if her date was coming at all. She ran back to Lily's room, hoping someone would be there with a computer.

OutoftheBlue: So sorry that I haven't been online. My friend had her baby.

ValentineGuy: Another baby or another friend.

OutoftheBlue: Another friend. An old friend. A new friend had the other baby. Sorry to be confusing.

ValentineGuy: So does that mean you saw HIM?

OutoftheBlue: It does.

ValentineGuy: So our hospital date is with HIM too?

OutoftheBlue: Um, yeah. Sort of. Now it seems like I'm using you or something. Maybe I am. Ick. I'm sorry. Maybe we should call it off.

ValentineGuy: Use me.

OutoftheBlue: Huh?

ValentineGuy: You heard me. I don't mind. I'm curious to meet this guy. Anyone who could have such an effect on you can't be all bad. It's cool.

OutoftheBlue: Are you sure?

ValentineGuy: Positive. See you at seven.

OutoftheBlue: Room 413

ValentineGuy: Got it. If I give you my number, will you call me?

OutoftheBlue: Maybe.

18

She'd decided to call her date for the Valentine's Day dinner without consulting anyone except God. It occurred to her that it didn't make much sense to meet someone for dinner and not even know his name. Once she'd heard his voice, she'd almost forgotten to ask his name.

He offered it willingly. "Samuel."

"Chenille."

It had begun, the official phone dance. It felt like high school, only without her mother banging on the door and threatening to unplug the phone. They talked too long and laughed too much, but she didn't regret it. At least not until she saw the circles under her eyes the next morning. Thank God for good makeup.

That was one lesson that Jean had taught her: once you pass thirty, you need a good bra and some real makeup. Chenille still used her drugstore stash too, but for days like today the real makeup bag was required. She considered a girdle too but decided against it. A good bra was one thing, but she didn't know this guy well enough for that kind of restraint. She had a few other tricks up her sleeve and in her clothing drawer, but that one would have to stay tucked away for now.

When she stepped out of the hospital elevator and saw the not-so-inconspicuous SWAT team of her friends and their spouses casing out the fourth floor for any signs of her date, she was glad she'd left the girdle at home. She would have sweat herself into a tizzy just watching them march back and forth.

"Which way do you think he's coming?" Doug asked, as he pushed Stephen back and forth in his stroller.

"For his sake, I hope he's coming some back way. You people are ridiculous. I'm going back to Lily's room." Jean waved for Nigel to follow, which left Doug on his own. He didn't last long, but assured Chenille that he'd be watching, pointing two fingers from his eyes to hers.

She shook her head, hoping that didn't mean that Flex was stashed in one of the ficus plants nearby. He'd probably scare poor Samuel to death if he put his mind to it. Sure enough, Raya showed up with some lame story about bringing baby clothes for Stephen to go home in, as though she hadn't bought the child a ton of almost-new hand-me-downs already.

"Now what's his last name again? We might need to google him while you're eating. You know, just to be sure."

Arrgh. Pre-date Google searches had probably saved some women from harm to be sure, but Chenille couldn't help but think that it'd probably soured some romances on the vine too. Sometimes too much information was just that. "I don't know his last name, okay? We didn't quite get to that on the phone—"

Raya looked faint. "The phone? Did you give him your number? I think I feel sick. Well, I'm going to pray. It's all I can do. You're a grown woman, you know."

Chenille got a kick out of that one. "You don't say."

Raya made a smacking sound with her lips and threw up her hands. "All right, Miss Smart Aleck, it's your life I'm trying to save. I'm out of here. Get going. It's three minutes 'til. Fluff your hair."

Now Chenille felt sick. She had tried to restrain the curly red monster otherwise known as her hair, and now here Raya was, telling her to feed the animal, to fluff it. "Do you want him to think I'm Ronald McDonald?"

"Basically, but really your hair looks best big. Trust me. I'd melt under that stuff, but it works for you."

One mad fluffing session and several strides later, Chenille found herself at the door of room 413. All of a sudden, she wondered if Samuel had arrived before her and gone inside or—

"Chenille?"

"Yes?" She turned, trying not to have a heart attack. He was definitely worthy of some type of cardiac event. His skin looked as smooth as his voice sounded. It was the color of Jay's best bread—white in the center and brown at the edges. That kind of tan didn't come out of a bottle. His eyes were wide set and piercing, like they could see for miles. Right now, he could probably see right through her. She extended a hand, but he gave her a hug instead. One of those church hugs, just around the shoulders. She wasn't sure why, but that made her feel better. Safer. "Samuel? Is that you?"

"It is. It's so good to finally meet you." He handed her a bouquet of wildflowers and leaned against the door frame.

Taken by the beauty and uniqueness of the flowers, Chenille didn't hear much of what he said. Beyond his handsomeness, there was something about him that was familiar. Hauntingly so . . . She handed him a box of candy that she'd picked up on the way. "Not quite flowers, but here."

228

The door swung open before Chenille thought to knock. Sergio greeted her with a wide smile and extended an arm behind him inviting her in. Chenille stepped toward him, holding out a cheese wheel that she had brought. She looked past him to see rose petals dusting a path to the table, lit by what seemed like a hundred candles, large and small. Megan was standing somewhere behind the glow, looking beautiful but tired. Chenille realized Samuel was still outside the door, resting against the frame and out of view.

Sergio turned to pick up a candle that had sputtered out.

Chenille paused to get control, both of herself and of the evening. She hadn't brought Samuel here to use him. She wouldn't. Maybe things had started that way, but now she really wanted to get to know him better. She turned back to the door. "Hold on, let me introduce you to my friend, Samuel—"

Her date gave her a confident smile before moving through the doorway and into the room.

As he did, Sergio dropped the candle he was holding.

Samuel dropped the candy Chenille had given him. A cherry cordial splattered on the carpet.

Chenille and Megan stared at each other in confusion as the two men approached one another cautiously, as if the other were breakable or make-believe.

Sergio spoke first. "Blue? Is that you?"

Samuel smiled back at Sergio. "Blue. No one has called me that in a long time. Most people know me as Samuel now. I know what you're probably thinking, that I hated being called Samuel when we were kids. That seems like forever ago. Look at you. A doctor. You really did it . . ."

Chenille didn't hear the rest. When they were kids? What was that supposed to mean? The room was starting to get hot and the scent of the roses was suddenly overpowering.

229

The two men grabbed one another in a desperate hug and fell silent for a moment. It was a sacred silence, like the hush after an announcement on the intercom that someone famous has died. Megan and Chenille looked at one another, but neither said a word. Whatever was between these men, it was something deeper than the relationships the two had with either of the women. That much was certain.

Samuel lifted his head and took a deep breath as if realizing where he was. A hospital. "So you went for the baby doctor thing, huh? You did right. I know I kept saying plastic surgery back then, but that was only for the money. There's more to life than that. I'm just glad to see you, bro."

Sergio nodded slightly, still in a dreamy place himself. "I hadn't heard from you in so long, and then there was that fire at your record company. I thought you were dead."

"I was dead, man, but not from the fire. I was just all messed up. But the Lord saved me, just like you said he would. I guess you kept praying after I asked you not to."

"I did. That was one request I couldn't honor, not even for my only brother."

So there it was. The only other man on earth that was interested in Chenille turned out to be Sergio's brother? Chenille knew that God was in control, but there had to be a place to file a complaint for this.

To make things worse, Samuel turned to her. He took her hand and asked, "Is this him, the one? It figures."

Chenille longed for her girdle. It seemed all her internal organs had pulled away from their positions and were heading full speed for her brain. "This is Megan. They're getting married . . ." It was all she could think of to say, especially since Sergio's eyes went back and forth from her to his brother. It was as if he'd forgotten that Megan was even there.

She hadn't forgotten, though. Megan looked every bit her

old self in a red surplice jersey dress and stacked heels. The only difference was her hair, which was more natural now and free-flowing in waves more than curls. She had a rose behind one ear. Like a car shifting gears, Samuel seemed to fixate on her, noting every detail. He squeezed Chenille's hand and took a seat, but she hadn't missed the way he'd scrutinized Megan.

Nor could she miss the way that Sergio was staring at her. There were places set for "Chenille" and "Guest." The seating had both couples across the tables from one another, but with Megan closer to Samuel, or Blue as Sergio kept calling him. The good doctor was close to Chenille.

"I can't believe this. Any of it," he said softly as Samuel pulled Megan into a discussion on life on the West Coast versus life in New York. Samuel was as enchanting as he'd been on the phone, but in the presence of Sergio, he seemed different. It was like another light being shone on what you thought was the perfect outfit. It still looks good, just not exactly as you thought.

As the other two continued in conversation, Sergio took Chenille's hand and kissed it. "Thank you. Thank you so much. This is the best Valentine gift I've ever gotten. You don't know how much your friendship means to me."

Oh, she could imagine. She was his best buddy in the world. "Thanks, but I really didn't plan this. I didn't know anything. Blue, I mean, Samuel was my date. I just—"

He held a finger to his lips. "Whatever. God did it, then, but he used you in it. My mother will be so happy to see him. Even happier than I am, if that's possible. And you were part of it. Thank you." He reached across and gave her a hug.

A hug that went a little long.

Chenille broke his grip just as dinner arrived: four heart-shaped steaks with salad, baked potatoes, and rolls. Sweet tea was the drink and strawberry shortcake the dessert. The menu was like something out of a fairy tale. If only the reality had matched it.

Chenille didn't eat a thing.

"You've got the wrong girl, man." Though they hadn't seen one another in years, it didn't take long for Sergio and Samuel to fall back into their places, with Blue talking out loud and Sergio talking inside his head. The difference now was that Sergio had God to talk to as well. Still, it was both wonderful and painful to hear the new, deep sound of his little brother's voice. They would go to visit their mother a few hours later, but for now it was open season.

Sergio kept ironing his pants, trying to take deep, full breaths. "No, Blue. You've got the wrong girl. Chenille is all wrong for you. Not your type. You belong with somebody like—"

"Megan? You might not have said it, but we're both thinking it. True enough, Megan and I used to hang out with the same crowd in LA, but we've both changed. All I'm trying to say is that I saw something between you and Chenille, and before I go after her—and I am going after her—I need to know if there could ever be anything between the two of you again." Blue sat down on his brother's leather sofa and laced his fingers behind his head. "Having a kid and getting saved has really chilled Megan out, I have to say. She seems so peaceful now. You need to let some of that rub off on you. Those deep breaths aren't fooling me."

Sergio clenched his fist. There was a lot he missed about his brother, but suddenly he couldn't remember any of it. "Look, it's complicated, okay. Just stay out of it. There was never really anything between me and Chenille. It was all in my mind. In my dreams. She's a good friend and I respect her very much. You should too." He gave his brother a stern look. It was obvious that his brother had come to faith, but Sergio still didn't know how he lived out that faith. The thought of Blue with Chenille, even kissing her . . .

Blue smiled. "Look at you. You're about to spit fire just thinking about me being with that woman. I know for a fact that there was something between you. That there still is. And that something is love. If you want to keep denying it, then that's on you, but I have to call it like I see it. Besides, Chenille and I were really having a good time the other night until you came to the door. Once she saw you, she just walked off and left me there. It's not like I'm saying I'm all that, but that doesn't happen to me often."

Sergio took a long look at his younger, yet taller brother. People said that Sergio had their mother's Brazilian beauty, with dark skin and black hair. A modern movie star on stilts, an older woman at the hospital had called him. His dimples and athletic frame had always gotten people's attention, even when they were kids. What remained of the attention after they saw Blue, that is.

With thick blondish brown hair and blue eyes, he had an easy sway to him, even as a little kid. Every now and then, Sergio had caught glimpses of Blue on music videos singing backup for someone; he was always the tallest one, singing with his eyes closed. Sergio wished his brother had kept his eyes closed on Valentine's Day. Instead, he'd seen all the things that Sergio didn't want to see. And now he was saying all the things he didn't want to hear. "You're exaggerating, of course, but you know that I am your big brother, after all."

Blue craned his finger in the air, signaling for Sergio to come toward him. Unable to resist, Sergio set his ironing aside and lunged at him. They ended up in the same arm-leg tangle they'd shared growing up. Sergio was thankful for Flex's killer workouts as he flexed and stretched, finally pinning Blue in a headlock.

Tapping the floor in surrender, Blue burst out in laughter. "What have you been eating? Super Wheaties? I used to beat you with one hand." He took a deep breath and got to his feet. "I'm serious about Chenille, though. Don't think you're distracting me with wrestling. You can try and fool yourself all you want, but I've read what she's written about you, so I know things run deep between you two."

He almost burnt himself then. Written? What did Blue mean? A few clicks later, he found out as his brother showed him Chenille's journal site.

As curious as he was, he didn't want to read it. "I don't want to pry," Sergio said. "This looks very personal."

Blue gripped Sergio's arm. "It is personal. Read it anyway. Looks like that's a new entry. You may have to go back some to see what I mean . . ."

Already his brother's words were melting into the background as Sergio settled on the words on-screen.

In the depth of winter, I finally learned that within me there lay an invincible summer.

-Albert Camus

It's snowing outside tonight. It's snowing inside me too. I hadn't known what to call it exactly, but from the time my husband died until a few months ago, I've been on ice. Frozen. I still woke up every day, still went to work, still ate my Cheerios and took my vitamin, but I was frozen just the same.

I was pruned away, cut back and peeled bare of all the love that had covered me. My friends brought

their love, bright and bold, and covered me.
Like a stick plastered with rainbow leaves in an
everlasting autumn, I staggered on. They brought
me fall, crisp and tart with the time and patience
they gave to me.

Soon, we began to take out Lyle's things, to
quilt together his shirts like promises, to make
lullabies out of his handkerchiefs. I took the
blankets to the babies, tiny babies like the one we
had lost, Lyle and I. Babies whose parents stared
at me with questions and fear as I wrapped and
rocked their little ones. I could only give them my
prayers and the meager tatters of my own thawing
hopes. Spring came then.

But it was a man, I know now, who kissed me back
to summer. I kissed him first, of course, shocking
us both. That was something Raya or Jean would
have done. Something powerful. Something strong.
It wasn't either. It was a needy, pitiful kiss
that bloomed only in the meeting of our lips. His
lips told me that he had been hurt too and was
still hurting, but that there was a place in him
where it was always summer, with fireflies so thick
you could catch them in your fists, and knee-high
sunflowers. I went with him to that place, to his
summer, and in a few seconds planted my own garden.
I must have tucked one of his flowers in my soul,
behind my tear jar, because summer stayed with me.

Tonight, though, there's just the cold. The
loveless freeze of grief and denial. I had told
myself that I was happy for him, that I wanted what
was best for him. I lied. I simply want him. Just

for me. Maybe by writing it, admitting it, I can move on. Maybe, somewhere out there, summer awaits me on another man's mouth, a man who is probably reading all of this.

Maybe and maybe not.

Either way, it's always best to begin at the beginning.

Blue chose not to fill the silence after Sergio read what Chenille had written. Sergio wished that he had. Instead, all he heard was the slow splash of his tears against his shiny, black shoes and the steady beat of his broken heart.

His phone vibrated in his pocket. It was Megan. She was having trouble with the baby's oxygen machine. Could he come? *Of course.* And could she come with him and Blue to see his mother? *Yes, that would be nice.*

Sergio spoke slowly as the reality that he was engaged to another woman rushed in and drowned Chenille's garden, washing their summer away forever.

Sergio had stayed with his mother as long as he could, leaving only to go to college. His mother had done fine with the help of friends and many different medications, but there were also times when she didn't want to take them. A condition like bipolar disorder made that sort of difficult to do successfully. His mother had made marked improvements through the prayer and fasting of her friends and church members, and would often call him to apologize for things he'd long forgotten but she'd only just discovered. Most times now, she was lucid and clear; it was the damage to her kidneys from all the drugs she'd taken that bothered her these days.

It seemed strange to be taking Blue to her now. Megan seemed to understand the implication of the trip and could hardly contain her excitement. Sergio returned her smiles, but it wasn't easy. He did love Megan to be sure, but not in the way he loved Chenille. Although it'd been many hours since he read Chenille's words, he couldn't shake them. He couldn't help wondering if he loved people who needed rescuing, all the while hoping to be rescued himself. He gripped the wheel tighter and shoved the thoughts away. One thing he'd always strived to be was a man of his word, and he'd given his word to Megan that he'd marry her.

Despite Chenille's fireflies and sunflowers, his word would have to stand. It was almost too convenient for Chenille to be saying all of this anyway. He'd laid his heart out to her. She'd thought his Christmas gift was a ring and been quick to reject it. To reject him. And she'd been wise to do so. They barely knew one another. Sure Megan had her problems, but Sergio was used to them. Chenille had told him that she just didn't have enough room left to love another man. Sergio believed her, both then and now. Their sunshine kiss was one thing, but building a marriage, a life, was something else altogether.

I don't want to be like them, Lord. I don't.

His parents had the kind of summer between them that Chenille described. Blue was too young to remember a lot of it, but not Sergio. One would stare at the other sleeping and almost be brought to tears. He'd crawl up into his father's lap, pushing back the bush of blond hair and staring into his blue eyes, asking what was wrong. "I don't ever want to lose her," his father would say. "Not ever."

And in the end, his father had done more than lose her, he'd thrown her away. Living with a crazy woman and raising two little boys had become too taxing for him. So he hit the road. And when Blue had hit the road with him, his brother discovered he had a voice better than their father's. They didn't write much or call, and Sergio had been glad. He didn't want to have to act as though things were okay. They never were. Love hadn't been enough for his parents. It wouldn't be enough for him.

Sergio glanced in the rearview mirror. Blue didn't look too happy about this trip, although he was really enjoying riding in the back of the car with Brianna.

"I'm Blue," he kept whispering. "I was little like you when I was born. I couldn't breathe either, but look at me now. You're going to be a beautiful, wise woman, just like your mother."

Maybe he had changed in more ways than Sergio had noticed.

Sergio looked over and saw Megan smile. "That brother of yours is some charmer," she said. "Chenille had better be careful or she'll be married before us."

For all his theories about the impossibility of him and Chenille ever being together, Sergio didn't want to think, even for a moment, about his brother ending up with her. Although maybe that would be the best answer. If Blue married Chenille, it would all be over. Whatever was between them would end.

Ever see Gone with the Wind?

He had seen the movie, several times, in fact. The portrayals of blacks in the film served as a depressing reminder of some of America's history, but Scarlett O'Hara's twisted love story never failed to capture his attention. Today, his own crazy love triangle needed his attention, though he wasn't ready yet to give it. "You all right back there, Blue? Mama was so excited on the phone. She's going to freak when she sees you, I just know it. It'll be great."

His brother's high-pitched baby talk switched to a deep-throated grunt. "Yeah. Maybe."

The light in front of them flashed red. Megan reached over from the passenger's seat and touched Sergio's arm. He paused to look at her, reading the call for restraint in her eyes. After losing her mother to AIDS recently, Megan believed strongly in family. One of the things she'd learned, she told him, was that maybe being right wasn't as important as people thought. Sometimes being there was enough.

Sergio shrugged her hand away as he started through the intersection. What Megan said about family was true, only he was the one who had been there, the one who had stayed through the neighbors' gossip and the teachers' calls, through the strange men. Not his father and not Blue. And that was okay. But the least his brother could do now was say hello and give their mother some peace before she died. Though Sergio had stayed, it was Blue that she cried over at night. His father too. He knew it then and he knew it now.

"I'm not goin' upstairs. Not tonight."

Sergio's little brother slammed his fist against the wall. "I'm not gonna climb up there and freeze and listen to them down here carrying on while we're up there, cramped up and cold, getting bit up by spiders. I ain't doin' it, and I'm gonna tell Mama so."

Sergio sucked in a hard breath, pulling back the words he wanted to say. He'd always known this day would come, the day that Mama would have to say things he'd waited to hear his whole life—all the time knowing it would be Blue, the little one, who would push her to it.

Little Boy Blue, born with no air, no newborn cry. They'd laid him aside for dead when some nurse noticed he'd pinked up and started moving. His father had caught him just before he rolled off the table. Nobody since then had ever doubted Blue was anything but alive. He never shut up unless he was sleeping or eating. He even talked in the bathroom.

From the day Blue almost died, his big brother had decided to be a doctor. A doctor who saved babies like God had saved Blue.

Another slam against the wall. "I mean it, bro. I'm going to tell Mama just what I think, what you think too. What you're just too scared to say."

Sergio settled down hard in one of the kitchen chairs, snagging his shirt against a nail poking up out of the table. He'd meant to get the hammer and beat it back that morning, but he ran out of time, what with making breakfast and trying to get Mama's supper started. He rubbed his arm where the nail had scratched him, wondering when he'd find time to patch the shirt before laundry day.

His father had taught him how to mend when he was six, because a man needed to know woman things and man things because a man never knew what he might have to do. His father patted Sergio's hand after his son had finished the last stitch. "Beautiful," he said. "Just like your mama." What he hadn't added—that all women weren't able to do women things—went unsaid.

It was then Sergio realized that his father would leave some day, that the sewing lesson was meant for his survival. And one day Blue would leave too. He and Daddy were alike in that way. They were like a drinking glass that overflowed when it had its fill—they could only take so much. He liked that about them, having an end like that. *Finite*, as his math book described it. But no matter how hard he tried, Sergio wasn't like the two of them. He'd finally accepted that there was no end to him. No beginning either. He just was.

Their mother's voice, smooth as butter, came through the screen door. "Thanks for the ride. See you tonight."

Sergio liked to hear her sounding happy, even though he knew that every sugary word brought the boys closer to a night in the attic. But Blue had scrunched his face tight. Sergio looked away from him, not wanting to find the piece of Daddy in those eyes. Blue forced him to see things for what they were, even when it came to Mama and the things Blue didn't know about. It had been a good choice to protect his little brother for so long from things that hurt.

The screen door smacked shut, punctuating the shift in their mother's mood. "What in the world are you two doing down here? Didn't I tell you we were having company tonight?"

Blue, three years younger and two inches taller than his brother, spread his legs apart, crossed his arms. "I'll tell you what in the world we're doing down here, Mama. We're looking for something to eat. Well, I am. Sergio's probably just trying to find some leftovers even though he made the meat loaf for tonight's bum, whoever he is."

He tugged at his little brother's sleeve. "Blue."

Blue waved his brother off. Together, they watched their mother's quivering face. Sergio pushed the cookie jar back on the counter and pressed his butt up against the silverware drawer. His mother had never gone for a knife with them, but she'd done other things almost as bad. And this wasn't just Blue talking tonight. This was Daddy talking. He was just using Blue's voice.

"Don't stop your brother, Sergio. He's a grown man of twelve. Thinks he can run me and my house. Let him have his say. Then I'm going to beat his tail." She reached for the handle of the silverware drawer but got a handful of Sergio's shirt instead. That seemed to surprise her more than Blue's hijinks. "Move, boy!"

Sergio may not have blond hair or blue eyes like Blue or Daddy, but this was one time he was going to have to disobey. He stood there and pretended not to hear his mother. Maybe there was some Daddy in him after all.

"You need to cook?" Blue said. "That's real funny, because you know what, Mama? I'm cooking tonight."

Sergio swallowed hard then, staring at the back door. Blue had lost his mind, and part of him didn't want to stick around to help him find it. His mother pushed him aside, dropping down and reaching into the low cabinet. She came up with a cast-iron skillet. "What are you cooking, Little Boy Blue? Tell me now. I want to help you."

Blue turned his back on her. Pulled open the refrigerator and grabbed a package of meat. Then he walked right up to her and snatched the pan out of her hand.

Sergio looked out the window. The worry was rising up inside him about where all this was headed.

His little brother didn't sound worried. "I took me a can of Manwich from the gas station. Your boyfriend saw me do it, but I guess he was too ashamed to stop me. Or scared I'll tell his wife something. He knows you got kids. He knows and he sits his behind at this table, eats all the food, and takes you in that room . . ." He was crying now. "He knows we're here."

An itch spread over Sergio's skin. He backed up to the kitchen door and rubbed against it, tried to sand down Blue's words so they wouldn't hurt him so bad. Or hurt Mama. Blue couldn't remember what was under all that cheap makeup and perfume. He was too young to remember who Mama really was. And Sergio was too old to forget.

She slumped against the stove, slid down the front of it. Her head rolled forward into her dress like a rag doll.

Blue stepped over her and put the pan on the stove.

Sergio pulled her up and glared up at his little brother. "You're taking this thing far."

"Am I? I don't think so. I ain't took it far enough." He turned the pan all around like Sergio had taught him when Mama wasn't home, stirring the hot meat through the center, scraping the sides.

She was lighter than Sergio thought she would be, his mother. In his father's arms, she'd looked so sturdy, so full. But now, it was like she was pouring through his fingers. Another try got her to the chair. Her bun came undone, and the long black hair she so often hid tumbled down. He couldn't help but touch it. "It's okay, Mama."

She didn't look up, just talked right down into the table like a kid in trouble at school. "It isn't okay, Sergio. I know it isn't. Looks like I've gone and lost my mind again. Must have. Don't know how long now. Do you know?"

"Yes, ma'am."

"Too scared to say anything?"

Too confused really. Daddy had said anybody with sense enough to know she was crazy wasn't very crazy at all. Sergio wasn't so sure.

Blue turned off the burner, leaned in toward them. The anger drained from his face. "What she talking about, losing her mind?"

He didn't know. Sergio had always tried to cover it, to keep things easy for his brother. But not this winter. This winter had been anything but easy.

Their mother looked up then, red-eyed and tired. "I told your daddy I could keep you two. I wanted to. I thought I could . . . I thought that if I did, he'd come back to me."

The other chair at the table cushioned Sergio as he fell into it. His mother's words were like a breath he'd been holding since their father left, since Sergio had stood on the porch holding Blue's hand, telling his father that he wanted to stay, telling himself that he had to.

Blue, the boy who never cried, started bawling, his body twisting up like a pretzel. He reached for his brother.

Sergio wanted to slap him. Why couldn't Blue have just let them go to the attic like before? Sergio would have bought him candy or something tomorrow. Their mother always left extra money after meat loaf nights. Always before. Now there would be nothing.

Blue howled like the cats outside at night. "Why did you even have us, Mama? Especially me. You had Serg. He's your favorite anyway. Why'd you have another baby?"

Sergio did smack his brother then, square in his ribbon lips. He knew this answer too, but he didn't want to hear his mother say it.

"I had you because your daddy wanted you. And I wanted him. It sounds bad to say it, but it isn't so bad. When I got you here, I wanted you too. Loved you the best I could."

Blue didn't say anything. He just stared at his brother.

Sergio had known this, and he could see that Blue had just realized it—and they could no longer be on the same side. Mama's side. It was the only side Sergio knew. His father had placed him there. Oh, he knew his mother may never love him in the way he wanted her to, but he'd learned how to make the love she had stretch and bend, how to tuck it under the edges of himself. Blue could never learn that. He didn't have it in him. And the love he wanted from Mama, she didn't have it in her.

Sergio turned away from his brother; it hurt to do it. Blue had been good to him. The quiet without him would drive Sergio crazy. But he knew.

Blue would go.

And he would stay.

A knock sounded at the door. His mother moved first, winding her hair into that knot. She touched Sergio's shoulder. "Go to the door, son. Tell him to go home."

Blue wiped his eyes. Sergio's eyes remained dry. "You get it, Mama. Blue and I have some things to do upstairs. Homework."

Mama curled his hands together and pulled them to her bright lips. "He won't stay long, I promise. I'm sorry that I'm weak, that I need to be with somebody. You boys are strong, like your daddy. You won't ever have to be like this. Like me."

Sergio followed Blue out the side door and watched him climb the stack of boxes to get to the attic. Sergio usually opened it for his brother, but not this time. He'd chosen his mother against Daddy and now against Blue. He'd let her pour in trouble way past full, drowning the three of them.

He watched Blue, happy that his brother had turned out strong. He would miss him, but it was better than having him turn out weak like Mama, needing to be with somebody even if they couldn't ever really love you. Better than being stupid enough to climb into an attic while the man from the gas station ate their supper. Better than being fool enough to stay even when Daddy came to save them.

Blue would turn out better than Mama. Better than him. Sergio took some comfort in that.

Megan was saying something. Sergio blinked back to the present. He shook his head to clear the memories. A quick look in the rearview mirror as he started through the green light revealed fear in his brother's eyes. In that moment, Blue finally looked like the younger one. Sergio reached back and punched him in the leg. "Come on, Blue. Don't be like that. She did the best she could."

Leather squeaked as his brother twisted in the backseat, covering his eyes. "I know that she did the best she could. I really do know. I had to get out there and live a little, see some things to understand. She gave us the best she had. What makes me sad is that you gave her the best of you too. Maybe too much . . ."

Blue stopped short of saying more, probably out of respect for Megan. For that at least, Sergio was glad that she had come. Otherwise, he regretted bringing her along. Engaged or not, this could go in a lot of different directions. Their family had never had reunions, only explosions. Dangerous explosions. Blue was a laid-back record producer now, and he was a doctor, but Sergio knew that being in their mother's presence could be a frustrating, even enraging experience. He'd had many years to learn how to deal with it. His brother had only the memories that sometimes seeped into Sergio's sleep and made him wake up sweating and tasting meat loaf.

Sergio dusted off his shirt as they pulled into the parking lot. For some reason, he always dressed up when he went to see his mother. He wasn't sure why. "Are you done trying to analyze me? I think you should have gone to med school for psychiatry. Don't worry, you'll get to disappear again and go back to your life soon. Just don't make it about me. It's not about me."

"Isn't it?" Blue laughed bitterly as he unstrapped the infant seat without being asked and lifted it gently out of the car. "It's always been about you, bro. Always. All I'm saying is, you did all the right things. You stayed with Mama. You became a doctor. Now, I think you're even getting married for her. Or to her."

Megan's mouth opened wide. She reached out and took the baby from Blue, then gave Sergio an exasperated look. When Sergio didn't find the words fast enough, Megan found her own words, formed her own questions. "I am not your mother." She glared at Sergio, and then Blue. "I have enough issues of my own." She turned toward Sergio. "Talk to him. I'll be waiting for you inside."

And she was waiting inside. Inside his mother's room. When he entered with Blue, his mother was laughing with both hands raised in the air. She had glaucoma now and couldn't see very well, but she loved strong voices. Megan had a good voice. Chenille did too. He remembered that from listening to her read to the babies in the NICU nursery.

That was a random thought.

"Mama! Hey, how are you—"

"Little Boy Blue? Is that you? I don't know anyone else who reeks of Juicy Fruit gum." Sergio's mother closed her eyes and reached forward from her bed with both hands as if she couldn't see at all. Her once-black silky hair laid against her pillow like corn silk She was sixty-two now, not a whole lot older than some of Chenille's friends. But it seemed that she had been old for a very long time.

His brother stepped forward cautiously. Sergio thought about giving him a shove. Megan must have read his mind, because she did shove him, right into his mother's arms.

"Yes, Mama. It's me. I–I'm sorry. We didn't come back. We meant to, and then Dad got that backup job. He talked about you all the time when he got sick. He wanted to come then, but the doctor wouldn't let him—"

"Shhh . . ." Though Blue was the taller of her two sons, she gathered him up into her arms onto the canopy bed that Sergio had bought her many Christmases ago. The home where she stayed had been nice about letting her keep it.

Sergio fought back tears as she checked Blue over, searching first for the scar his brother had earned falling out of their neighbor's barn. "I see you put cocoa butter on it like I told

247

you. You always did have good skin. Your hair doesn't feel right, though. Are you using cheap shampoo?"

Blue laughed at that. "It's forty bucks a bottle, Mama. It's anything but cheap."

She huffed. "What something costs has little to do with its value. Your father could sell raindrops if he wanted to; doesn't mean they were worth buying. But they're probably worth more than that expensive pine tar you're putting on your hair now. Sergio, come over here and put your hand in your brother's hair. The boy's a porcupine."

Sergio didn't move. "I believe you, Mama."

Evidently Megan didn't, because she went over and shoved her hand into Blue's scalp, wiggling her fingers like a shampoo girl. "Okay, I'm with your mother, Blue. That stuff is rough. It may not be the shampoo, though; could be the gel. It'll eat your hair up if you're not careful."

His mother looked confused, tucking a handful of white hair behind one ear like a column of snow. "Men are gelling their hair again? Hmph. I have been in here a long time." She turned to Megan. "Buy him something from the health food store. And make it fruity. He always liked the fruity. I know he won't listen to you now, but after the wedding, you can tell him what to do—"

Blue's head shot up. "No, Mama. She's—"

His mother shook her head. "I know, I know. New wives are shy. I was too, right, Sergio? Oh, maybe you don't remember all that. Sometimes I think that you were born right along with us, that you were there raising us up. Now what were you saying?"

Megan took her hand. "Mrs. Loyola, don't you remember me? Megan? I'm not marrying Blue, I'm marrying Sergio. I'm sure you remember. Sergio and I were engaged for a long time. You came to see my dress and everything?"

Sergio sat back and watched, though he knew he should have stepped forward, should have said something. But he couldn't think of anything to say. All of them looked so right together, so much like a family, like the family he'd wanted so badly. He felt as though he'd been invited to dinner at a friend's house, only to arrive and find that no place had been set for him. As his mother tried to grasp how Blue's girlfriend could be marrying her other son, Sergio backed out of the room.

He'd thought that love wasn't enough, that friendship, common goals, and family would be a better foundation for a marriage. He knew now that wasn't enough either. He wanted, needed, both. He wanted to be someone's invincible summer.

He pushed the door back and stepped into the hall.

"Ow."

He turned quickly at the sound of the voice, a woman's voice.

Chenille's voice.

The breath left his body at the sight of her. Her hair was tousled like copper wire, and though she'd done a good job with her makeup, she'd definitely been crying.

Her eyes were wide at the sight of him too. "I–I talked to Samuel last night about him seeing your mother today. I thought he might need some support afterward so—"

Sergio kissed her quiet. It wasn't gentle and melancholy either, like the kiss at the hospital or at her office. It was a passionate, burning question: *Do you want me?*

Yes, Chenille's mouth answered back before she caught herself and pushed him away. She looked angry. Hurt. "What are you trying to do to me? Okay, I probably shouldn't have come, and maybe if I'm honest I was coming for the both of you, but don't toy with me. I can't—"

His hands were in her hair now, pulling away the band that held it up. He showered her neck with kisses, ignoring the nurse who passed by, snickering under her breath. "I read what you wrote. The invincible summer. Did you mean that?" He kissed her again before she could answer. He knew he should stop, that someone, probably both of them and Megan, would get hurt, but watching his brother's prodigal homecoming had been too much. Right now, he needed to know if she wanted him.

Just him.

Chenille pulled back. Her face tightened. "You read that?"

He took her hand and placed it on his face. He covered her hand with his and nodded. He had read it. He felt it too. Their summer was warm on his face as she touched him.

"I am so sorry. I never should have posted that. Did your brother read that too? I was so upset. I wasn't thinking. And Megan?" She pulled her hand from his face. "Tell me that she didn't read it too?"

The door opened behind them. Megan emerged smiling with her daughter on her hip. "Hey, Chenille! Blue didn't say you were coming. What's up out here? And what was I supposed to read? Whatever it is, it's going to have to wait until you both come in here with Blue and his mom. They are cracking me up." She patted Sergio on his arm. "Your mother is something else. She didn't ever seem to like me before, but she's sure enjoying me today. You might want to talk to them about switching her meds. My mom was bipolar, and she got like that sometimes with a new prescription."

Sergio hung his head, then cast Chenille an apologetic glance before turning back to Megan. He felt like an idiot watching the woman he was supposed to marry smile at him about his family's antics when it would have taken only a coat of lipstick to give away what he'd really been up to. He was both thankful and angry that Chenille had gone without her usual red shine and opted for clear lip gloss instead. Even that should have looked strange, but maybe Megan only had eyes for Blue and his bushy hair.

"I've got to go," Chenille said. "Megan, call me about your dress. It's almost ready."

Megan's brows furrowed. "The dress? Oh yeah. Okay. I'll call you." The baby began to cry and cut them off.

Sergio turned and walked back into the room with Megan. He leaned down and took the baby from her, rocking as he did with the babies at work.

Megan paused before they opened the door and gave Sergio a weary smile. "Tell Chenille that's a nice shade of lip gloss. I don't like it so much on you though."

"You can't take it down, Aunt Nilly. For real, you can't."

She could and she was. Chenille sat in front of Raya's office computer reading again her "Invincible Summer" post on her blog. It was time to delete the whole thing. What had she been thinking that night? Not much, evidently. Lyle had always reminded her that words had power and one should be careful in how she used them. If she'd never been clear on that one before, it certainly hit home now, just like Sergio's kisses had hit home, knifing right through her soul.

Despite Lyle's death, she was still a married woman at heart and unused to dashing cold water on her passions. Or anyone else's. But she was going to have to learn how, starting with deleting her online journal. Jay was jumping up and down like a praying mantis, trying to convince her otherwise.

He unplugged the keyboard and went from playful to serious. "Okay, for real, Aunt Chenille. You can't stop. You were telling some real truth on that thing. And not just about love either. I know you thought you were talking about you, but it wasn't just about you. I was feeling you on a lot of it. Elena and a lot of our friends too."

She slumped in her chair, not knowing which was worse, the thought of Sergio or a bunch of hormonal teenagers reading her personal thoughts. Okay, so Sergio won that one, but not by much. As a thought came to her, she covered her eyes. "Okay, please, whatever you do, tell me that your mother didn't read it." She opened one eye to watch for his response.

He tapped his teeth together and pulled his lips into an apologetic grin. "Well, see . . . I was reading it and we were at Aunt Jean's house—"

"Oh! Oh . . ." Her voice went from high to low. She didn't want to hear any more. "They were all there, weren't they? And they all read it?"

Jay bit his lip. "Dad printed it out and put it up at his gym, if that gives you any indication, but that's beside the point. That was a great post, but it wasn't just that one, it was the others, the ones about the Irish bread I made or stuff we did here on some days. You made me look at things from a different angle. You're good at that—you do it with business, with clothes, with friends. Please, don't stop doing it. Like that guy in the comments said, I need your view."

Chenille put her hands in her lap and tried not to cry. She was unsuccessful in that attempt. Her "view," as Jay called it, had messed up a lot of stuff. Sergio's brother had filled her voice mail with messages. She'd given herself until tonight to summon the courage to answer them. And Sergio? Well,

252

she hadn't talked to or heard from him at all, and as things stood, she thought that might be best considering he was marrying someone else. Her stomach hurt to think of it. She pushed Jay's fingers from the keyboard. His fingers snagged on her new turquoise ring.

Looking down at the ring stopped her short, made her think about Jay's gift to her and how much the blue stone he'd given her had meant to her. She'd started out with plans to make it into a necklace, but when she, Lily, and Jean were done, there was a ring, necklace, and earrings, all set in sterling silver. She wore the ring the most, reminding her about the blessing of having been blue, having been winter. Now God would have to be the one whose kisses she craved. Jesus would have to be her invincible summer.

Her first love.

She smiled at Jay at the thought of first love, remembering how hard things had been for her and Lyle at first. There'd been his close-knit Italian family and her close-mouthed Irish one and the two of them stuck in the middle. Add a strict church, lots of loose friends, and hard times, and things had been up and down for a while. She was very thankful that she'd come to her senses and seen Lyle for who he was. Were Jay and Elena going through some of these same struggles now? They were only eighteen, but these days, eighteen wasn't as young as it used to be.

"I'm sorry I got your finger. I guess that was to remind me that you gave me something and perhaps in some way, my blog gave you something back. What bothers me is that maybe I took away some things too. Some things just might not need to be said for the world to see."

Jay shook his head. "Love always needs to be seen. It's what makes life matter. It's the difference between summer and winter. God is love. That's what I got from what you wrote. I saw my life before I knew Christ and my life now. I have really been blessed, but sometimes I let myself forget how much. It was also special that it came from you, because without you sharing my picture at your staff meeting, things might have turned out very different. All I'm saying is, if it was okay to hold up my picture and tell my story, isn't it okay to tell your own story?"

Chenille closed her eyes. Jay had a point, but he was forgetting something. The story wasn't only hers, and it was that part, the side of the story that didn't belong to her, that was getting all turned around. She thought again of how Sergio had kissed her . . . and how she'd kissed him back. She smiled before navigating back to her blog page. "I think Lyle told his story and now I've told some of mine. Though it would be tempting to keep writing, knowing that you and so many others are reading and enjoying it, I think I will take this to my paper journal, to my secret place in God."

The boy rested against the edge of the desk, nodding. This was something that he seemed to understand.

With trembling fingers, Chenille typed her last post, apologizing for anyone she had hurt and praying for anyone she had helped. She proclaimed her summer love for Jesus and her thanks to her friends, all of them, for bringing her through the seasons of her grief. She'd had a good man, and if she never had one again, she'd be content, or at least try to be. She'd hold on to Jesus with both hands and keep her eyes and heart open, even when parts of her wanted to wither and hibernate, avoiding hurt and pain.

As she published the post, there was a painful silence, both in the room and in Chenille's heart. She wasn't sure why this had turned into such a big deal, but now it was God's deal, and she'd have to leave it there.

Jay shrugged his shoulders. "That was another great post. And it's hard to argue with. I'm going to run down to the bakery for a while. Want anything?"

She shook her head. Usually she had no problem making a suggestion for some delight to bring back for her: cannoli, tiramisu, baklava . . . Today though, she felt full. Satisfied. "No, thanks. I have some things to do for your mother anyway. I'd better get busy."

She sat at the computer for a moment offering up prayers for both strength and forgiveness. A few months ago, she'd wondered if she could ever love another man. Now, she found herself loving someone else's man.

They're not married yet, Red.

Lyle. There he was, when she least expected it.

And he wasn't alone.

"Special delivery," someone said behind her.

She turned to see a man holding a vase, thick with yellow roses. A single sunflower stood tall among the others. The flowers covered the man's face, but she knew his voice. Sergio. Chenille steeled herself against the sight of him, praying that neither her words nor her body would betray her.

As he set the flowers on the table, she saw the same caution in Sergio's eyes, and something else too—regret. He cleared his throat. "Don't worry, I'm not going to kiss you or anything. In fact, I came to apologize for that, if that's possible. That was totally inappropriate—"

I loved it. I love you.

"It's okay. What I wrote was pretty inappropriate too. I just shut my journal down. I hope that you and Megan, even Samuel, can forgive me. I was so caught up in my own emotions that I wasn't thinking about what someone else might think when reading it. I just felt an overwhelming need to—to—"

His shoulders relaxed. "To what?"

To tell the world that I loved you. That it wasn't just some crazy kiss, but a real, wonderful thing.

"Nothing, I just needed to express myself," she said softly. "Thanks for the flowers and for coming by. Thanks for everything."

He rubbed at his face, smoothing stubble Chenille had never seen on him. She wished she wasn't seeing it now. As she looked closer, she saw his eyes were a little bloodshot, his cheeks more drawn than the last time she'd seen him. Defying her vow to keep space between them, she stepped forward before she knew it, touching the side of his face. "Are you all right?" she asked.

Sergio placed his hand on hers and closed his eyes. He purred like a cat. "No, I am not all right. I won't ever be."

Chenille pulled her hand away. "Of course you will be. You'll see." She looked around the room at the clock, trying to remember when Raya or Jay would be returning. She hoped it was soon. This was too much. Way too much.

Laughter rang from his mouth then—the bitter, ironic kind of laugh—with a dryness in it. "My mother asked that we move up the wedding. Once we convinced her that Megan wasn't marrying Blue, of course. I won't even get started on that one. Anyway, I went today to give my vote on Megan's bouquet. You know what I chose?" He waved his hand across the flowers. "Yellow roses. The florist looked pained when she explained that yellow roses meant friendship. Megan didn't even seem surprised. It was as though it confirmed something that she'd been thinking too."

Chenille put a hand to her throat, trying to keep it close to her mouth in case she got the urge to say something she might regret later. Her heart raced in her blouse, but she fought that too, forcing herself to listen. Sergio needed her friendship now probably more than he'd ever needed her love.

He continued. "So the lady told me to close my eyes and think of love and to open my eyes and pick a flower." He pulled the sunflower out of the bouquet. "Here is what I chose, what I choose. You." He bowed on one knee.

Chenille's hand on her throat was joined by her other hand. She felt like choking Sergio and herself. "Get up! You're getting married. What are you thinking?"

He smiled up at her. "I'm thinking that if I don't really love Megan, I shouldn't marry her. And I'm not going to. I decided that much at the florist. She took it pretty well. She sort of helped me admit it. I think she has a thing for Blue, if you can believe that. Anyway, now I'm here with you. Now what's to be decided is if I get the sunflower."

I will not cry. I will. Not. Cry.

And she didn't. Not yet anyway.

"Here's what I need to know. Do you really love me or is this just another way of grieving for you? You told me before that there wasn't enough room left in your heart to love another man. Is there enough room now? I'm pretty flexible and not afraid of small spaces."

So much for the not-crying thing. She moved closer to him and held his head to her waist before reaching down to kiss his head. "I didn't think there was room when I told you that. What I didn't know is that love makes room. The more love you give, the more love you get, the more love there is. You made room for yourself. I can't lie, though. I will always love my first husband."

Sergio stood and held her close. "Good, you keep on loving your first husband. I'm not him and I'm not going to try to be. I want to be your last husband. Your invincible summer."

As she buried her face into Sergio's chest, Chenille heard

the beginnings of applause from the doorway. She turned to find all her friends and quite a few of her work acquaintances packed into the hall.

Jay held up both hands. "I know you want to keep your love private and everything, but it looks like God had other plans."

Chenille nodded and resumed her embrace. God had other plans indeed.

Epilogue

Four months later . . .

"You're looking good, little bro." Sergio stared at his brother in the full-length mirror. He looked more than handsome in the Armani tuxedo that Nigel Salvador had lent him. But it wasn't just the tux. The joy on his face was what caught Sergio's attention.

Blue retied his bowtie for the seventh time. "You don't look too shabby yourself, Doc. Can you tie this for me? It's like I can't hold on to it."

Sergio took a deep breath before tying his brother's tie in a few deft moves. Hanging out with Chenille's friends had taught him new tie techniques as well as giving him a new wonderful family to add to his own. He spent time with Nigel helping with his Veterans with a Vision ministry, each time learning something more about being a man and a soldier in the army of God. Doug LaCroix's missions programs had given him a window into the hurting world for a few days at a time. Flex taught him how to be friends, showed him the power of prayer. Even Jay always had something to teach, like a new recipe so easy that Sergio could master it.

In the end, though, it had been Blue who had made the most difference in his life. It was Blue who'd said what needed to be said on that day Sergio had set out for the florist: "You're trying to marry Mama. Or someone you think is like her. But you're wrong. Megan isn't like her. Megan is strong. She doesn't need your pity. If you don't really love her, leave her alone."

And his brother was right, even if he did have an ulterior motive behind his words. And a very good one, at that.

Raya pushed aside the curtain to their dressing room. She wore a blue gown and held a clipboard. "You two look great. And just in time. We're on, gentlemen. Love awaits you."

Like they'd once done in a silent, dark attic, the two brothers made fists and stacked them on top of each other a few times, ending with a finger snap. "Dap," they'd called the handshake back in their old school. Brotherhood is what they called it now.

As they emerged from the dressing room, Blue whispered into his brother's ear. "Thank you. For everything."

There was a lot more behind those few words, and the brothers both knew it, but they only spared the time for a quick hug. There'd be time for them to talk later. Right now, they had two beautiful women to marry.

Sergio smiled when he heard the strains of soft music from the sanctuary. Rico, Erica's father, who'd finally called and let Sergio hear his music, played the guitar softly in the church. Jessica, his girlfriend, was on the program as well.

Raya ushered them through the sanctuary's back entrance, and they took their places on the altar: Sergio on the right and Samuel on the left. Only his brother and his soon-to-be daughter (he didn't like the step thing) still called him Blue these days. He smiled too big for the name to stick anymore. The sight of Brianna eating more flowers than Raya's sons were sprinkling on the ground made him smile even bigger. Brianna reached out for Blue and cried when he passed by. Laughter bubbled through the crowd as he backtracked and gathered the little girl in his arms.

Their mother sat on the front row, looking stronger and more beautiful than she had in years. She'd let Jean dye her hair auburn for the wedding and she sat tall on the pew like a queen on her throne. She whispered to everyone who would listen, "Those are my boys up there getting married. Aren't they handsome?"

Looking over at his brother, Sergio had to agree. Until he saw his bride, that is. He wasn't sure of the dress or the cut, but as Chenille came down the aisle, Sergio knew for sure that there must be more of those satin and lace dresses somewhere in heaven. It matched the June sky perfectly and was beautifully simple. It reminded him of a dress he'd seen at a Renaissance festival in college. In her hands, Chenille held a bouquet of fresh sunflowers, cut this morning from the garden the two of them had planted last spring. He took her hand as she arrived beside him.

He squeezed her hand and stared deep into her eyes. There was laughter there. There was love there too. She designed maternity clothes now for her own company, Forty Weeks. Garments of Praise made and distributed her designs. They'd found their partnership at last. Once the wedding was over, Sergio and Chenille were headed to South Dakota to work with women and babies on the Indian reservations there.

As Megan started down the aisle toward Blue, the smell of the meat loaf his mother had insisted on making for the reception downstairs escaped the basement oven and filled his nose. Jessica, Erica's mother, half read and half sang Chenille's "Invincible Summer" post. Even now, so much later, the words shook Sergio to his core. He reached for the hand of his bride just to be sure that he wasn't dreaming. Her smooth, steady hands in his confirmed it. Sergio closed his eyes for a second and sighed in relief. Though so painful at the time, Chenille's post had saved each of them from more than just heartache. If not for her honesty, none of them would have found the love they now knew.

And for that, Sergio was thankful, because after today, he'd have summer forever.

Acknowledgments

It's hard to believe that this is the fourth book in the Shades of Style series, mostly because I've had such fun people to work with. It's also because Jesus has been my help each and every time, teaching something new about himself and about myself along the way. I thank him for that.

I also thank my family: my dear husband, Fill, and my children, Ashlie, Michelle, Fill Jr., Ben, James, John, and Isaiah. Each of you inspire me.

To my pastor Kent Nottingham, his wife Debbie, and the Calvary Chapel Tallahassee community, thanks so much for the prayers while I wrestled this book to the ground. You are a blessing to me.

Special thanks to my editor, Jennifer Leep, for believing in me and allowing me to grow. Kudos to everyone at Revell who worked so hard on this book and all the others: Barb Barnes, Cat Hoort, Cheryl Van Andel, Erin Bartels, Lonnie Hull DuPont, and so many others.

For Claudia Mair Burney, I owe you one. Again. Thanks for the reads and the words of encouragement.

For each of the readers who write to me about these books, thank you. I keep every one of your notes.

Mom, thanks for sharing these books with all your friends . . . and for being you.

To everyone I forgot to name, thank you for your friendship and your support. I appreciate it.

marilynn griffith
words with heart... and sole*

Dear Reader,

Thanks so much for joining me on Chenille and Sergio's journey. I'd loved Chenille's first husband so much and so long that I wasn't sure how this one would wrap up, but I was wonderfully surprised. I pray that you were too. Thank you so much for reading these books with me. I hope that you love the folks at Garments of Praise as much as I do. They will always be with me. Thanks for all the emails and prayers. Keep them coming!

Blessings,

Marilynn

Discussion Questions

1. Though Chenille's life has been tightly woven with her friends' lives for a long time, things change for her in this book. How does she deal with the new directions in her life? How do her friends handle it? What would you have done differently?

2. Chenille is a big believer in loyalty and faithfulness. She cares a lot about being true to her friends and the love she had for her first husband. How did she handle it when the time came to be true to herself? Have you experienced the same conflict?

3. Though Chenille regrets the entry in her online journal, young Jay and many other people, including Megan and Samuel, were greatly impacted by her words. Do you think Chenille was wrong for what she posted? Do you journal privately? Would you ever keep a blog?

4. Although losing her son was one of the great tragedies in Chenille's life, helping mothers and babies turns out to be her passion. Have you ever had God take something that hurt you and allow you to use it to help others?

5. All of Chenille's friends are very different, yet they all love her very much. Can you relate to the way Raya, Lily, Jean, and Chenille interact with each other? Are you and your friends more subdued with each other? More honest? What one thing can you take from the friendships between these women and apply to your own relationships?

Marilynn Griffith is a freelance writer who lives in Florida with her husband and seven children. When she's not helping with homework or trying to find her husband a clean shirt, she writes novels and speaks to youth, women, and writers. If you enjoyed this book, please drop Marilynn a line at marilynngriffith@gmail.com.

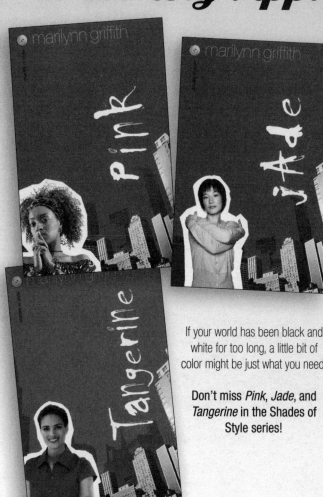